STORM RIDERS

T0281868

STORM RIDERS

JAMES HITT

THORNDIKE PRESS
A part of Gale, a Cengage Company

Copyright © 2022 by James Hitt.
All scripture quotations, unless otherwise noted, are taken from the King James Bible.
Thorndike Press, a part of Gale, a Cengage Company.

LIBRARY OF CONGRESS CIP DATA ON FILE.
CATALOGUING IN PUBLICATION FOR THIS BOOK
IS AVAILABLE FROM THE LIBRARY OF CONGRESS.

ISBN-13: 978-1-4328-9271-5 (softcover alk. paper)

Published in 2023 by arrangement with James Edward Hitt Jr.

Printed in the USA
1 2 3 4 5   27 26 25 24 23

STORM RIDERS

AS TRUE AS —

One early afternoon, I was lounging at the bar nursing a whiskey when he pushed through the swinging doors. A shaft of mid-morning light followed him inside, illuminating swirling dust motes. I lifted my glass and offered a smile. As usual, he appeared grateful for my favors. Since his wife passed on, I provided his only female companionship. My attention involved nothing more than kindness. He was well past sixty winters, and I sympathized with his loss.

We never knew his real name or we had forgotten it, so we called him Pappy because of his white hair and beard. Though colored like me, his lighter skin pointed to a mixed parentage. As a border town, El Paso encouraged a wilder element, and rumor said when he first arrived twenty years before, no man dared insult him. He was fast with a gun and faster to take insult. Now too old for such shenanigans, he continued to carry a sidearm, so ancient the ivory handles had turned a light brown, matching the color of his skin.

The Four-Square Emporium made most of its money from an assorted crowd. While a number of white boys frequented the establishment, especially at night, Mexicans and colored men like Pappy comprised the majority of the clientele. Even during the middle of the day, we kept the interior of the Four-Square dark. We seldom cleaned the front windows, heavy with dust. A single kerosene lamp hung from the ceiling, the wick kept low so the tables around the walls lay deep in shadows, which attracted customers rather than repelled them. In the evenings, when the girls came out — and we hired the best-looking girls in southern Texas — the darkness concealed the men from their wives and sweethearts.

As for me, I billed myself as "The Black Lily" and belted out songs. Though past thirty, I knew the boys, colored and white alike, still considered me handsome, yet I never sold my favors like the chippies. Still, I liked the way we lit the saloon. The shadows made me appear younger, which in my business was good business.

Other than me and the bartender Jake, whose wrinkled face said he was older than

God, the place stood empty as usual for that early in the day, and the thump of Pappy's boots echoed off the walls. He laid a book on the bar, my copy of *The Life of John Westley Hardin as Written by Himself.* The printer released it the previous year, after Hardin's demise. After reading it, I loaned it to Pappy, which was another reason we got along. I read books. In those days, most women, regardless of color, didn't read unless they read the Bible or *Ben-Hur.*

"I thank you very much, Lily Darlin'," he said.

I laid a hand on the book. "Was Hardin as dangerous as he claims?"

"I didn't really know him. We spoke a few times. Seemed a nice enough fellow when sober. As for being dangerous — I've known a lot of men who fit that description. When I was trailin' herds to Sedalia, Wichita, Dodge, I met most of the famous ones — Hickok, Bat Masterson, Wyatt Earp. Hell, Earp ran Hardin out one of those towns, though I forget which one."

"How is it a colored fellow like you met so many of these gunmen?"

"In those days, a third of the drovers were colored fellows, freed slaves looking for new lives, though that wasn't exactly the case with me. I was punching cattle as early as

9

'58, and believe me, those were hard, bitter days. Skin color didn't mean much under those circumstances."

"Who was the most dangerous man you ever met?"

Without hesitation, he said, "His name was Waco — Waco Joseph Callahan."

"I don't think I've ever heard of him."

He reached into his coat pocket and brought out another book with paper covers, an A.D. MacPherson Wild West Dime Special. He dropped it on the bar. Of all the companies that printed dime novels, A.D. MacPherson produced the cheapest. The covers curled at the edges, the spine cracked, the pages loose. One more reading would find it in tatters.

"Last week, I picked this up at the general store. I read it straight through that night." With his index finger, he tapped the book, *The Comanche Kid on the Trail of the Six,* number four in the series with the promise of more to come. The cover drawing showed a man in a saloon much like the Four-Square. He held a smoking .45 in one hand, a tomahawk in the other, and a half-dozen bodies lay scattered at his feet. He wore a rawhide-fringe shirt, breeches, and a feather in his hatband. His facial features said he was a full-blooded heathen and took special delight in dispatching the white villains.

"Go on, take it. It's yours, darlin'," Pappy said. "Enjoy it, though it is mostly a pack of lies."

"The Comanche Kid?" I viewed Pappy with a jaundiced eye. "Is he this Waco-whatever-his-name? You're saying you met him, too?"

"No, darlin', I didn't meet him. I was there the day he came into the world. We rode together. He was as close to a son or a brother as I'll ever have."

"I thought he was a made-up character. You know, like Deadwood Dick."

Jake ambled a few feet closer, moving so slowly I swear I could hear his joints creak. His ancient eyes perused the cover. "Long before I ever seen a penny dreadful, I heard stories 'bout the Comanche Kid, though I figured most of them was bullshit."

I laid a hand on Pappy's arm and searched his face for any hint of duplicity. I saw none.

To Jake I said, "Pour my friend a drink. I'd like to hear his story."

The ancient bartender brought a glass from under the bar and poured two fingers of whiskey, the most Pappy allowed himself on any given day, and a cheap price to pay for hearing a good story. He didn't appear to take offense at my insignificant bribe.

11

He sipped the whiskey, distillery made, and rolled the shot glass between his palms. "In my whole life, only one other person knew the whole story. She's gone two years now. As a matter of plain fact, I've wanted to tell it for a long time. I just doubted anyone would listen."

"Is it true, this story?"

"As true as my memory." He took another sip of whiskey, enjoying its taste, one of the few pleasures left to him. "I witnessed a lot with my own two eyes, and what I didn't, people with no reason to lie filled in the missing pieces. I forget a lot these days. By noon, I can't remember what I had for breakfast. Don't matter. I remember every detail of the time I rode with Waco. Even now, twenty-year past, I see him as clear as I see you."

Outside, clouds moved in. The shadows within deepened.

"I was a kid, no more than thirteen, when I ran away from my master in Louisiana. He may also have been my Pa, though he never claimed such. At any rate, I wound up in the Texas Panhandle where slaves and cotton didn't matter. A white rancher, Captain Callahan, hired me. He didn't care where I came from. He only cared his riders give him an honest day's work."

For the next hour or so, Pappy told his story, his deep bass transporting me to a vision of yesteryear.

CHAPTER ONE

The day his Indian mother gave birth to Waco Joseph Callahan, no one bothered to ask him if he wanted to come into this world, and his half brothers, Flynn and Dermot, dearly wished he hadn't.

When Waco turned three, the fraternal twins made their first overt attempt on his life. A case might be made that they were too young to understand the consequences of their actions. I assure you, at nine years old, they understood only too well. When alone, they called him "half-breed" or simply "breed." Occasionally, they boxed his ears, though never to the extent any marks showed. They put scorpions in his path and often set him near the corral where they hoped a mustang might kick him in the head.

Blue Feather, his father's second wife, worked in the kitchen slicing wild onions while her boy played outside near the window, although "play" may be the wrong word. In a normal sense, Waco seldom played. He observed. Because of Waco's stoic demeanor, Flynn claimed the kid was touched in the head. "Breeds ain't like real people," he told Dermot. "They're half one thing, half another. Drives them crazy."

For one so young, Flynn was a cocky kid. His intense blue eyes, his curly blond hair, his slender build hinted at the handsome man he would become. Half a head shorter than Flynn, Dermot possessed the same hair and the same build, yet the way he seldom looked a fellow straight in the eye implied a weakness of character.

Flynn spotted the rattler, four feet long and full-grown, its belly swollen with a gopher or jackrabbit. The reptile slithered twenty feet from the baby, headed in the opposite direction toward an outcropping of rock. Flynn swept up a rake that leaned against a corral fence and snatched the diamondback on the prongs. With a wide swing, he tossed the creature at Waco.

The serpent landed smack in the kid's lap. Instead of reacting, Waco remained still, his expression free of fear. Around the ranch, rattlers were as common as horseflies. Even at his young age, Waco may have understood the parental warnings concerning rattlers.

Don't antagonize them. Leave them alone, they'll leave you alone. It fears you more than you fear it.

The snake slunk away, paying scant attention to the kid who followed it with his eyes.

Blue Feather charged out the door clutching a butcher knife. With one swipe, she severed the rattler's head from the body. With three quick stabs of the blade, she dug a hole and shoved in the head. With a sweep of her hand, she covered it with earth. Blood poured from the rattler's neck, pooling in the sand. She seized the carcass, which trembled as if still alive, and carried it inside, pausing at the door to glare at Flynn and Dermot. That night, the family dined on rattler. The way that Indian gal simmered the meat in herbs smelled delicious.

So, what saved Waco? Perhaps the manner in which the creature landed, its head bouncing off the ground, knocking it senseless. Or perhaps the toss disoriented it. Or — and here's what fueled concern for the brothers — perhaps the blood of Waco Callahan was the cause. He was part Comanche, a half-breed as his brothers claimed, though we ranch hands never uttered the term, knowing if his father, the Captain, overheard, he would send us packing.

What we saw that day and in the years that followed led us to believe the kid possessed a special ability over the creatures of the wild. I know my musings sound like supernatural hogwash. Understand, we were a bunch of waddies living fifty miles from the Texas–New Mexico border and on the edge of the Llano Estacado, often called the Staked Plains, bounded on the north by the Canadian River, on the east by the Caprock Escarpment, a precipitous cliff of more than three hundred feet, and on the west by the Mescalero Escarpment and the Pecos Valley. To the south where the Bar 4 C lay, no natural boundary existed, only a general blending of the landscape. Not much grew on this vast tableland except grama grass and scrub oak.

White man's influence ended where the Staked Plains began. Though the ranch lay outside, we were no less isolated than the Indians. Our nearest neighbors lived twenty miles south, the other thirty miles east. We never saw newspapers. Half of us could only make our mark. While the boss owned twenty or thirty books, other than him, only I could read. Because the Captain took pity on my ignorance, he schooled me. Turned out, I took right to book learning. Even so, isolated as we were, we were ripe for superstitions. We focused those on the kid.

I don't know who told the Captain about the snake. Blue Feather may have seen the incident from the kitchen window or one of my companions carried stories. Whatever the case, that evening before dinner, while the rattler meat simmered on the stove, the boss hauled Flynn and Dermot to the barn. He hadn't removed his belt, the usual punishment for transgressions. Instead, he swept the bullwhip from the peg, snapping it once, the coiled rawhide raising dust that swirled before settling to earth. He intended the sound to unnerve the boys. The Captain stood perhaps five eight or nine and was broad of shoulders, his arms all muscle. Pox marks scarred his cheeks. When he angered, his eyebrows merged, and his eyes took on a wild gleam that spoke of untapped violence.

Flynn backed away until stopped by a stall. "I was just trying to throw that rattler as far away as I could. It slipped off. Honest, Pa. Tell him, Dermot. Tell him it were an accident."

His brother nodded, his blond hair dropping before his eyes. "He's telling the truth, Pa. I swear it. He's telling the truth."

The Captain cracked the bullwhip once with such precision the tip touched Dermot's chin, laying open skin half an inch long. The boy grabbed his wound, and blood ran through his fingers. The Captain flicked the whip again as Flynn threw up an arm, the lash peeling flesh from middle knuckle to wrist as neatly as if his father used a cut-throat razor. Flynn shoved the wounded hand under his other arm.

With deliberate slowness, the Captain curled the whip, his voice without rancor. "This one time, I'll accept it as a careless accident. If I believed you did it on purpose, I'd lay your backs open. But from this point on, you best understand if anything happens to Waco — if he gets trampled by a horse or a herd of buffalo or if another snake lands in his lap — I'll figure you two had a hand in it." He set the bullwhip on the peg. At the barn door, he again faced his sons. "I do not think less of you two than I do of Waco. The three of you are brothers. Equals. I will play no favorites. What I want is simple. I want you, Flynn, and you, Dermot, to be men to ride the river with."

We heard that expression every time the Captain hired a new wrangler. Such an individual embodied courage and honesty, yet beyond that, the phrase suggested a nobility of character. None of us reached such lofty expectations, the boss included, yet to him, the words were as important as any in the Good Book. Often, he lectured his sons, including Waco, on the values inherent in that phrase. The Captain invariably revisited the same point. "If you don't try to live up to them words, you ain't worth a glob of spit."

The boss earned his title "Captain" in the War with Mexico when he led a company in the battle of Buena Vista, during which he engaged along with his troops in hand-to-hand fighting even after he suffered a shoulder wound. Enos, who became the punchers' cook, and MacInnis, another puncher, returned with him, and out of respect, continued to call him by his rank. He carried his military code of honor into the civilian world.

Before you lay too much blame on the two brothers, you best understand the circumstances. I knew their mother, Margret, whose bosom always preceded her into a room. I will not say that was the reason the Captain married her, for she owned a pleasant if unremarkable face. In those days in the Texas Panhandle, women were in short supply. When the Captain brought her home, I was only a youngster myself, fifteen or sixteen, she a year my senior. Still, I daydreamed of her as I suspected did the other dozen riders.

Then, seven years later in the middle of a bitter autumn night, the constant wind whipping from the north, she crept out of the house, saddled a horse, and headed north. When the morning sun rose and we discovered her gone, the Captain and I rode after her. We followed the trail, as plain as if she painted it, which led us to the banks of the Prairie Dog Fork of the Red River. Her mount loitered at water's edge, the reins secured under a rock. We found her half a mile downstream entangled in the roots of a scrub oak that hung out over the water. We buried her beside the river.

When I looked at her life with a dispassionate eye, her decision appeared somewhat understandable. She came from a St. Louis family that resided in a mansion overlooking the Mississippi. Now her shrunken world revolved around a one-room sod house, her only companions a bunch of ignorant cowboys, a husband seldom home, and two colicky kids. We never saw her smile, and she moped around with a hangdog look as if the world had played her a dirty trick.

As we headed back to the ranch, we were on guard. In those days, the Quahadi Comanche roamed the Llano Estacado, an area the size of New England. A nomadic tribe, they knew every water hole, canyon, and cave. They moved from place to place on a whim. One day they might reside in Palo Duro Canyon, a day later the headwaters of the Pease River. They could break down their village and travel seventy-five miles before the sun set, which made any invasion by the army an exercise in futility. Intelligence would locate them, but by the time the troops arrived, the Indians would have moved. It was a task akin to chasing ghosts. During the late spring through early fall, they stormed from the Staked Plains on lightning raids. Twice we found our riders dead, their bodies pierced with arrows. On another occasion, a horse returned without the rider, for whom we searched for days without finding a trace.

An hour from the banks of the Red River, we spotted buzzards circling ahead. We drew our pistols and approached bent low in our saddles.

Coming upon a patch of matted grass, we discovered a Quahadi boy with a Tonkawa arrow buried in the right shoulder. His chest shuddered in labored breathing. His eyelids fluttered. In his right hand, he gripped a hunting knife. We dismounted and approached. The Captain holstered his weapon and took possession of the blade.

The Indian lad opened his eyes, gray rather than the customary brown. I doubt he had passed his fifteenth year, yet he was my height. His aquiline nose and complexion lighter than mine presented clear evidence of mixed blood, although his dress said he was pure Comanche. He wore moccasins, leggings, a loincloth. A necklace of bear claws adorned his chest, a copper bracelet his right wrist, a crude antelope carved into the surface. Upon seeing us standing over him, he must have experienced a surge of apprehension, though he failed to react in any discernable way.

"We mean you no harm," the Captain said.

I doubted the Captain expected the Comanche to answer. Few of his tribe understood our language.

His voice weak, the Indian replied in stilted English. "You take knife."

The Captain uttered an incredulous laugh. "I'll hold it 'til we both feel comfortable. In the meantime, let's see about getting that arrow out."

The Indian boy cast his gaze on me. I held my pistol, and the Captain nodded for me to put it away, which I did.

"Son —" he drew out the word — "I have

no quarrel with your people. If you desire, we will leave you with your weapon and pony. We will leave food, water. Yet if we do, I fear you will die. On the other hand, if you let us, we will do our best to help you."

"How I know you speak truth?"

"You are alive."

I assumed that mollified him since he offered no further objections. The Captain rolled the boy on his side. Sure enough, in back the arrowhead bulged without breaking the skin.

"What is your name?" the Captain asked.

"Quanah."

"Well, Quanah, I must push the arrow through. You understand?"

"Do it."

The Captain pushed the shaft until, in a spurt of blood, the arrowhead emerged. Once he cut away the barb, he pulled the shaft free. Quanah registered his pain with a grunt and a tightening of his mouth. While all this took place, I constructed a fire, laying the blade of my knife in the flames. When it turned orange, the Captain seized the hilt and laid the metal against the hole in back, the skin sizzling. He applied the same to the front, at which point the boy sagged, and his eyes rolled back in his head. Afterward, the Captain bound the injured shoulder and, cutting rawhide into strips, fashioned a sling. He propped Quanah against a saddle, so he rested more comfortably.

The lad's pony had wandered off fifteen or twenty yards. I threw a loop over it and tied him with our mounts. I hobbled them amid grass and near a stream.

For the first two days, the Indian lad floated in and out of consciousness. On the second day, the Captain hunted, leaving me to play nursemaid. The boy awoke once and scanned the immediate vicinity.

"Where is white man?"

"The Captain is hunting. He'll return soon."

"You brown like me, yet you with white man."

"The Captain judges a man's heart, not his skin color."

"What happens when I can ride?"

"He will send you on your way. He honors his word."

He grunted, a response I perceived as neither positive nor negative, simply an acceptance of the situation. I understood. His life lay in the hands of the Great Spirit or Fate or whatever deity in which he believed. He could do nothing. When I came to know the Comanches better, I discovered in them a belief in predestination, not the same professed by Christians, rather a more practical conviction in which, when facing the inevitable, they accepted it with courage.

Minutes later, he retreated into the land of dreams. The Captain returned, having bagged three prairie hens, which we roasted over an open fire. Catching the drippings in a tin cup, he concocted a broth that, once it cooled, he fed to Quanah, who roused himself enough to drink. For the next twenty-four hours, the lad hovered between life and death, often closer to death, his breathing shallow, his fever high.

On the fourth day, as the sun peeked over the horizon, Quanah sat up, alert, the fever broken.

The Captain offered him our last bird, passing it to the boy, who ripped into the meat before tossing the bones in the brush. Finished, he wiped his fingers on his loincloth and rose on unsteady legs. "I go."

The Captain handed him his knife. "We will accompany you for a while, if you don't mind."

We packed up camp and lifted Quanah aboard his pony. He sat tall and straight, although as I steadied him, I sensed the strain in his coiled muscles. We traveled two

cook as well as our doctor, making use of her knowledge of herbs and roots and other heathen potions. She carried a knife in her belt, ready to use it either on the food or on us if we gave her any trouble, which we never did. Around her, we followed her rules, if for no other reason than she provided a protective shield against the heathens.

Did the Captain love Blue Feather? I'd seen the ways other white men treated their Indian women. Blue Feather ate at the table with him and the boys. The couple shared the same bed. When they conversed in English or Spanish, they did so with a comfortable intimacy. What I'm trying to say, not too well, is that he treated her the way a man should treat a woman. The fact she was a squaw didn't matter.

Despite his advanced age — he was in his late thirties when he brought Blue Feather home, she twenty years his junior — the Captain possessed a youthful vigor. He rode the same hours as we, worked as hard or harder than any of us. Two or three punchers were faster and more accurate with sidearms, yet none could match his abilities with a rifle. Once, he brought down a horse thief at half a mile, which I witnessed.

One morning before daybreak, we discovered three mustangs missing from the coral. The Captain and I mounted our own ponies and took out in pursuit. We picked up tracks easily enough. Perhaps because the thief stole only three horses, he believed we would overlook his transgression. Perhaps he believed that our time chasing him was worth more than the horses. The Captain took the thievery as a personal affront.

Near sundown as we topped a ridge, his dust revealed the fugitive's presence in the valley below. Though he must have known we trailed close behind, he refused to release his prizes. Had he done so, he could have avoided any chance of capture. With night approaching, he must have believed he would elude us.

The Captain dismounted, removed the rifle, a Sharps, the best single-shot, breech-loading rifle available, a .54-caliber rimfire, Model 1866 with a Buckhorn rear sight attached to a forty-four-inch octagon barrel. The weapon weighed nine pounds, but once the Captain tucked the stock into his shoulder, the weapon never wavered.

He inserted a shell and closed the breech. Lying flat on his belly, he ripped loose a handful of prairie grass, tossing the blades in the air to gauge the direction and strength of the wind. He planted his elbows in the earth and squeezed off a shot, the boom shattering the silence.

Smoke obscured the target, then the breeze whisked it away. It must have taken two or three seconds for the bullet to reach the rider, who tumbled from his mount. The horses trotted a hundred yards farther where they halted at a spring.

We rode down the slope to discover the thief still alive. The bullet had punctured a lung. With every breath, blood surged over his lips. We could do nothing for him. The slant of his eyes and the darker hue of his skin suggested a mixture of Mex and Indian. Slight of build, wiry rather than thin, he wore puncher's gear right down to his chaps, his only heathen regalia a pair of moccasins. For a quarter hour, he kept his eyes closed. Near the end, they opened, and he stared at the Captain as if he offered salvation. His lips moved without sound. After three tries, he spoke one word, "Nana." With that, he offered up a last sigh, and the lights in his eyes dimmed.

"Vaya con Dios." The Captain whispered the words, as lonely and sad as anything I'd ever heard.

We rounded up the horses and hobbled them. Afterward, we buried the man in soft sand and piled on rocks so he would be safe from scavengers.

That night we made a dry camp beside the grave. Although exhausted, neither of us fell asleep right away.

I said, "That was the greatest shot I've ever seen."

The Captain rolled on his side away from me, pulling the blanket up around his neck. "I only meant to wound him."

The Captain took the man's death hard, mainly I believe, because in him, he recognized some part of Waco. In those days, the world wasn't kind to half-breeds. Many of them, outcasts by whites and Indians alike, turned to thievery to survive. If the fellow had ridden up to the house, asked for a meal or a job, the boss would have given either or both on the spot. Many travelers survived because of the generosity of people like the Captain.

CHAPTER THREE

I could tell a hundred stories that covered the following twelve years, stories chock-full of adventure, but that would take the rest of my life. Suffice it to say, we existed on the edge of the frontier where death lurked behind the next bush or in the next arroyo. We persevered against the elements and against others of our ilk. Under such conditions, people not only learn to survive, they learn to prosper, none more so than Waco. During this period, one incident in particular has meaning above others because it sheds light on Waco and our belief in his supernatural abilities.

At four, Waco received a rare gift from his father, a pony. The boy possessed a natural ability and rode with the rhythm of an accomplished rider. By twelve, he was all legs as kids that age tend to be and had outgrown the pony. When he asked for another mount, his father told him, "We got no spares. We got three dozen waiting to be broke. Find one to your liking. Break it, if you can."

The next morning, the kid sprinted to the corral before any of us were out of the bunkhouse. He dropped his lariat around the neck of a stallion, wide in the withers, a mixture, part mustang, part something else, each half derived from magnificent stock, and frankly, the most beautiful animal I ever saw, his coat a pure black, black as his heart. That damned animal had yet to kill anyone, though not from lack of trying. When he tossed a rider, he bucked and stomped in an effort to grind him into dust.

I passed the corral as the lariat settled over the beast. Snorting, he pulled back, ready to kick out with his forelegs. Waco kept his voice low, soothing, confident. He continued talking as he drew closer, coiling the rope until he stood within inches. From his pocket, the kid withdrew a cube of sugar, holding it in his palm. Not me, not any of the boys, would have pulled such a stunt, fearing the creature would take fingers along with the treat. Yet, after a quick sniff, the beast snatched the sugar with a flick of his tongue.

With the black devil distracted, Waco made a hackamore with the rope, secured it over the animal's nose, and sprang aboard. Before Waco settled, the steed bucked and bucked again. I ran forward yelling for the kid to jump clear. I flung open the gate to go to his aid. Instead, the horse dashed past, so close the kid's knee knocked me on my backside, dust rising around me, blinding me, choking me. I retained enough sense to close the gate before any of the other stock escaped. In the passing of seconds, that creature carried Waco far out on the prairie, heading toward a rise we called Powder Hill.

The boy and stallion flew on the wind, their bodies in harmony, running wild under the morning sun, the world open before them. Tearing up the long slope, they arrived at the crest where that black devil sped toward the edge, which ended in a sheer drop of over a hundred feet. The beast, hearing the soft words of his companion, feeling the tug of the hackamore, slowed before coming to a complete halt less than ten feet from eternity. Waco leaned forward and stroked the beast's neck. The animal's sides heaved, his legs trembled.

The kid slid to the ground. From his shirt pocket, he drew another sugar cube, offering it to his new friend. The kid nuzzled the horse's nose, and the creature made no objection. "They call you devil horse, and so we will make sure they remember. Diablo. That's the name for you. There's not another like you. Together, we'll show them a thing or two."

Waco waited another five minutes until he and Diablo regained their breath, then took his time riding back down the hill. They were halfway to the ranch before the Captain and I arrived, sending dust swirling around us. We needn't have hurried.

"How did you manage it?" his father asked. "That bronc laid out plenty of punchers including your brothers."

"He just needed a friend, Captain, not a fella trying to break his spirit."

CHAPTER FOUR

Whenever Flynn and Dermot, eighteen, full-time punchers, watched their half brother riding the range with Diablo, they experienced outbursts of jealousy.

"We softened that cayuse," Flynn said to his brother. "We did the work. Me, especially. I rode it a dozen times."

As usual, Flynn exaggerated. He never "rode" Diablo. No one had, except for the kid. With the help of others, Flynn made it into the saddle on four different occasions rather than the dozen he claimed. Each attempt concluded with Flynn eating dust.

He spit. "Hell, I got more right to that horse than Waco."

With his curly blond locks, his piercing blue eyes, his chiseled features, Flynn had grown into a man who women found handsome, although as I have said, women were a rare commodity in our part of the country. Flynn courted Miriam Wilson, who lived with her family thirty miles southeast. He bragged of taking her to the barn and parting her legs.

Every morning when he woke at home or on the range, Flynn combed his hair, smoothed his golden mustache. He gave himself a bath once a week whether or not he needed it. He refrained from chewing tobacco, so his teeth kept their brilliance. Whenever he passed mirrored glass, he took a long drink of himself. On days he shined his Sunday-go-to-meeting boots or the metal finish of his Winchester, he stared at his reflection, which stared back with equal appreciation.

Despite his good looks, despite his success with women, he believed the world owed him. Exactly what I doubted he could have set to words. In him existed a discontent that often jaundiced his outlook. Over the years, his resentment of Waco sprouted like jimson weed, if for no other reason than the kid was an equal heir. "After the Captain kicks off, I don't cotton to sharing the ranch with a stinkin' breed. If he wants land, let him join his Injun brothers on the Staked Plains. He can share a tipi with that mother of his."

All this led to that morning in March '72 when events changed our perspectives of

Waco in unexpected and indelible ways. By then, he and Diablo had partnered close to a month. When the day ended, Waco watered Diablo, fed him oats, rubbed him down, all the while whispering to the animal as if imparting a philosophy of life. More than once when I passed them, that creature had its ears perked, listening.

Let me say now that we lived in such an isolated area that history passed without so much as a nod. Even the War between the States meant little. The white men in the Panhandle owned no slaves. The struggle to shore up that peculiar institution held no interest for them. Granted, we suffered privations during those years. Toward the end, flour and cartridges all but disappeared, and many a day passed without coffee or strong brew passing our lips.

It all changed once the war ended. The East wanted beef. We had plenty.

Preparing for a cattle drive, a formidable task, required all of us, including the kid, to work from dawn to dusk, sometimes longer. That year Waco, still too young, would not participate in the drive, yet he worked the roundup as hard as any. None except his brothers resented his appropriation of Diablo. In fact, we admired the kid. He showed plenty grit educating that horse.

As usual, the crew rose early and were saddling up when Flynn chose to make his move. I believe he wanted an audience. A cold wind blew from the north, and we buttoned our coats and tied down our hats with kerchiefs or secured them with bonnet strings fastened under our chins. Tumbleweeds rolled past in increasing numbers. We ate sand.

While Waco led Diablo from the stable, Flynn strode toward the corral, Dermot following as usual. The Captain was there, tightening his cinch. Sensing trouble, we watched Flynn cross the yard, climb through the railings and glare at Waco with contempt. "You've had this critter long enough. I put more effort breaking it than any puncher here. I broke him, not you."

Six years older than his half brother, Flynn stood a head taller, sported wider shoulders and more muscled arms. If it came to a fight between the two, we saw the outcome as obvious. Yet none dared interfere. The Captain believed arguments between brothers should be settled by them. He would step in only if things got out of hand.

Flynn snatched the reins from Waco. "He's mine. You got nothing to say about it."

Waco showed neither anger nor resentment. "He is not broke, Brother. Do not do this."

"You gonna stop me?" Flynn uttered a guttural laugh. "I would like to see you try. Indeed, I would."

He slipped a boot in the stirrup and threw a leg over Diablo. Before his rear touched the saddle, Flynn flew over the head of that black devil. He hit the dry, cracked earth with a resounding thud, his breath expelled in a whoosh. The animal reared, his forelegs crashing down, a metal shoe splitting Flynn's right cheek from eye to jaw. The creature reared again, intending to crush his skull. None could prevent it.

Except Waco.

He grabbed his brother by the coat collar and jerked him from under the hooves as they thundered down, the ground trembling with the impact. Waco threw himself forward, his hands held skyward. The kid spoke heathen words, his tone soft, melodic, commanding. Diablo settled to earth, his frame shuddering, his eyes wild. Waco stroked the creature's neck, and the beast pressed his muzzle into Waco's shoulder.

We carried the unconscious Flynn to the main house and laid him on the kitchen table. Blood pooled on the oak surface and dripped on the floor. At that point, we were uncertain about the extent of his injuries. For all we knew, Diablo had taken an eye along with half a face. Blood hid the socket. The Captain summoned Blue Feather, who approached with needle and thread.

By then, Flynn regained a measure of consciousness. "I'm gonna killed that damn horse." His voice was half threat, half sob. "I'll kill it, I tell you! I'll kill it!" Flynn balled his hands into fists as Blue Feather leaned over to inspect the laceration. "Get this squaw away from me! She ain't touching me!"

Blue Feather straightened, her expression emotionless, yet below her placid exterior, I sensed anger.

The Captain stood at the foot of the table gripping two bottles of whiskey he'd purchased at Dobson's Trading Post. "You will scar. There is no argument there. Blue Feather sews you up, maybe it won't be so bad. Maybe she can save that eye. It's your choice." He uncorked a bottle and handed it to his son. "Get drunk. It'll ease the pain."

Flynn finished the bottle and started on the second before he passed out. With a rag soaked in hot water, Blue Feather cleaned the wound. Afterward, she poured liquor over it. The pain aroused Flynn from his stupor. The Captain forced more liquor down his son's throat. With Flynn once more in the arms of Morpheus, Blue Feather pierced his flesh over a hundred times before she severed the thread with her teeth and tied off the end.

Three days later, Flynn climbed out of bed before sunrise. When he struck a lucifer and lit the lamp, he spotted his blurred reflection in the shaving mirror on the wall. The injury rose like a bloodied snake, his right eye drooped like melted candle wax. We heard his roar in the corral.

Sweeping his pistol from the bedside table, he stormed from the house. He threw open the barn door to discover Waco waiting.

Flynn curled his thumb around the hammer of the .44. "Out of the way, breed, or so help me God, I will put a slug in you, too."

The two faced each other inches apart. Waco stood his ground.

"You try," Waco said, "and I will open you from belly to chin."

His words were cold as winter wind.

Earlier that same year, the Captain had given Waco a Bowie knife for which he had sent all the way to Dallas. The perfectly balanced blade was over nine inches in length and close to two inches in width. The kid had carved his initials, WJC, in the ivory handle. He had owned knives before, although none this fine. He practiced every day, hours on end, tossing the weapon at targets, until if the mark lay within range, he couldn't miss. That knife became an extension of his arm: once he tossed it, his hand still guided it. From ten feet, he could skewer a snake. Once we witnessed him bring down a jackrabbit in full flight. After that feat, as we slapped him on the back and congratulated him, he said without humor, "Never happened before. Probably never will again."

Now Flynn glanced down to see the sharp point of that Bowie knife digging into his shirt.

With his left hand, Waco seized his brother's revolver. Flynn gripped it more tightly. Waco pricked him hard enough for him to feel the point. Flynn released his hold on his weapon and stepped out of the knife's reach. Waco slipped the knife in his belt and opened the rolling gate of the six-shooter, ejecting the cartridges one by one, each striking the ground with a muted thump. "You know what you are, Flynn. You are an idiot full of sound and fury, signifying nothing."

"What the hell does that mean?"

"You should read more, Flynn. You might learn you a thing or two from Shakespeare."

"It's just a damned horse." A sob escaped Flynn. "I'm your brother, for God's sake."

"You call me 'breed,' and now you plead 'brother?' Which am I, Flynn?"

They stared at each other a full minute before Flynn said, "I've always hated you."

Waco tossed the pistol at Flynn's feet, dust enshrouding the weapon. "Anything happens to Diablo, I will not kill you. As you say, you are my brother. Understand, I will take something from you. Fingers. An ear. Your hair."

Waco dangled his arms at his side as if inviting attack. Flynn knew better than to try. He was too weak from his injury, the kid too fast with the blade.

Flynn swept up the empty pistol and dragged himself from the stable, his boots kicking up dust that lingered in his wake.

CHAPTER FIVE

In May of '72, we started six thousand longhorns for Abilene. By then, Flynn had grown a full beard to cover his disfigurement. No hair grew on the damaged skin, so he greased his whiskers, pasting the hair over the scar. Because of his blond hair, the red gash showed through. His right eye drooped. Often, he fingered the scar, assessing its length and breath. When he talked with women, he faced them obliquely, as if he hoped they wouldn't take note.

We reached Abilene on the sixteenth of July. Three times we battled stampedes and once an outlaw band that tried to take the herd. Each incident cost us, and still we made the stockyards with a little over five thousand head. Once the boss paid us off, we yahooed the town, losing most of our wages at roulette or faro.

While we were on the drive, a most curious event happened back at the ranch.

Only one wrangler other than Waco stayed behind, MacInnis, stove up with busted ribs he suffered in a spill. His hands were knotted, and his bones never stopped aching, yet he could still toss a rope. Blue Feather attended the house, and Waco kept the cellar stocked with meat. Every few days, he and Diablo rode out on a hunt, never failing to bag prairie hens or a deer.

At the beginning of June, he rode five or seven miles beyond Powder Hill before he brought down a wild turkey. As he tied the dead creature to his saddle horn, he spotted buzzards riding the air currents. If they circled, the creature still lived. Curious, he headed Diablo in that direction.

Ahead lay a shallow wash. Since he had little or no idea as to the creature or the danger it represented, he removed the Sharps and dismounted. "Stay here, big fellow," he said to Diablo.

Reaching the bank of the dry wash, he discovered a common prairie tragedy. A young wolf lay twitching, blood staining its fur from two punctures on its right flank. The only reason it still lived was its size, the largest of its species Waco had ever seen — at least 140 pounds, clearly a male. The animal was broad across the shoulders, and his entire body rippled with muscle. Although his eyes remained open, the animal appeared incapable of movement. The gray fur contained streaks of red, which suggested mixed parentage.

As Waco approached, the beast bared his fangs, displaying a set of clean, sharp incisors that could crush a man's arm or leg. For the moment, he lacked the strength to do more than threaten.

Three feet away lay a rattlesnake in separate pieces. The wolf dog had won a victory, but the exertion spread the poison more quickly. Otherwise, the animal, a beautiful creature with so much life in front of him, might have survived. Waco didn't want him to die alone. Murmuring soothing words, he squatted and passed his palm along his neck, feeling his warmth, his tension.

He whistled. Diablo loped to the wash's edge. The kid snatched the canteen from the saddle horn and filled his palm with water. Most of us would never have proven so bold. We would have feared the animal would take our hand with the water. The beast growled, but catching the scent of water, darted out his tongue and licked the palm dry. Twice more Waco performed the charity.

Although certain he was too late, Waco pulled from his saddlebags leaves of a plant white people called Black Samson or Black Susan. The Comanches, too, knew its uses. It combated everything from colds to rheumatiz. The leaf also had the power to draw out poison from a snakebite. He wetted the leaves before laying them over the punctures.

He had come upon the dying animal near noon. By six, long after the wolf dog should have breathed his last breath, he clung to life. Waco unsaddled Diablo, fed him oats and rubbed him down with a stiff brush. He cleaned the bird, and building a fire from cow patties, cooked it. He cut pieces from the bone, ate some, then held out a piece to the wolf dog, who snatched the meat. By the time the fowl surrendered its last morsel of sustenance, the kid and the wolf dog had consumed equal shares. The buzzards disappeared, looking for a more accommodating meal.

When Waco offered the beast more water, he lifted his head and drank with far less difficulty. The kid harbored no illusions. This was a wild beast, an enemy of man, a killer of cattle. Once he discovered the creature, he should have put him out of his misery. No one would understand saving his life. He didn't fully understand either, except in some undefined way they shared an affinity. A white man would have scoffed at such an ill-defined explanation, but Waco's Indian blood gave him special insights. White men called them heathen superstitions.

Once the light died, the kid tossed his bedroll on the ground, circling the area with horsehair rope, a surefire way to keep rattlers from crawling in with him. The instant he laid his head down, he fell asleep. Twice during the night, the wolf dog tried to rise, his efforts waking Waco. Both times, the animal fell back. Around one in the morning, Waco tossed more brush and cow patties on the embers until flames shot sparks into the night air. He gave the animal more water.

An hour before dawn, Waco climbed out of his bedroll to discover the animal had slunk away, perhaps to die alone. The kid experienced a sense of loss.

He threw more cow patties on the embers, intending to make coffee. The flames blazed, casting light farther from the perimeter. Less than ten feet away, the wolf dog watched, his body tense, ready to bolt. With slow movement, Waco pulled from his shirt pocket two pieces of beef jerky. He chewed on a piece and held the other out, intoning words, gentle, soothing, hopeful. The animal

51

approached, sniffing the air until he stood within an inch of the dried meat. With a snap, those monstrous jaws closed on the jerky.

The beast backed away a dozen paces before he settled down, the jerky held between his front paws as he chewed, his gaze never leaving the kid.

Diablo stirred, pawing the ground. Waco climbed the bank, and removing his hat, poured in the last of the contents from the canteen. Diablo lapped the water until it was gone.

The Bar 4 C comprised over two thousand acres. The wranglers rounded up close to five thousand head, yet half that number still roamed free. Because water could be scarce, the Captain had dug two wells and installed pumps connected to underground springs. One lay less than three miles north, servicing the ranch and any Comanche who wandered by. Once Waco saddled Diablo, the kid headed there, sure the wolf dog would go his own way. By the end of the day, the animal would have only a vague recollection of him.

Instead, the beast loped along in the wash. When Waco drew rein, the wolf dog stopped, his keen eyes weighing the kid's every move.

"What is you want, feller? Are you measur-

ing me for your next meal? Or are you looking for more handouts?"

With unexpected speed, the animal darted
off and disappeared in the brush.

"So much for saying 'goodbye' or 'thank
you kindly.' " The kid laughed at his foolish-
ness. What the hell did he expect?

He nudged Diablo, and they trotted on
toward the well. He would refill his canteen
before he resumed hunting. Once he bagged
a deer or a couple of prairie hens, he'd head
for home.

The cry of a turkey disturbed the peace.
Waco figured coyotes had made a kill, yet
they hunted in packs and usually at night.
No yelp of victory followed. Instead, when
he came within sight of the well, he understood the bird's fate. The wolf dog waited
by the trough, the trophy in his mouth.

Waco dismounted and squatted beside
Diablo. Again, he uttered heathen words.
Comforted, the wolf dog took a tentative
step, then another until he dropped the bird
at Waco's feet. For the next four hours,
Waco stayed at the well. He carried a copy
of Shakespeare's tragedies. His back
propped against the trough, he opened the
book to *Hamlet,* his favorite among the col-
lection. He had read all the plays at least
once, some, like *Macbeth* and *Lear,* three or

four times. Flynn could read little beyond his name. Dermot was literate enough but uninterested. Among all the ranch hands, only Waco, his father, and I cottoned to books.

At noon, he made a fire and cooked the turkey. Tearing off the meat, he gave half to the wolf dog. Sometime past noon, Waco said, "I can call you wolf or I can give you a name. That's what white men do, give things names as a way to own them. They have a legion of names."

The animal perked his ears at the word "legion."

"I do not wish to own you, but 'Legion' it is. What do you say to that?"

Waco uttered a soft laugh, and the beast closed in until his head rested within inches. Reluctant to touch the creature, Waco feared he might take any move as aggressive. Instead, the kid held out his hand for the wolf dog to sniff. Only after Legion nudged the hand did Waco stroke the animal's neck.

"I see now that Diablo, you, and I are alike. We're half-breeds. Well, Old Son, if it means anything, we've got each other. Together, we'll show them a thing or two."

We returned from the trail drive in August, knowing that our world had changed in very fundamental ways. The Captain, richer by $25,000, upped our wages from ten dollars a month to twenty-five. He also expressed plans to build a larger house, one fit for him and his family. The only one among us who didn't share in our collective joy was Flynn, whose anger over his disfigurement grew exponentially. We couldn't remember the last time he smiled or enjoyed the most fundamental pleasures. As we shared drinks in Abilene's Trail Street Saloon, Dermot confronted Flynn. "Damnit, Flynn, you're alive. Ain't that enough?"

"It's all Waco's fault." Leaning over the bar, he stared down its length to his father. "You know it, too, Capt'n."

With Flynn's remark, all eyes turned to the Captain who lowered his beer mug and met his son's gaze. When he spoke, his tone said patience, but those who knew him understood anger lay just below the surface. It lay in the way he pronounced certain words, drawing them out so the listener could not fail to understand. "Waco kept Diablo from killing you. Had you said to me what you said to your brother, I would have let the horse have its way."

Flynn worked his features into a sneer, yet he could not hold the gaze of his father. He stared at his drink before finishing it.

"Come on, Dermot, let's get out of here. I got money. Let's find a whorehouse."

The Captain said, "Flynn, I once warned you about Waco. I still mean it. Nothing happens to him. If it does, you answer to me."

Flynn inflated his chest. "You think that scares me?"

"It should."

If Flynn ever thought about making another attempt on Waco's life, which I doubt, he discovered his chances reduced even more when, three miles from the ranch house, the kid rode up astride Diablo, the wolf dog loping at his side. Including the Captain, ten of us covered in trail dust, worn to the bone, gawked at the animal beside Waco. The sight woke us from our lethargy. Flynn clawed for his pistol.

The kid cradled the Sharps against his chest, his thumb curling around the hammer. "Stow it, Flynn."

Sensing Flynn's attitude, Legion bared his fangs and growled. Waco said a heathen word, and the creature fell silent, his bestial eyes locked on Flynn.

"So all of you know, my companion is Legion. Best no one gets in his way."

"Is that a threat?" the Captain asked.

"No, sir. Only a suggestion. He cottons to

56

me and Ma. That's all."

"You realize that's a full-grown wolf, don't you, Son?"

"He's part wolf, part dog, Captain. A mixture, like me." Waco focused his cold eyes on Flynn. "A breed."

CHAPTER SIX

Over the years, many tales circulated of Quanah Parker and the Quahadis, who earned a reputation as the most violent and warlike of the Comanche bands. They pillaged and murdered with impunity, and they knew survival tricks even the most experienced frontiersman refused to try. One such story claimed that, if they ran low on water, they drank the stomach contents of dead horses. Another claimed they roasted babies and ate them.

Although Quanah's mother, Cynthia Parker, was white, the Quahadis elected him chief, a unique event in their annals. Countless times, he exhibited his courage in battle. Though only in his early twenties, he defeated the invaders at every turn. Of all the Plains tribes, the Quahadis accumulated the most wealth, which they measured in horses.

In 1871, the government assigned Colonel Ranald Mackenzie and the Fourth Cavalry to combat the menace. In autumn, they ventured into Quahadi country. Believing he had the Quahadis trapped, Mackenzie marched his troops deep into the Llano Estacado, following a trail that led to the Freshwater Fork of the Brazos River, which meandered through a thirty-mile shallow valley called Blanco Canyon. Mackenzie discovered only a vacated encampment. On their second night in Blanco Canyon, when the vast bulk of the men slept, a string of piercing yells sounded throughout the camp followed by screams and gunshots. Quahadis galloped among the tents. Behind them came the thunder of six hundred army horses, loosed from their iron pickets.

Amid this stampeding hoard rode Quanah Parker, his face smeared with red and black paint, a devil straight from hell. Waving his pistol, he rode a pure black steed. Those who witnessed the spectacle that night would assure you that horse snorted fire. Oblivious to the bullets that cut the surrounding air, Quanah wheeled his mount and shot a young private, blowing the man's brains over the exterior of Colonel Mackenzie's tent.

Quanah had won a glorious victory, albeit a Pyrrhic one. The government reinforced Mackenzie with three thousand additional men, the largest force ever employed to hunt down and destroy an Indian band. In September of '72, Mackenzie and his Fourth Cavalry again invaded the Llano Estacado, killing fifty-two braves and wounding countless others. They also captured an entire herd of ponies. The Battle of the North Fork of the Red River, as it came to be known, the worst defeat in Comanche history, signaled the beginning of the end of the empire of the Quahadis.

We discovered the details a day after the battle when the Captain, Waco, and I encountered Quanah as we rounded up stray longhorns intending to brand them. No sooner had we built a fire and placed the branding iron in the flames than the Quahadis showed up. Legion knew of their presence before they arrived. So did the kid.

"How many?" the Captain asked.

"Twenty. Maybe more."

"Keep working." The Captain scratched his grizzled beard as if considering a move in a chess game.

They galloped into our camp, their faces full of war paint. Quanah in the center, his figure towering over the other braves. He had grown into a man who, much like the Captain, radiated confidence. His height and steel-gray eyes set him apart from other members of his tribe.

Three of the warriors sat bent over their ponies. Quanah gave an order, and braves laid their wounded on the ground.

"You once saved Quanah." He leveled his finger at the prone warriors. "Can you save these?"

During the Mexican War, the Captain had seen many who suffered injuries. He'd repaired a few himself and seen others at work. He kneeled beside each brave, inspecting the wounds. Afterward, he faced the Comanche chief. "The one shot here" — he placed his palm against the brave's stomach — "I can only make him comfortable until his spirit departs. The two others have bullets I must dig out."

"Will you do this for Quanah?"

"No need to ask." The Captain turned to Waco. "Put a kettle on the fire. I will need hot water." He pointed to me. "I have long johns in my saddlebags. Tear them into strips."

While we waited for the water to boil, the Comanche chief took a moment to appraise Waco. "The Little Captain has grown."

This was not the kid's first meeting with Quanah Parker. When he was eight, Blue Feather had returned to her people for a visit and taken Waco with her. From the mo-

61

ment of his arrival, the Comanche boys taunted Waco about his white blood. They played tricks on him and excluded him from their games. These abuses came to a head when a group of ten or twelve enclosed him within a circle. Though only a child, Waco showed no fear.

Of all the Quahadi boys, Straight Lance was the wildest, the toughest, the most willing to challenge Waco. A year older and a head taller, he bragged of his strength. In fairness, he bullied only Waco, never his own kind. "You are half white, half devil."

Waco looked into the eyes of his tormentor. "Is Quanah Parker half devil? He has white blood, too."

Straight Lance thumped his chest. "In his heart, Quanah all Quahadis."

With both hands, he shoved Waco, who landed on his backside.

Quanah Parker strode into the center of the boys. Naked to the waist, he wore a breechcloth over leggings, his only adornment a necklace of bear claws.

Waco feared he would support one of his own. Instead, he faced Straight Lance. "When I lay dying, this boy's father returned me to life. Without him, there would be no Quanah Parker."

After that, a group of seven boys included

Waco in their play, although Straight Lance and his followers continued to ignore him. When Waco returned two years later, he encountered much the same attitudes. Those who accepted Quanah's endorsement welcomed him, those who followed Straight Lance avoided him.

Now five years had passed since Waco had last seen the Comanche chief.

The kid sat beside the fire, one arm around Legion who remained on alert, his ears perked, his nostrils flaring. The Quahadis radiated a peculiar scent of the outdoors, of brush and of the earth, not offensive, only different, unfamiliar. Waco whispered a word, and the wolf dog sat.

" 'The Little Captain' is a fine name because it honors your father." Quanah allowed his gaze to fall on Legion before returning to Waco. "There comes a time we must step out of our father's shadow. You deserve a true Quahadi name. From this point forward, we will call you Brother Wolf. It is a name our people will come to honor."

He announced this to his warriors, who grunted approval. By now, most had dismounted, their fierce countenances replaced by more stoic expressions. Quanah ordered scouts to patrol the area to give us plenty of warning if the army showed up.

While the Captain worked on the brave who suffered the arm injury, he asked Waco to clean the wound of the brave with a bullet in his leg. When Waco pressed a cloth over the entry hole, his fingers touched a lump in the man's thigh. He slipped his knife from its sheath, held it over the flame for a few seconds and sliced an inch-long gash in the skin. A bullet slipped out, and Waco displayed a misshapen .44 slug in his open palm.

"A ricochet." He passed the spent bullet to the brave. "A treasure to pass to your grandchildren." I also removed from the Captain's saddlebags a bottle of whiskey he'd purchased at Dobson's Trading Post. The boss drank nary a drop while we worked. He carried it for medicinal purposes. I passed the bottle to Waco, who poured the liquid over the open areas of the wounded leg. It must have burned like blazes, but those heathens were experts at hiding their emotions.

The Captain dug for the slug buried in the shoulder of the other warrior. When he freed it, the hole was three inches wide, and the man had lost enough blood that it pooled under him. The Captain poured whiskey in the hole. Afterward, he bandaged the wound.

Quahadi sentries rode into camp and informed us they'd spotted army scouts. The Indians helped their wounded comrades on their ponies, even the warrior who was belly shot and dying. They refused to leave anyone behind, and for that, I admired them. Friendship and loyalty were not solely provinces of civilized man.

Before he mounted, Quanah offered his hand to the Captain, which surprised me. It was common knowledge the Comanche chief hated whites, yet he respected my boss as he did no other. With a glance at me, he nodded. Last, his gaze settled on Waco. "Be brave, Brother Wolf. I have seen the future. You have many trials ahead."

Since that day, I have often wondered at those words. Had he seen Waco's future in a peyote-induced dream or was it a prophecy by a shaman? Or, because of Waco's origins, did he make an obvious observation? Half-breeds had a rough time in the world, accepted neither by whites nor Indians. Quanah himself was an exception. Waco did not have the Comanche chief's advantages of growing up submersed in Quahadi culture. Waco straddled two worlds without a foothold in either.

Covering their tracks with brush, the Quahadis rode off.

We saw neither the cavalry nor their Tonkawa scouts, although Waco assured us they were within hailing distance. "The clatter of their horses is deafening."

We figured the scouts had spotted us. They must have believed if Quanah Parker and his band had come across us, we'd be dead.

Quanah Parker and the Quahadis escaped that day, but in June of '74, they suffered their worst defeat. A young Quahadi medicine man, Isa-tai, convinced the various tribes his magic made warriors impervious to white man's bullets. As a result, five hundred Comanche, Kiowa, and Cheyenne warriors swept down on Adobe Walls, a deserted outpost of four sod houses, where twenty-nine buffalo hunters congregated. The hunters, armed with Sharps .50-caliber rifles that could bring down a full-grown buffalo at a thousand yards, took cover inside the structures. The battle lasted four days. The hunters counted four dead, the Indians close to a hundred. The Quahadis retreated to the Llano Estacado, where they faced a bleak future.

In mid-October, the winds swept down from Canada, harbingers of a severe winter. Not only were the Quahadis fighting a defensive war, they had lost their food supply with the disappearance of the buffalo. To ease their suffering, the Captain pulled together twenty-five head of prime longhorn to deliver to Quanah Parker's band. He asked MacInnis and me to accompany him. We needed a fourth.

"I ain't handing cattle over to a bunch of ignorant redskins," said Flynn.

"If the army caught us, they'd toss us in the stockade and throw away the key," said Dermot.

When he heard his brothers turned down the job, Waco went straight to his father. "Take me, Captain. It's been a long time since I visited the Quahadis."

Once we gathered the longhorns, we headed them north. The second night, we housed them in a box canyon and erected a wall of brush to keep them contained.

As we ate a meal of beans and hardtack, Waco looked east, his expression intense, concerned. "Riders."

"Quahadis?" asked his father.

"Cavalry."

That night we saw their campfire half a mile away. An hour after daybreak, the ground mist heavy, we crossed paths with a sergeant and his squad of ten men. "Hold up there." He hailed us from twenty yards.

Emerging from the mist, they approached

in two columns, a Tonkawa scout guiding a squad of battle-hardened troops who wore clothing made for the trail rather than regulation uniforms. Wide-brim hats blocked the sun from faces and necks, loose-fitting coats kept them warm without impeding movement. Soft, non-regulation pants with extra pockets provided storage. Their weapons appeared as if they'd cleaned them that morning.

The sergeant offered a cursory salute to the Captain. "Good morning, sir."

His jacket displayed his stripes. His wore leather breeches to protect his legs from thorn bushes, his boots knee high to protect against rattlesnakes. He carried a repeating rifle, the breastplate so worn the engraved curlicues were mere suggestions. His side-arm was a non-standard Colt .44. "Can I ask what you're doing out here, sir?"

"I would think that is self-evident. We are rounding up strays. I am Captain Callahan of the Bar 4 C."

The sergeant waved a thumb northward. "You are dangerously near Comanche country."

"I am well aware of that." The Captain focused a hard stare on the man, the kind he often used on his sons when chastising them for a perceived sin. "You are trying to make a point, I believe."

"Only that you seem to have no fear of the Comanches. Why is that, sir?" His attention shifted to Waco.

"That boy is my son. His mother is part Comanche. So you are correct. I have no quarrel with them — nor with you."

"I meant no offense, Captain. I am only doing my duty — following orders."

"Which are?"

"To patrol the southern border of the Llano Estacado. We are to keep the hostiles from breaking containment. To make sure no one goes in or out."

The Captain touched his hat brim. "Then I wish you and your men good luck."

The sergeant laid spurs against his mount. The others fell in behind. The Tonk scout, a gaunt man well into his forties, remained until the last soldier passed. "I have been told a white rancher befriends the Quahadis."

"If you believe it is me, you should tell your sergeant."

"Had I done so, we might all be dead. The Quahadis wait within the mist. Twenty or more. They have been watching since yesterday. Of this, I have informed my sergeant."

After the Tonk departed, the Captain said, "He believes we are villains."

"Are we villains, Capt'n?" MacInnis looked in the direction of the departed scout.

"Regardless, I will not allow women and children to starve."

Not long after, we came across unshod pony tracks of five or six riders rather than the twenty the Tonk scout claimed. Then again, the Comanche had ways to disguise their numbers.

Neither the Captain nor Waco had any idea where to find the Quahadis. They found us. Three armed warriors, silent and ghostlike, materialized out of the mist alongside us. Legion perked his ears, announcing their presence, and Waco signaled the wolf dog to be quiet.

We spent the first night on the Staked Plains camped within sight of a salina, a salt lake. These depressions contained water for six or seven months, and for the rest of the year formed dry beds. This one, fast drying up, held a pool in the middle. We camped downwind, and the odor of salt hung in the air. As we drifted off to sleep, a crane passed overhead, its wings snapping like breaking tree branches. Landing in the salina, it trumpeted a call. To settle the cattle, upset by unfamiliar odors and sounds, Waco rode among them and sang, starting with the soft and melodic "Lorena." Before he finished the last note, I was asleep.

The following day, we reached Blanco Canyon where Quanah Parker and his people encamped. Their village, which comprised over a hundred tipis, bristled with life. We drove the cattle into a makeshift pen of rocks and brush. Once we settled them, Quanah Parker himself strode over.

The Captain offered his hand. "I am glad to see you are in good health, Mister Parker."

"It is good to see you, too, old friend." Quanah nodded a greeting to me. His gaze fell on Waco astride Diablo, Legion at his side. "You have grown, Brother Wolf. Are you a man yet?"

Waco took no offense, his answer as simple as the question. "Man or boy, I am who I am."

Pleased, Quanah smiled.

The Captain wandered away with Quanah, leaving MacInnis and me to unsaddle the horses, which gave us a good view of all that followed.

Waco went in search of those he knew from his previous visits. Before he traveled ten paces, Straight Lance and three of his followers blocked his path. "You come again to my village. You seek to buy our loyalty with cattle."

Waco understood the warrior meant to push him into a fight. To Legion, he said, "Sit. Stay."

The wolf dog obeyed, his ears at attention as he watched the other three boys.

"Legion will not interfere as long as it is a fair fight."

"Your animal knows the difference between what is fair and what is not?"

"Strike me. Legion will do nothing."

Straight Lance remained skeptical yet reluctant to call him a liar.

Waco dropped his arms, leaving himself vulnerable. "Come, strike me."

With an open palm, Straight Lance knocked Waco back a step. Legion remained on his haunches.

"Are we to fight then?" Waco asked.

"You are shorter than me. I am stronger. A victory over you will be without honor."

"True, you are taller. Stronger? There is one way to see."

"Then we fight."

"And the rules?"

"We do not bite. That is for women."

Each stood his ground, reluctant to begin, wary of each other.

A part of me wanted to rush over to protect Waco, which would have gone poorly with the Quahadis, not to mention the kid. He would never have forgiven me.

Straight Lance grew impatient, one of the few times I recognized an emotion in him or any Quahadi. He clenched his jaw and charged. He was faster than I expected, more agile. Their bodies slammed together. As they fell, Waco shifted his weight so they landed side by side. Scrambling to his feet, Waco threw a right, a solid punch that drove his opponent back to the ground. Stunned, Straight Lance wiped his lips, smearing blood. Rage twisted his face.

Waco back stepped, giving Straight Lance a chance to get to his feet, which I saw immediately as a mistake. He should have pounded the Indian until he couldn't get off the ground.

Waco threw two more punches, so fast they were blurs, each a rock-hard blow. Again, Straight Lance launched himself, a forearm catching Waco under the chin, sending him to the ground. Straight Lance hauled him to his feet and circled his arm around Waco's neck, cutting off his air. The warrior's grip was steel, unmovable, unbendable. Waco flung an elbow into the ribs of Straight Lance. He threw another and another, each a solid wallop. Straight Lance held on.

73

A voice cried out, "Enough!"

Straight Lance released his grip.

Waco dropped to his knees, gasping for air.

Quanah Parker stepped between the boys. "Brother Wolf and those with him are guests. Have you no shame —"

Waco scrambled to his feet. "No, sir. No, sir. Straight Lance — he was showing me ways the Quahadis —" he wanted to say "wrestle," but couldn't remember the word in their language "— the way the Quahadis defend themselves without weapons."

Quanah cast his gray eyes on Waco. "A lesson in the ways of the Quahadis, is it?" Turning to Straight Lance, he used his thumb to wipe blood from the boy's lip. When he spoke again, his tone was playful, ironic. "And Brother Wolf showed you the white man's way of defending himself. It is always important to learn new ways of fighting. Still, there will be no more lessons today or tomorrow — or any day."

Quanah left them.

Waco rubbed his neck where the muscles were already sore. "You had me beaten."

Straight Lance touched his bruised ribs. "Someday when we meet on the battlefield, I will kill you. When that happens, I know I have killed a warrior."

"That will not happen."

"You believe you are a greater warrior than Straight Lance?"

"It will not happen because I will never make war against the Quahadis."

The next morning as we climbed aboard our mounts, Quanah came to say farewell. A stiff wind blew from the north, whistling down the long valley and rippling the river water. It carried the scent of snow. We wrapped ourselves in coats and tightened the drawstrings on our hats.

Quanah clutched a buffalo robe close to his body. "This war goes badly for us. Let us hope the four of us meet again, if not on this side, then on the other."

CHAPTER SEVEN

In June of '75, Quanah Parker signed a peace treaty, whereupon the government resettled him and his people in Oklahoma Territory. A small band of Quahadis, less than a dozen warriors along with their women and children, led by Straight Lance and his father, Lone Wanderer, refused to surrender. They were the wildest and fiercest of the Quahadis, unrepentant marauders who, because of Quanah's relationship with the Captain, refrained from raiding the Bar 4 C. But how could you trust such heathens? Fearing the truce might not last, we persevered with patience and hope but kept our rifles and six-shooters within easy reach.

In late December, the Captain sent Waco and me to the north range to bring strays into the grazing area where the low-lying hills provided protection from the winds. In four days, we rounded up over eighty head, including calves, holding them in a ravine where we roped off the only exit. Our frosty breaths roiled the air. We drank coffee to warm our innards before we went off to find more strays. Less than a mile from camp, we encountered three warriors bent over a carcass of a cow. When they spotted us, two seized their bows, ready to defend their prize.

Waco reined in. "I see you, Straight Lance."

"I see you, Brother Wolf."

The kid nudged Diablo, Legion scurrying along beside them. The heathens still appeared wary of our presence. I do not mean to imply they feared us. For the past six months, the Army had pursued this last free remnant of the Quahadis. These fugitives trusted no one.

We dismounted to meet them on equal footing.

The warriors who accompanied Straight Lance showed the ravages of hunger. Their cheeks were sunken, their facial bones skeletal. Even Straight Lance appeared smaller, his once impressive bulk diminished. They looked more like beggars than warriors.

Straight Lance drew himself to his full height, a bloody knife in his hand. Because of the animosity between him and Waco, I stayed alert for trouble. Legion sensed the tension, too, his muscles tensed, his gaze fixed on the Quahadis.

"You wish to deny us food?" Straight Lance gripped the knife tighter.

Waco glanced at the dead beast. "Too much goes to waste by butchering it here. A mile back, we have more."

"We know. We have watched you."

"How many do you need to see you through the winter?"

"We take what we want."

"Yes, you can take what you want." A note of exasperation infected Waco's voice. "You once pointed out that I am only half Quahadi. This offer comes from my Quahadi half."

Straight Lance dropped the knife to his side. "We are no good with cattle. The soldiers would see us. They have many patrols."

Waco cast a glance at me. I understood his unasked question. "Suits me," I said.

"In three days, we will meet you at the headwaters of McClellan Creek with enough beef to see you through the winter. As for this one" — he pointed at the dead longhorn — "take what you can. Do not overburden yourselves."

Without a word, the warriors resumed

carving up the animal.

As Waco and I rode away, I said, "When we have not returned in the next couple of days, the Capt'n will start to worry."

"There's nothing we can do about that."

From the stories we heard, the entire band of renegade Quahadis, men, women and children, probably numbered between twenty-five and thirty souls. We pulled six longhorns from the ravine. Before sundown we traveled twelve miles and camped that night on the edge of a dry salina, the earth cracked, the salt showing in patches. Despite the cold that surrounded us like death, we went without a fire, afraid we might cross paths with an army patrol that would question our reasons for being so far from our range. We had our story of chasing strays. If they saw through our ruse, they'd arrest us. At the very least, they would turn us back.

After a cold supper, Waco and I turned in, pulling our bedrolls close, Legion between us. The wolf dog radiated furnace heat. I slept like the dead until morning when Waco climbed from under his blankets and stretched to unkink his muscles.

We spent a second night on the Staked Plains battling the cold, the threat of snow hanging in the air. On the third day with the shadows lengthening, we reached the headwaters of McClellan Creek, a marshy area that, this late in the season, separated into dozens of stagnant pools. There Straight Lance and his braves waited among a clump of trees.

That night after a meal of cooked beef, we slept with our backs to the blaze. Up to this point, the army had yet to invade this part of the Llano Estacado. The Quahadis were not so naïve to think their security absolute. They set out a guard whom Straight Lance relieved in the middle of the night.

Once we awoke and ate, Straight Lance stood and wiped his greasy fingers on his breeches. We stood with him. He faced Waco, and I feared more harsh words might ensue. Instead the Quahadi brave said, "I have misjudged you, Brother Wolf. In your heart, you are Quahadi."

The warriors rode off with the cattle. They never said thanks, except with their relaxed postures and less aggressive expressions. I admired them even more.

As we turned our mounts for home, I did so with a sense of pride. We had provided the Quahadis with food to make do until summer. Our actions should have appalled me. We gave aid to fugitives who raided and killed in ways I could scarcely fathom, their cruelties too numerous to list. Yet they suffered, too. The white man had killed hundreds of their people, destroyed their food supply, stolen ancestral lands.

Trail weary and bedraggled, we returned home after nine days, smelling food from a hundred yards out as we arrived for supper. We reached the house and dismounted. The Captain, Flynn, and Dermot met us on the porch. Blue Feather watched from the doorway.

"Where the hell have you been?" The Captain stuck his thumbs in his belt as he appraised us. "We've had riders out looking for you."

As Waco explained the circumstances, the veins in Flynn's neck turned rigid. "You gave those renegades our beef. You young whelp! That's money out of our pocket. I ought to horsewhip you."

"You wish to try?"

Flynn had six years on Waco. Taller by three inches, heavier by at least thirty pounds, he was a full-grown man, while the kid still had growing to do. Flynn harbored plenty of hard muscle, his thick build made for rough-and-tumble brawling. From his posturing, he was certain he could defeat the youngster. I thought so, too.

Flynn grinned. "You ain't going to interfere, are you, Capt'n? He's had this coming for a long while." He pointed at Legion. "Is this a fair fight or are you going sic that mongrel on me?"

Waco gave a command, and the wolf dog sat on its haunches. Waco's gaze never left his brother. "The only mongrel you have to fight is me."

The Captain glanced from Dermot to me. "No one durst interfere. Is that clear?"

He didn't have to warn me. I wasn't about to step between wildcats who wanted to tear each other apart. Yet I feared for Waco. Flynn would have no compunctions about maiming or even killing his half sibling.

With his fists at his side, Waco stood, waiting, anticipating. Moving in, Flynn hurled a roundhouse right. The kid sidestepped and delivered a left hook that connected with the scar, splitting it open. With a roar, Flynn swung on his heels and threw a body blow that caught Waco in the ribs and drove him back. Flynn charged, head down.

Although stunned, the kid once more slipped the larger man's grasp. As Flynn stumbled past, Waco kneed him in the face. Flynn straightened, blood streaming from his nose. He swung a wild backhand that caught Waco in the face and staggered him. Flynn seized him in a bear hug. For several moments, they drifted this way and that like dancing sleepwalkers. Waco was trapped, his breath cut off, his bones crackling.

Flynn had won. The Captain strode forward ready to call a halt to the fight. Before he uttered a word, Waco slapped his palms over his brother's ears three times, so hard each blow sounded like wet towels striking flesh. Flynn let go and covered his ears, leaving his middle open. The kid delivered a series of blows, so fast and so many I lost count. Gasping, Flynn collapsed to his knees.

The rage had built in Waco for too long, and too long he had suppressed it for the fight to end there. He threw an arm around his brother's neck, interlocking it with the other arm. Flynn struggled to get to his feet, and even when he did, the kid tightened his grip. In less than a minute, Flynn closed his eyes, his frame sagged, held up only because Waco refused to release him.

The Captain jumped forward. "That's enough, Son."

Waco held on, twisting right and left as if to rip his brother's head from his shoulders.

"Waco! That's enough!" The Captain shouted the command. It wasn't that the kid failed to obey his father. He had lost all semblance of rational thinking. His rage blotted out the world.

It took the Captain, Dermot, and me to pull the kid off Flynn. Even then, he fought us. To this day, I believe, if he'd reached Flynn again, he would have killed him.

As Waco slipped my hold, Dermot tackled him around the ankles. Waco hit the ground face first. I pounced on him, grabbing an arm, Dermot the other. He kicked and bucked like an unbroken mustang. When he finally ceased struggling, his father said, "Son?"

The kid offered no further resistance.

"It is over." Waco sounded himself.

The Captain glanced at Dermot and me, offering a nod. We released our holds and climbed to our feet.

I cast a glance at Blue Feather and realized she had saved our hides. She had a grip on Legion, stroking his neck, whispering to him, his ears perked as if he understood every word. If she had not stepped in, the wolf dog would have jumped us to protect Waco. The animal could not have understood we only protected his master from himself. Though Flynn was a mean, conniving son of a bitch, he and the kid shared the same blood. Guilt would have weighed too heavily.

Dermot and I picked Flynn off the ground

and carried him into the house, where we lowered him into a chair. By then he had opened his eyes, though I doubt he knew where he was or what had happened. Blue Feather left Legion by the door, went out of the room, and returned with a pan of water, a dishcloth hanging over the rim. She dipped the cloth in the water and cleaned Flynn's injuries. The touch of cool water roused him.

Waco stood over his brother. When he spoke, he sounded on the surface unemotional, but anger lingered among the words. "Never come at me again, Brother. The next time, there may be nobody to pull me off."

CHAPTER EIGHT

By '76, the cattle buyers had reestablished in Dodge City, where a railhead waited. In that year, Waco turned seventeen. The seeds of his legend had already sprouted among us, among the Indians, among anyone who resided in the Panhandle. The stories of his supernatural affinity with animals had grown until people who never met the kid believed he spoke the language of the beasts. For decades afterward, I heard many stories of his exploits. During the late '80s, a whole series of fanciful dime novels flooded the East, most exaggerations, if not bald-face lies.

The seeds of the legend fully bloomed in March when the Captain sent Blue Feather and Waco to Dobson's Trading Post on the Texas side of the Red River to purchase flour, salt, and other foodstuffs for the upcoming trail drive. We also needed cartridges, knives, extra Winchesters. The

Captain ordered Dermot and MacInnis along for protection. He knew the caprices of human nature, that men often looked for scapegoats and easy targets. A woman and a boy with skin that showed a darker hue offered easy marks.

In those days, Waco had yet to carry a six-shooter, relying instead on his Bowie knife and the breech-loading Sharps his father had passed along. Already his prowess with the Sharps exceeded the Captain's. Twice I saw him bring down a deer at more than half a mile, one in full flight. As good as the Captain was, he couldn't lay such a claim.

Sitting erect, Blue Feather drove the wagon. Waco rode Diablo, the wolf dog Legion trailing at his side. Dermot and MacInnis lagged behind the wagon on the lookout for trouble. Two days before they reached Dobson's, a cold wind charged down from Canada. The four travelers bundled in heavy coats. At night they gathered around fires, the wind cutting through MacInnis and Dermot as if they wore nothing at all. Waco and Blue Feather slept warm, the wolf dog nuzzling between them, their bodies sharing heat under thick Indian blankets.

An hour before sundown on the fourth day, the travelers observed the white plume from the smokehouse a mile before the buildings came into view. Dobson never let the flames die, keeping them going all through the night as he roasted beef, deer, and prairie hen for travelers eager for better food than jerky and hardtack.

At the trading post, the two whores, Ginger and Molly, lounged in front. Molly, a Bull Durham held between her lips, leaned against the building. She wore a low-cut dress, her large breasts on partial display. She was still under thirty, but encroaching wrinkles showed around her mouth and eyes. Women wore out fast on the frontier, especially whores because of the abuse their bodies and souls absorbed every day.

Both women struck poses. Ginger, a redhead and the better-looking of the two, eighteen at best, had worked at Dobson's for over a year. She rocked in a rickety chair, crossed her legs and hiked her skirt above her shapely ankles. Molly bent over pretending to brush dirt from her dress and displayed more of her breasts. She removed the cigarette and tossed the remnant to the wind. With indolent eyes, she appraised Waco who, though clean shaven, already projected the demeanor of a man. "Hey, Kid, would you like company? Ginger and me can provide a stirring good time."

Waco dismounted and tipped his hat. "Thank you kindly, ma'am. I grant you ladies are handsome beyond all necessity. Unfortunately, the Captain has given strict orders where to spend the money."

Molly laughed. "Do you always obey your daddy?"

"In this case, I think it prudent."

The trading post, a sod structure, was set back five hundred feet from water's edge. Emile Dobson, the trader, had learned a bitter lesson when in 1866 he constructed his business on the banks of the Red River. Heavy rains brought the bloodshot water rushing through the door, covering his goods in rust-colored silt. He rebuilt, and within a year, his trading post grew into the most frequented business along the river. Not only was he honest, but he served the best homemade brew in Texas and kept his whores clean and presentable.

Waco waited for his mother to climb down from the wagon. The two entered the trading post. Dermot and MacInnis took care of the mounts. Two other mustangs waited at the hitching post, their reins looped through iron rungs. The animals hung their heads, their hot breath roiling the evening air. Despite the chill, sweat glistened on their flanks.

Blue Feather pushed her way through the door, Waco following, and beside him, the massive mongrel. In a far corner, a potbellied stove provided the only light. Otherwise, the interior lay in deepening shadow. In her hand, Blue Feather clutched a list of supplies. Sown into her buckskin dress, she carried over $500. She may not have been able to read, yet the Captain trusted her with money more than any man, including his sons.

The moment Waco spotted the two men at the bar, their bottle empty, slivers of brown liquid coloring the bottom of their glasses, he sensed trouble. Perhaps it lay in the way they eyed his mother as she handed the list to Dobson, who studied it, his bald head lowered as he attempted to read the Captain's writing. Satisfied, he disappeared into the storeroom.

Both hardcases were in their late thirties with grizzled beards and sombreros pulled low, hiding their features. Their pants revealed slick butts, their coat collars and sleeves ragged around the edges. The men carried holstered .44s, their ivory handles brown and cracked. They put their heads together and whispered as they eyed Blue

Feather. Anxiety registered in their tense bodies.

Waco stepped away from the door, Legion close at his heels, neither making a sound as they blended with the shadows.

The drifters turned their full attention on his mother. Wranglers found Blue Feather a handsome woman. Though not as physically endowed as the first Mrs. Callahan, Blue Feather, with her high cheekbones and dark eyes, projected a patrician appearance, though I doubted she would have understood the term "patrician." Cowboys watched her on the sly, never making full eye contact. Occasionally, they remarked to one another on her graceful movements, her refined haughtiness. Those qualities plus her tendency to intimidate kept punchers at a distance.

The two hardcases didn't know her. They saw a squaw with a list, which meant she carried money or something of equal value. They finished their drinks and ambled down the bar until one stood on either side. The taller man grabbed her arm and whirled her so she faced them. He sported a hawk-like nose, and his Adam's apple bobbed when he talked. "You know, Rogers, it don't seem right, an Injun squaw parading around in a white man's store. Ought to be a law agin it."

"I think she has money she has stolen, Smith." The shorter one wore a belt buckle covered by a concha, the shell-like silver ornament that riders from South Texas often exhibited. "Maybe we should hold it for its rightful owner?"

The taller man, Smith, laughed, his lips curling over his gums to expose a missing front tooth. "Let's see what you got there."

He seized a breast.

His mother made no move or showed any expression except a subtle change in her eyes, a defiant hatred.

Neither man noticed the kid emerging from the shadows until he stood within five feet and cocked his Sharps.

The two men shifted their gazes to Waco.

Smith narrowed his eyes. His hand inched for his pistol. "That's a one-shot weapon, boy. You can't get both of us."

Legion growled, exposing his razor-sharp teeth.

"You'll be dead," Waco said. "My mother will dispatch your friend."

Rogers flinched, his eyes widening. "The squaw has a knife in my back."

Right then, Dobson returned from the storeroom toting a shotgun. He planted his elbows on the counter to steady his aim.

The double barrels were thirty inches in length, and the weapon weighed at least twelve pounds. A slight man, barely five feet, Dobson exhibited a toughness that belied his size. He cocked the left barrel followed by the right. "Lay them sidearms on the counter."

"What the hell?" Smith said. "You ain't taking the side of a squaw and a half-breed."

Dobson tapped the counter with the stock of the shotgun. "Unbuckle your belts. Put them on the counter. You got five seconds before I cut both of you in half."

As the hardcases unbuckled their belts, Dermot and MacInnis came through the front door.

"What's going on?" Dermot asked.

With lightning quickness, Waco slammed the stock of the Sharp into Smith's face, cracking his nose. Smith collapsed spread eagle on the dirt floor.

Rogers held up a hand as to ward off an attack. "I didn't lay hand on her. What Smith did is his business."

Waco drew his Bowie knife and leaned over the fallen man.

"You can't kill him." Dermot wrinkled his brow. Sweat moistened his forehead and beaded his blond mustache. "Tell him he can't kill this feller, Blue Feather."

With a quick pass of the knife, Waco sliced the man's lower lip more than an inch in length and clean through to the inside of the mouth. Blood spewed across the floor. The wound would scar, forever reminding the man of his transgression.

With slow precision, Waco wiped the blade on Smith's coat, leaving dark streaks against the cloth. "Make sure these two get on their way."

"Yeah — sure." Dermot reached for the pistols on the counter.

Waco laid his hand on them. "These no longer belong to them."

"This is dangerous country for unarmed men," Dermot said.

"They have rifles on their saddles. That's more than they deserve. This one" — Waco nodded to the man on the floor — "pawed my mother like she was meat."

Without another word, Dermot motioned to Rogers who lifted Smith, still groggy, his eyes unfocused, blood streaming from his nose and lip. Together they dragged him through the front door.

Dobson lowered the hammer of each barrel of the shotgun before he placed the weapon under the counter. "Please inform Mister Callahan I do not tolerate such behavior. When those two wandered in, I should have sent them on their way. Because they flashed money for a bottle, I overlooked their manners."

Waco again placed his hand on the pistols. "I would like one of these, Mister Dobson, if that is all right with you."

"I have no call on them. They're yours, son. However, I will take them in trade and offer you a better outfit."

Once again, he disappeared in the storeroom and reappeared carrying a belt, holster, and pistol, which he spread out on the counter. "I have never seen a rig like this. The man who sold it to me said the holster was molded wet to the gun." He slipped the Colt .44 into the holster made of thick, hard leather. The hammer and trigger were clear of impediments. "It has a seven-and-a-half-inch barrel. The total length is over twelve inches. It weights two and a half pounds, which gives it stability. Put it on. See how it fits."

Waco buckled the belt around his middle. The holster tilted forward a fraction of an inch. When Waco drew the pistol, it sprang out as if possessing a life of its own. Waco twirled the pistol once before he dropped it in the holster.

Dobson pointed to the confiscated weapons. "I will take these two in trade. You throw in an additional ten dollars, that rig is yours."

"It is worth a lot more than you are asking," said Waco.

"That it is. Now why would I take so little for it? It must be worth sixty or seventy dollars. Perhaps more. It's simple, my boy. The man who sold it to me had been a town marshal down around Val Verde. No longer had use for it. He was crippled with rheumatiz. I've had the rig for over six months. I have shown it to a dozen punchers, not a one interested. They had their own and weren't willing to pay my price. You have no six-shooter. As for these" — he patted the confiscated pistols — "punchers are always looking for a cheap second gun. I can sell each for ten dollars. Throw in your ten, I've made a fifteen-dollar profit."

"I'm afraid I can't take it, Mister Dobson. I have no coin at present."

"I hear you are going on the drive with your pa. Is he paying you wages?"

"Same as any rider."

"See me when you get back." Dobson waved a thumb over his shoulder. "Take it down by the river. Try it out."

A nod from his mother gave the kid all the permission he needed. With a wave, Waco signaled the wolf dog, and they left

Blue Feather to oversee the supplies. By the time Waco stepped outside, the troublemakers, Rogers and Smith, heading west, were mere shadows in the darkening landscape. The taller man, Smith, listed right.

"We had to tie him on," Dermot said. "You ruined that man."

"He is fortunate."

"I don't see how."

"I would have killed him. You saved me from going completely heathen. Be sure to tell Flynn how close I came."

"You're bluffing. You weren't really going to kill him."

"Believe what you want."

With Legion at his heels, Waco headed for the river, where last light reflected off ripples. The underbelly of clouds glowed orange. Dermot trailed behind. At river's edge, Waco inadvertently kicked a metal cup, the side bent, the rim crooked. Red mud caked to a rock-solid hardness filled the inside. Snatching the cup, Waco threw it out over the water that ran swift on each side of a sandbar. Ten yards out, it dropped in the mud, half its bulk sinking out of sight. Thinking it a game, Legion jumped into the water to retrieve the object. Waco called him back. The beast dashed ten feet upstream where he sat and watched.

Last light glinted off the rusted metal. Waco drew the .44, cocked it, and fired. The bullet struck with a distinct ping, ricocheting into the far bank. He waited for the smoke to clear. The sun sank behind the horizon, only seconds of daylight remaining. Waco squeezed off another shot. The cup leapt six inches from the mud before it tumbled back.

"Damn!" Dermot said. "That's as good a shooting as I've ever seen."

"Shooting a pistol is like pointing a finger. Anybody can point a finger." Waco ejected the spent shells and replaced them with fresh rounds.

Dermot hooked his thumbs in his belt, his expression one of exasperation. "Things come too easy for you, kid. Fellows like me struggle to break a horse while you feed an outlaw stallion a couple of sugar cubes, and he's yours. You tame a wolf that's a closer friend than any human. You plug a target I can barely see."

"Nothing comes easy. I'm a breed, remember."

"You never heard me use that word."

"Not aloud."

"I'm not Flynn."

"You're his shadow."

CHAPTER NINE

Dobson kept a corner empty in the store-room where, for a slight charge, travelers bedded down. Because of the trouble with the drifters, he dispensed with the charges on this occasion, using the accommodations as another form of apology. Throughout the night, the wind howled around the trading post. Waco rolled up in his bedroll, his mother in hers, Legion snuggled between them. Before daybreak, they awoke. The wind had died, the cold remained. Within the confines of the storehouse, their frosty breaths lingered in the air. By first light, they were a mile west of Dobson's.

From the start, Waco battled an uneasy feeling. He wished now he had taken the rifles from the two hardcases.

For most of the day, they traveled through rolling hills, none higher than fifty feet, the horizon often closed off to their sight. Waco, Diablo, and the wolf dog rode point. With less than an hour of daylight remaining, Waco drew rein, stood in the stirrups, and peered north. The rest of the caravan halted.

Dermot rode up beside him. "What is it?"

"Smoke."

Dermot sniffed the air. "I don't smell nothin'."

Waco shifted in the saddle to face Dermot, whose blond hair crept from under his hat, individual strands highlighted by the dying sun.

"Stay here," Waco said.

Dermot called after him. Waco gave no indication he heard.

Within minutes, he came upon a faint glow that tinted the crest of a hill. His Sharps cradled in his arms, Waco slid from the saddle and sprinted up the incline, then threw himself to the ground. Legion lay next to him. The kid peered over the top.

Twenty yards away, Rogers and Smith abided in the firelight, their attention concentrated on a Comanche warrior, Straight Lance, who lay with his hands and feet tied, his only clothing a breechcloth and moccasins. His dark hair hung loose, damp with perspiration. A headband circled his head, a single eagle feather attached.

The curled tip of a running iron rested in blazing embers. These days, only rustlers used running irons to change legitimate brands on cattle or horses. Blisters showed on the naked chest of the Quahadi brave.

With a gloved hand, Rogers grasped the straight end of the iron. He stirred the embers, and the sparks shot into the dark sky. He removed the iron. The tip glowed orange. Grinning, he guided the curved end toward the warrior's left eye. The exhausted brave showed no fear.

Waco cocked the hammer of the Sharps, and Rogers lifted his gaze. The boom of the rifle echoed through the night. The slug lifted Rogers and slammed him into Smith, sending both to the ground. Revolver in hand, Waco dashed down the slope, ready to plug Smith if he made a move. The collision had knocked him senseless. Dark patches discolored the skin under both eyes. The sliced lip leaked blood.

Baring his teeth, Legion stood over the fallen man.

Waco unsheathed his Bowie knife, and with a quick pass, severed the bonds securing Straight Lance. He helped the brave stand. A half-dozen blisters marred the perfect symmetry of his chest. He swayed, ready to collapse, yet he drew himself straight, his teeth clenched.

Smith extended a hand for a Winchester a

foot away. Legion sprang forward, his jaws closing on the man's wrist. Smith screamed as bones snapped.

Waco said, "Enough, Legion."

Releasing his hold, the wolf dog stood vigilant, snarling.

Waco snatched the Winchester, passing the weapon to the Comanche, who tossed it aside. He staggered to the pile of his weapons and returned with a knife.

The Comanche touched the blade. "Is this man mine?"

Though Straight Lance spoke in his tongue, Smith must have divined his intent. His moans grew louder.

Waco said, "My camp is south. Come with me. We need to attend to those burns."

The Indian fixed his cold stare on Smith. "He bragged of killing my people, of taking scalps of children."

"Kill him quick then. Let's be on our way."

"Not so quick."

Smith watched in wide-eyed terror. "You can't let him do this! You got white blood in you. This ain't right!"

Straight Lance ripped off one of Smith's boots and Smith kicked out. Straight Lance caught the leg, and with a swipe, cut the tendon that connects the foot with the leg, the blade penetrating until it scraped bone.

He repeated the maneuver on the other leg. Blood poured from the fresh wounds. All the while Smith implored Waco to put a stop to it. Straight Lance seized a handful of the man's hair and drew his blade across the hairline. Smith screamed until he passed out. Straight Lance sliced and pulled and sliced until the scalp snapped free. With contempt, he tossed the scalp in the fire where the blaze curled the skin and shriveled the hair.

Sickened by the sight, Waco turned and whistled. Seconds later, Diablo came over the crest of the hill and trotted down the slope. Waco unsaddled the ponies of Rogers and Smith. With a slap on their rumps, he sent them fleeing into the night. Afterward, he collected the Winchesters of the men and climbed aboard Diablo.

Straight Lance found his pony a few steps from the firelight. Grasping the mustang's mane, he pulled himself aboard. He rode stiffly, the blisters leaking a brownish fluid. A hundred yards before they reached camp, Waco called out. When he entered the firelight, Dermot and MacInnis had their rifles cocked.

"We heard a shot." Dermot shielded his eyes against the glare of their firelight. "Is that a Comanch with you?"

Waco passed the rifles to MacInnis before he dismounted. Straight Lance had grown so stiff that Waco helped him from his pony. Blue Feather ground up leaves of Black Susan and stirred in axle grease. By firelight she spread the mixture over the blisters. Straight Lance displayed no emotion, his gaze fixed on the darkness.

"What happened?" Dermot asked.

"The two men from Dobson's used a running iron on him."

Dermot stared into the darkness as if he feared the villains lurked in the shadows.

"They won't be coming," Waco said.

"You killed two white men to save the life of a renegade Comanche?" Dermot said.

"I killed one. I gave the other to Straight Lance."

Dermot swallowed. Sweat beaded his forehead.

Waco smiled. "Looks like I have turned pure heathen after all, Brother."

CHAPTER TEN

By the next morning, the cold spell had broken. Once the sun cleared the horizon, the travelers removed their coats. In this wild country, roads were little more than cow tracks, the grassland often waist high, the land flat. Ordinarily they made less than fifteen miles a day, and since they carried a wounded man in the back of the wagon, Blue Feather kept a slower pace, which brought forth a complaint from Dermot.

"Dammit, at this rate, we won't be back at the ranch till next year."

MacInnis spit, a glob of tobacco juice discoloring the grass. "What's the hurry, Dermot? You got a pressing appointment?" He ran an arm across his mouth, smearing juice on his sleeve.

"I don't cotton playing nursemaid to a Comanche," Dermot said. "It ain't a proper thing for white men."

"I'd stow such talk if I was you." MacInnis rode up beside Blue Feather and tipped his hat. "A good morning to you, ma'am, and a fine morning it is."

Around noon, Waco spotted dust approaching from the northeast. He called for Blue Feather to halt the wagon. Legion bared his fangs.

Dermot reached for his pistol.

Waco jerked the weapon from his brother's hand.

"What the hell?" Dermot said.

Standing in his stirrups, Waco held the .44 above his head and called out in his Comanche tongue. "I see you, my brothers."

Bows drawn, arrows notched, five warriors rose out of the grass. Legion growled, but another word from the kid silenced the animal.

MacInnis curled both hands over his saddle horn, keeping them clear of his revolver.

Minutes later, five additional mounted warriors arrived, dust rolling over them as they formed a half circle around the wagon. Waco recognized the leader — Lone Wanderer. He wore his grizzled black hair long and unbraided. He carried a breech-loading rifle at least twenty years old, the varnish long ago worn from the stock.

Waco had met him twice when he accompanied his mother to the Quahadis. Lone Wanderer tolerated Waco but kept his distance, as if he believed his white blood might be infectious. Now he met Waco with a stern, unforgiving expression. "You have stolen my son."

Straight Lance slid from the wagon, his bare chest exposed, his wounds already healing because of Blue Feather's ointment. "I am here, my father."

From the front of the wagon, Blue Feather climbed down and faced Lone Wanderer. Not a word passed between them. He had sold her to the Captain for a half-dozen horses. That sounds harsh, yet she agreed to the bargain. As I said before, the Captain treated her with the same respect as the first Mrs. Callahan.

His expression stoic, Straight Lance moved stiffly because of the crusted injuries. "Brother Wolf saved me from white men who did me harm. Blue Feather attended my wounds."

"White men did this?" Lone Wanderer cast his eyes on Dermot and MacInnis.

"These men took no part," Straight Lance said.

"And those who did?"

"They provide a feast for the coyotes and

vultures."

Straight Lance's pony was tied to the wagon. With a tug, the young warrior freed his mustang and leapt aboard. The effort opened two wounds. Blood trickled down his chest. He urged his mount in close to Waco. "For as long as the wind blows, we are brothers." He plucked the eagle feather from his headband and passed it to Waco.

Waco stuck the feather in his hatband. "Our bond is a gift I will cherish."

The Comanche wheeled their mounts and rode off. Those in the grass disappeared as if the earth swallowed them.

Waco dropped the .44 back in his brother's holster. "You almost got yourself killed."

MacInnis spit. "Goddamit, Dermot, you almost got us all killed. When it comes to dealing with Comanches, best you listen to Waco."

From that point on, the stories spread. Dermot and MacInnis told the punchers, who in turn passed it on, embellishing it each time they told it. Soon white people laid a moniker on Waco — "The Comanche Kid." I truly believe he appreciated "Brother Wolf" because the title denoted respect. "The Comanche Kid" implied scorn, as if by associating him with the Quahadis, he was less than human. Whatever people chose to call him, the name carried a measure of awe. Even though not yet eighteen, Waco had twice bested trail-hardened villains, the second time sending them to their maker. The bodies disappeared, consumed by predators. Only bleached bones endured, their location a mystery to all except Waco and Straight Lance. Even their names, which we suspected were false, would soon be forgotten, yet their demise cemented the legend of Waco Joseph Callahan, Brother Wolf, the Comanche Kid.

Waco led his group to the ranch without further incident, arriving at suppertime the fourth day from Dobson's. The Captain met them on the porch of his new house built on the foundation of the old, with four bedrooms, one for each of the boys and one for the Captain and Blue Feather. It had a wood floor and a brick fireplace with a chimney. The Captain hired an engineer from Dallas who drilled a well and installed a water pump in the kitchen. None of us had ever heard of such a thing.

Even before Waco dismounted, the Captain waved the kid into the house. Once in the living room, he faced his wife and son. "I can see by the look on Dermot's face, you had trouble."

In a few words, Waco related his run-in

with the hardcases at the trading post.

"That ended it?" his father asked.

"No, sir. That came the next day."

Once again, Waco recounted the events. The Captain listened, his expression never changing until Waco ended with the last bit of information.

"You gave a white man to a Comanche?"

"Smith bragged about taking scalps of Quahadi children. It was my brother's right."

"Your brother?"

"For as long as the wind blows."

"What of Flynn and Dermot? They are your brothers."

Blue Feather uttered a despairing grunt. Exasperated, the Captain frowned. "What is that supposed to mean?"

Waco tapped his chest so he drew the Captain's attention. "You know as well as I, Flynn and Dermot bear me no love."

For a moment, the Captain appeared at a loss. When he found his tongue, he pointed to the holstered pistol. "Where did you gain the weapon?"

"I made a deal with Emile Dobson. It was a fair trade."

"And what do you purport is its use?"

"Shooting snakes. There are some about the ranch. I am sure they will be on the trail to Dodge, too."

The Captain reached for a bottle on the table and uncorked it. He poured whiskey into two glasses and handed one to Waco.

The kid had never tasted liquor. "I am half redskin. From what I understand, it is against the law to offer me liquor."

"Either share the drink or lay it aside — your choice — but you do not have the right to talk down to me, Son."

Waco lifted the glass in a salute and drank the contents in single swallow. The whiskey burned his throat. The Captain held out the bottle offering a refill. Although a mildly pleasing aftertaste lingered, Waco waved it off, not trusting his voice.

"Good whiskey should be sipped," The Captain said. "The manner in which you drank was callous, infantile, the same way you talk of killing a man. Killing can become too easy if we justify it so casually."

"You miss the point, Captain. I did not kill a human being."

The Captain sipped his drink. "You killed a man to save another's life — that I under-stand — though people like us pay a price."

"People like us? Have you forgotten I have Comanche blood running through my veins?"

111

"You're my son," the Captain said. "That is the only blood that matters."

CHAPTER ELEVEN

Each son had his own room furnished with a fine feathered mattress and soft pillows, yet Waco slept in the stable, curled up in his bedroll, Legion nuzzling him so they warmed each other and protected Diablo. Waco remembered his brother's threat. Perhaps that is why he learned to use his new 44. In the evening he took himself four or five hundred yards from the cattle where he set pebbles on rocks. Every time his revolver leapt from its holster, he shattered a pebble. He was the closest I ever saw to damned near perfect.

Flynn saw, too, and ran his fingers over his raised scar. He was twenty-three now, and in the years since Diablo inflicted the wound, his hatred of the mustang and of Waco had grown. The beating at the hands of Waco only added to his bitterness. We saw it — so did the Captain — in his son's narrowed eyes, the hard set to his mouth,

113

the hateful glances. Flynn no longer courted Miriam Wilson, who married a merchant from Dallas and moved away. We were unsure who broke it off, although most assumed the girl. For Flynn, Miriam's desertion added another grievance against Waco.

Despite his open hostility, Flynn knew better than to act against his half brother. His father's warning stood front and center. Even more compelling, Waco's ability with a six-shooter far outdistanced Flynn's, who tried to downplay Waco's talent. "Sure, he's fast and can hit what he aims at. Still, there's a big different between shooting a target and facing a man straight on."

When Dermot reminded him of the death of the two hardcases, Flynn shrugged. "Doesn't count. He shot 'em from ambush. Face to face — that takes a real man, not a boy."

At the time, they rode herd with MacInnis who seldom hid his thoughts. "Goddamit, Flynn, when did you ever draw on a feller? You're full of horseshit."

Flynn glowered at MacInnis. "You looking to get fired?"

"The Captain hired me. He'll do the firing, not you." MacInnis spit and wiped his grizzled beard with his sleeve.

"You worthless old —"

Before Flynn concluded his sentence, Mac-Innis galloped ahead, leaving the two brothers eating dust.

In the weeks following Waco's return from Dobson's Trading Post, he worked harder than anyone rounding up cattle, branding strays, bedding them down at night. We slept beside the herd never seeing the inside of a building for close to a month, and we smelled worse than the cattle. Most days we struggled before dawn until after dark. By day's end, exhausted, we ate and fell into our bedrolls, fast asleep the moment our heads touched our saddles. Not Waco. Before he fed himself, he groomed Diablo and paid attention to Legion. Except for the night riders, the kid was the last to sleep, the first to wake, so conscientious he made his brothers appear lazy, especially Flynn, who was quick with a complaint. The day was too hot or too dusty, the cattle stupid, the ramada decrepit. When trouble found him, it was because the lariat was frayed or his saddle worn or the mayflies too thick. While branding a calf, Flynn pulled the iron too early and had to brand the animal twice. "Goddamn fire ain't hot enough. MacInnis built it. It's his fault."

Dermot untied the calf, and with a slap, sent it to its mother that waited fifty yards away. "You're always blaming somebody, Flynn. It ain't never your fault. Just stow it, will you?"

Flynn waved the branding iron at his brother. "How'd you like me to bend this over your skull? Just say so. I'd be more'n happy to oblige."

CHAPTER TWELVE

On the first of June 1876, we began the drive five hundred miles north to Dodge City, pushing close to four thousand head, which meant we would reach our destination early to mid-August. Liquor, gambling, and whores awaited at trail's end.

We had to get there first. Stampede was always our biggest fear, that once the cattle started running, our mounts would stumble, and we would fall under the hooves of the thundering herd. Anything could set the herd running — a pack of lobo wolves, a clap of thunder, a gunshot. From morning to dusk, we drove the cattle until we exhausted them. At night, riders circled the herd singing soft lullabies. Most of us had trouble carrying a tune. We hit all the notes, usually off key. Though only seventeen, Waco sang in a deep bass. He knew all the words to "Lorena," "The Unfortunate Lad," "Amazing Grace," and he sang with quiet authority. The times I rode nighthawk, I didn't mind so much as long as the Captain paired me with the kid. I swear, his soothing vocals not only calmed the cattle, it relaxed me to the point I dozed in the saddle.

Among the bulls, we had two troublemakers, Curly, so named because his horns twisted at oblique angles, and Walleye, given the moniker because an opaque film colored his right eye. When a stampede happened, no matter which way the herd bolted or which segment started first, those two found their way to the front. If a rider came abreast, he'd turn those critters until the cattle milled about exhausted. Once the stampede ended, we'd hear Waco again, his easygoing tones providing instant comfort.

Stampedes happened in short bursts. The dime novelists would have you believe stampeding cows, if unchecked, would run for hours. In reality, after a mile or so, they spent their energy, but if we failed to turn them, by the time they halted they would be spread out over the prairie. In that case, we would lose three or four days rounding them up and getting them moving again.

One morning over breakfast, all of us exhausted after such an incident the night before, a young puncher commented that every morning he prayed to God to keep him safe from a stampede. He asked Waco if he prayed. The puncher's expression was guileless.

If Waco took offense, he never let on. "What will happen, will happen, though we have some control over our lives."

"How so?"

"Say I am sitting under a tree during a storm. Lightning strikes the tree and kills me. I can do nothing about the lightning. It goes where it wants."

He left the remainder of his story un-stated, yet we understood his point. It wasn't the lightning at fault, rather where one chose to sit.

We reached the Red River on the tenth to find it swollen, water jumping its banks. We waited three days before the water reverted to its placid state, and we crossed into Oklahoma Territory, Cheyenne country. At dusk as we gathered around the chuck wagon, Waco informed the Captain that we had company coming. "Six riders coming from the east."

"Indians?" asked the boss.

"Cavalry."

Sure enough, twenty minutes later with the darkness approaching, a corporal and five recruits drifted into camp, the insignia on the caps and jackets stating they were property of the Fifth Cavalry from Fort Davis. Their mounts, which bore the army's brand, appeared as bedraggled as their riders, covered in trail dust, their faces wan, their expressions bleak. The soldier boys carried breech-loading Springfield rifles strung across their saddles.

The corporal halted the riders and regarded the Captain who stepped forward.

"We seen your dust," said the corporal. "We hoped you was white men."

A third of our crew were colored fellows like me, most former slaves. Unless someone brought it up, it seldom became an issue. Funny thing about working side by side with men, white or colored. On a trail drive, the only thing that counted was character.

"Light," the Captain said. "Have some grub."

For the next hour, they sat around the campfire sharing hardtack and beans. Corporal Haley, who hailed from New Jersey, fought at Shiloh, yet he counted his time in the West in months, not years. None of his young charges had fought Indians.

So what? we asked. The Plains Indians had never bothered us.

"The commander ordered us to escort ranchers and homesteaders to the fort, if that is their wish." The corporal stared into the fire. "The Cheyenne and Sioux joined forces. They wiped out General Custer's whole command at Little Big Horn. Over two hundred and fifty men, skewered, scalped, mutilated. The whole West is ablaze. No white person is safe. It's our job to wipe them heathens from the face of the earth. They're filth, vermin."

When Waco could no longer abide the vitriol, he stepped into the light. The feather in his hatband shimmered in the soft breeze. While the rest of our crew sported beards or handlebar mustaches and muttonchops, Waco was clean shaven, which only exposed his origins all the more. In addition, his youthful features belied his maturity. In a clear voice free of anger, he said, "The Cheyenne and Sioux, the Arapaho and Pawnee, the Comanche and Apache see the world the same as you. They believe they only will be safe if they wipe out every white man west of the Mississippi."

The corporal jumped to his feet, his empty plate clattering to the ground. "Listen, you half-breed son of a —"

The Captain stepped between the two men. "He is my son. No man dares insult him."

"Please step out of the way, Captain."

121

Waco kept his hands to his side, his tone soft, disarming.

"If I do, you'll kill him."

"If that is his wish."

The recruits, a bunch of scared kids, looked to each other, not knowing what they should do. The Captain set them straight. "This is between these men. No one durst interfere." He stepped away. "It will be best if you move on, Corporal. However, if you draw on my son, he will put three in your belly before you clear the holster."

"He can't be that fast." The slightest of tremors shook the corporal's voice.

Although Flynn was out night riding, Dermot sat among us, ready to duck if the shooting started. "The Captain ain't exaggerating," he said. "I've seen the kid shoot. We all have."

Often when dark fell, the wolf dog disappeared, hunting we figured. Now, as if sensing trouble, he materialized from the shadows, growling, his teeth bared.

"You have proven hospitable." The corporal's pitch rose half an octave higher on the last word. "I won't spoil your good intentions."

He ordered his boys to saddle up. When they mounted, the corporal's steed must have felt his tension and pawed the earth.

Waco strolled over. Knowing the kid's temper, we feared the confrontation about to escalate.

Instead, Waco laid a hand on the horse's neck, calming the animal. "Before sundown, I saw smoke to the northwest."

The corporal winced. "If there is trouble in that direction, that must be our destination."

"Keep to the gullies, the dry washes. Stay away from ridges."

"Why do you tell me this?"

"Regardless of what you believe, I wish you no harm. Best to remember this is their homeland. They know every inch of it."

"They're savages."

"They say the same of you." Crouching before the fire, holding his palms to the flames, Waco showed his back to the soldier boys. "They know you are here. There have been at least three braves watching since you rode in."

"Why didn't you tell me?" The corporal looked right and left, peering into the darkness. "If we'd known, we could have taken prisoners."

"As you were quick to point out, I am a half-breed. Those braves are full-blooded Cheyenne. I couldn't have caught them any more than I can catch the wind. If you had tried, you would have dead soldiers to attend."

"You talk as if you love them."

"I do not hate them. I do respect them. Lack of respect will get you killed."

The corporal faced forward, and with a kick, urged his mount into the night.

Once the soldiers were out of hearing, the Captain asked, "Will they survive?"

With a stick, Waco stirred the embers, sending sparks into the dark that the air quickly extinguished. "If they travel northwest, they are dead men riding."

For the next week, we encountered no obstacles except the bleached bones of bison that often lay in piles nine hands high, blotting out the earth. The cattle, as if spooked by the bones, passed to either side of such mounds, careful to avoid any contact. Since we departed the Bar C 4, we crossed paths with buffalo only once, a herd of five, an ancient bull and four cows, back lit by the dying sun.

We made good time, covering a bit under eight miles a day, always on the lookout for trouble. Only Waco witnessed the smoke, yet none, including Flynn, doubted his word. We shifted our gun belts and holsters to the left so, if trouble found us, it was easier to draw our six-shooters. At night, we doubled the riders, so no one faced the darkness alone.

On the fifth day after the solders departed our camp, the Cheyenne showed up. An hour after dawn as the sun peeked through a haze, they waited on a crest a quarter mile northwest, ghostly outlines astride their ponies. We counted ten.

The Captain cantered up beside Waco. Since we commenced the drive, the Captain had lost weight. His eyes sank into his skull, and his cheekbones showed most prominently, both of which contributed to create a haunted countenance. Yet, he burned with the same ardor as ever. This was his drive, his cattle. He might ask others for advice, but he made the decisions.

"They have been there for five minutes now." The Captain removed his hat and ran a sleeve across his forehead, encrusted with dust, the morning heat and humidity bringing its discomforts. "What is it they want?"

"Suppose I go see." Without waiting for permission, Waco rode off toward the Cheyenne.

The kid may have been impetuous. He wasn't foolhardy. He carried the Sharps across his saddle, the .44 in his holster. Holding a hand aloft, he reined up before the Cheyenne. With his ears perked as to

125

better understand the palaver, Legion remained by his friend's side.

Their leader, an ancient dog soldier, exhibited scars, evidence of a life spent as a warrior, his facial wrinkles so deep a person could hide the tip of his finger in the crevices. A breastplate made of wood covered his upper chest. Metal bracelets circled his upper arms. White streaks decorated his shoulders and exposed belly. His skin set him apart from his companions. Like me, he was a darker brother of mixed breeding, a former slave who escaped his masters. In his case, he joined the Cheyenne in their struggle against white encroachment.

Those who followed the old warrior were children, the oldest fourteen if that, the youngest twelve, yet all shared an unhealthy gauntness, so thin bones pressed outward against flesh. Every boy wore either a jacket or a cap with the insignia of the Fifth Cavalry sewn into the fabric. Six carried breech-loading Springfield rifles, the metal surfaces darkened with soot to prevent sunlight from giving away their presence. Bandoliers circled their shoulders and chests.

Before he spoke, the old warrior studied Waco, Diablo, and Legion. "I have heard of you, Brother Wolf." He spoke English without accent, yet he sounded as if speaking it made him uncomfortable. A scar circled his throat, an old rope burn given to him in his youth. "Stories tell of the boy who conquers what others fear. I see now the stories are wrong. You are no boy."

"And you are Raven. Even south, in the land of the Quahadis, yours is a name to reckon with."

Raven flashed a hint of a smile as he basked in past glories. Such reverie lasted a moment before he returned to the present. "You pass through our land. You will pay for the privilege. Twenty cattle."

"Twenty?"

"You have endless numbers."

"I will speak with my father who makes the final decision."

Waco wheeled Diablo to ride back to the herd when Raven said, "My scouts witnessed you turn the soldiers out of camp. They heard your words."

Flynn and Dermot joined their father.

"Why didn't you stop him, Capt'n?" Flynn's tone verged on insolence. "You don't send a redskin to deal with a redskin."

"Watch your tongue, boy." The Captain gritted his teeth and remained silent until Waco drew rein before them. "What do they want?"

"Twenty head."

Flynn snorted. "We give every beggar that comes along twenty head, soon we ain't got a herd. Hell, the four of us could run 'em off."

"What do you think, Son?" his father asked.

The kid leaned forward, an elbow on the saddle horn, his gaze settling on the Cheyenne who waited motionless, frozen in the mist.

"There's ten of them. Their leader is Raven."

"That black devil!" The Captain removed his hat to run fingers through his hair. With the hat to shade his eyes, he peered at the Indians. "He must be seventy, if a day."

"The rest are boys," Waco said.

Flynn spit. "So, what's the problem?"

"The young warriors had caps and jackets of the Fifth Calvary. They carried six rifles between them."

"Corporal Haley's outfit," the Captain said.

"Flynn's right," Waco said. "We could drive them off. It would be a mistake."

"Mistake, hell!" Flynn curled his fingers over the butt of his .44. "We've got the numbers. I say we let 'em eat lead."

The kid cast an angry glare at his brother

before returning his attention to his father. "I judge them to be two or three days from home. They are not accustomed to dealing with cattle. We give them what they ask for, they will take five, six days to reach to their village. By then, we'll be too far up the trail for them to come after us. Sure, we can drive off that bunch. If we do that, they will return with more warriors than we can handle."

As long as I had known the kid, he spoke more words in that speech than any other time in his life. He made plenty of sense. The Captain thought so, too. "Include Curly and Walleye. Those bulls will delay them all the more." He turned his mount toward the herd. "Good job, Son."

Flynn and Dermot cast glances at each other, angry at losing the cattle, angry their father praised their half brother. The boss expected an employee, whether a rider or a son, to give a full day's work without complaint. If a cowpoke did an outstanding job, he might get a grunt or a nod. "Good job" were words seemingly missing from his vocabulary. Yet the kid deserved the compliment. If Flynn had his druthers, we would have chased off the Cheyenne, we might even have killed most, yet I believe such action would have resulted in losing the herd.

The kid and I rode out with the cattle. Once we reached the Cheyenne, we drew rein beside Raven while his charges took over. As Waco surmised, they knew little about managing the dumb beasts, and the Indian boys galloped in all directions as the cattle wandered off.

"Once you round them up, keep them in a tight group," Waco said. "You ride point, your warriors on either side and at the rear. By tomorrow, you will be trail hardened."

"You did not bargain," said Raven. "I expected you to bargain."

"As you pointed out, we have plenty. Keep the bulls alive. Let them mate. In the spring you will have the beginnings of your own herd."

"We have many mouths to feed."

Raven's tone reflected a sadness, a loss. He knew of Custer's defeat, yet he must have understood that soon an endless stream of better-armed and better-equipped white invaders would descend upon his land. The Cheyenne way of life would vanish as had the Quahadis'.

So, we rode back to our cattle. When we reached them, we looked to the ridge where only the mist remained. The only evidence the heathens existed was our missing cattle, the absence of the beef proving far more precious than their value on the hoof. We never encountered another Cheyenne.

CHAPTER THIRTEEN

From early to late summer when the Texans made their drives, Dodge City averaged a killing a day. To restore order, the city council appointed Wyatt Earp marshal, with Bat Masterson and his brother Jim as deputies. They began by closing off most of the town to drovers. Only Front Street remained wide open, and it contained enough saloons to accommodate a thousand of us.

The first night after we bedded the herd in the stockyards, the boss paid us half our wages, and we flocked to Front Street. Waco came with us, Legion trailing at his heels. We wound up at the Bella Donna Emporium, the first we encountered, a "joint" the locals called it, a low-class dive that sold rotgut whiskey aimed for quick drunks. We gathered together tables, bought whiskey. The bartender, a surly-looking fellow with a wild mustache and puffed-out cheeks, spotted Legion and yelled for us to get that mangy animal out of his establishment.

"If he goes, we all go," said MacInnis.

The dollar signs rolled around the bartender's head, and he decided he could stomach the dog's presence.

"Just make sure he don't drop a mess in here."

MacInnis scratched his grizzled stubble. "No worry there. He prefers a cleaner abode to take a shit."

So, our evening began with a good laugh. We started drinking at six. By six-thirty, the world had grown fuzzy. Except for Waco. He ordered a beer, taking nary a sip. Twice he filled his palm for Legion. The kid kept us from the tables and prevented the whores from pilfering our coin. He was seventeen, yet he looked after us.

The night was going fine. Though a little drunk, we stayed away from gambling. Four punchers went off with whores, banking the bulk of their earnings with Waco. Dodge City tolerated prostitution. The good people understood at the conclusion of an arduous drive, drovers needed a release. We had spent many months suffering the celibacy of the saddle.

As I negotiated with a whore of a darker hue, three buffalo hunters stomped through the swinging doors, their clothes slick with grime and dried blood. Like all their kind, they smelled of dung and death, which was the reason the inhabitants of Dodge referred to buffalo hunters as "stinkers." The last to enter, a mountain eighteen hands tall, a quarter of that in girth, shoved an Indian woman before him, a rope knotted around her neck and secured to his waist.

A white woman's dress covered the Indian gal, the garment torn in a dozen places. Layers of dirt discolored the fabric. Bare flesh showed from her thigh past her waist. Another rip exposed part of a breast. Bruised skin marred her left cheek. At first, I judged her to be in her thirties, but the dirt and disheveled hair disguised her true age. When they halted at the bar, she stood close enough I realized she was a child, no more than fifteen.

The big man slapped the counter, which shook from one end to the other. "A bottle each for me and my brothers."

The bartender sauntered down, a twist to his mouth. "As I live and breathe, Bull Bryson. It's been a month of Sundays since you boys dropped in. Howdy, Crawley. Pearly."

He nodded to each brother, a smaller, younger version of the Goliath, if not in stature then in appearance. Crawley displayed a full beard, dark, wiry hair sprouting in all directions. Perhaps a year or two older than Waco, Pearly displayed a more controlled growth. Because his hair was lighter, the contours of his jaw exposed a chin that sloped into his neck, making it impossible to tell where one began, the other ended. All three shared another physical feature. Stringy hair hung from under their hats obscuring their foreheads, so it appeared their hairlines began at their eyebrows.

The bartender placed a bottle before each man. They popped the corks, which bounded across the sawdust-covered floor. Tilting the bottles, they drank.

The bartender leaned his elbows on the countertop to study the girl. "You know, she might clean up good, Bull. Want to sell her? I need fresh meat for my stable. My stock wears out fast."

Bull laughed. "Hell, I just bought her this morning. A sky pilot sold her to me. Said she needed taming, which we aim to do. Job commands it. 'He opened their ear to discipline, and commandeth that they return from iniquity.' That's what we're going to do. Make sure she understands iniquity." He jerked the rope. The youngster fell into him. He grasped a breast and ran a tongue over her cheek. "We're gonna have her tonight. After that, assuming we don't cut her throat and your price is right, might be we can do business."

Waco shoved his chair back, his expression stoic, almost disinterested. I knew better. I pulled the flap from the hammer of my .44. The whore edged away. She had seen enough trouble to recognize the signs.

The kid crossed the room, positioning himself behind the buffalo hunter, which shielded him from Crawley and Pearly. Waco crowded close, his shoulder poking Bull, who laid his palms flat against the bar to confront the kid. The buffalo hunter appraised Waco through narrowed lids. "I don't like being crowded, 'specially by breeds." He sniffed like he smelled shit. "I caught your stink the minute I came in. You sodomite, you abomination in the eyes of the Lord —"

The action happened so quickly that those who watched witnessed only a flash of light as the kid buried the Bowie knife in the man's right hand, cutting through flesh and bone before plunging into the wood. Bull screamed, his free hand seizing the hilt. Waco jammed his .44 into the man's side.

His brothers clawed for their pistols.

"Tell them to drop their weapons." Waco grabbed Bull's shirt and pulled him from the bar, stretching his arm, the blade slicing through more flesh.

Blood flowed across the pine countertop. "Do as he says!" Bull bellowed, his face twisted in pain. "Get rid of 'em! Goddamit, now!"

Still, they hesitated.

The kid said, "I will put a slug in him, then I'll get one of you, probably both."

The saloon had gone silent, everyone frozen.

"Do it! Do it!" Tears ran down the giant's cheeks and merged into his beard.

As ordered, Crawley and Pearly relieved themselves of their pistols and knives, their weapons clattering on the floor. Waco slipped the revolver from Bull's holster and stuffed it in his own belt. With a jerk, he freed the knife.

Clutching his wounded appendage, Bull slid down the bar until he sat on the floor. Blood soaked into his already-stained leather shirt.

Right then a dour fellow with a star pinned to his chest entered the establishment. His handlebar mustache drooped but failed to disguise he was in his mid-twenties. The manner in which his coat hung with such precision, an inch below his hips, the cut of his vest, the watch fob hanging from his pocket, suggested a local businessman. The .44 strapped to his leg told a different story, as did the steely eyes, the set of his jaw, the tensed body.

The marshal's gaze fell on Waco before lighting on Bull. "What's going on here?"

Waco dropped his pistol in his holster. "This fellow did not understand our country rid itself of slavery."

With a pass of the knife, he severed the rope that bound the girl.

"And you believed it your duty to teach this gent a history lesson." Earp smiled. "That's mighty white of you."

"We didn't do nothing." Bull spoke between clenched teeth. Blood streamed between his fingers. "It was him that started it."

Earp focused his attention on Crawley and Pearly. "Take him to Doc Adams. If I catch any of you in town tomorrow, I'll shoot you myself."

Crawley ran a sleeve across his nose. "You got no right to talk to us like that, Marshal."

"This is Dodge City, mister. It's my town." His anger lay on the surface. Word had spread, and no one dared to anger the marshal. The man who did might wind up with a cracked skull — or worse. "Now get him out of here."

The men eased toward Bull. Crawley glanced at the weapons at his feet.

Earp shifted his coat so it freed his pistol. "Touch that six-shooter, mister, and say hello to hell."

That ended it. Crawley and Pearly lifted their brother. Staggering under his weight, they dragged him from the saloon.

Waco faced the bartender. "If I ever hear you've bought another woman, Indian or otherwise, I'll be back. You do not want that."

The blood drained from the man's face. He kept a scattergun on the wall behind him, yet I don't believe he considered going for it. He'd seen what the kid did to Bull, and he knew the kid had friends in the room. With a rag, he wiped the countertop. "No, course not. I was only considerin' out loud."

Earp hooked his thumbs in his gun belt. "It might be best if you moved on, youngster."

"Are you running me out?"

"You'd be doing me a favor if you parted company with Dodge. I was hired to cut down on the killings, not add more. You stay, and those stinkers will come after you. They'll kill you or you'll kill them. Either way, the dead pile up."

"Then I won't burden you," Waco said.

Since the ruckus began, the silence in the saloon was deafening. Once Earp vacated the premises, a slow rumble filled the room. In all that time, the Indian girl watched without moving, waiting for the events to play out. Her expression showed a hint of perplexity.

Waco snatched a bottle of water used for chasers and handed it to the girl. She drank until she emptied it.

"Do you speak English?" Waco asked.

She acknowledged his question with a nod.

"Best you come with me," he said.

He led her through the swinging doors and down Front Street toward the stockyards. At the end of the street, he glanced over his shoulder. Shadows crowded in. When he failed to spot her, he feared she had fled. Then he realized she followed within arm's length, more part of the darkness than he. Legion brought up the rear.

Their camp lay a quarter mile from town, and when they reached it, he found his father and MacInnis bedded down.

The two men climbed to their feet and listened as Waco explained the situation.

"What about the girl?" he asked.

"I could not leave her in Dodge on her own."

"No, of course not." The Captain laid a hand on the kid's shoulder. "You're a good man, Son. You did what needed to be done." He glanced again at the girl. "Grab some clothes, pants, and a shirt. She can't ride far in what she's wearing. Take the pinto from the remuda. The mare's size will make it easier for her to ride. Take what grub and cartridges you need. We'll see you at the ranch when you get there. Go now. And for God's sake, watch your back."

CHAPTER FOURTEEN

The dealer dealt all five cards before Flynn swept them from the table to discover he held a pair of black aces. For most of the night his luck had run to the bad — he was forty in the hole. A player to his right, a sour-faced storekeeper named Zinman, threw in a silver dollar. His stack totaled over two hundred dollars. Flynn called and discarded three cards. The dealer dealt him another ace and a pair of deuces, a full house, his best hand since he'd taken a seat at the table more than an hour before.

Flynn bet five, the dealer folded. Zinman flicked the bottom edges of his cards, a nervous habit he employed every time he had a good hand. He had drawn a single card, which meant he hit a straight or flush. Flynn wanted to laugh aloud. The man raised ten, Flynn pushed in his last $23. Zinman matched the bet. With a shout of triumph, Flynn spread his cards on the table. He reached to rake in the pot when the merchant showed four jacks.

Flynn muttered "Goddamit" under his breath.

The man stacked his coins. "Come back tomorrow night, cowboy. I love taking your money."

Pushing his chair back, Flynn strolled to the bar from where he watched his tormentor in the mirror, its surface clouded by smoke from cigars, pipes, and Bull Durhams. Already another player had taken the vacated chair, and Zinman jabbered on about his poker prowess.

Dermot elbowed his way to Flynn and ordered a beer. Once the bartender set it in front of him, Dermot drained the glass. With a sleeve, he wiped the foam from his trimmed mustache. "The kid is in great trouble." A whore sidled to Dermot, pressing a breast against his elbow. Her red lips and overpainted cheeks appeared garish in the harsh light. He threw her a cursory glance. "Later, honey."

As she wandered off, Dermot inspected her swaying backside. A head shorter than Flynn, he possessed the good looks of Flynn before that devil horse forever scarred him. The moment he hit town, Dermot rushed to the tonsorial parlor, where he purchased a haircut, a shave, and a bath. Over the years, he developed an easy affability with women. Since the mauling, Flynn found himself tongue-tied around females, and his brooding nature acted as another wall. At trail's end he paid for favors, although he seldom found the experience enjoyable, more like a chore that, once completed, provided a sense of relief rather than pleasure.

"So, what did the kid get away with this time?"

"That's just it, Flynn. I mean he's in a peck of trouble." Dermot related the story he gathered from a puncher who witnessed Waco's encounter. Flynn paid attention, even though Dermot probably embellished the narrative with a few details of his own.

"The marshal ran Waco out of town."

Flynn sipped his drink as he considered the story. Fact and cow shit. Secondhand stories often mixed the two on the way to embellishing the facts. He downed the last of his whiskey. "Where are these buffalo hunters?"

"Last I heard, they was getting the big one patched up. Waco 'bout cut that fella's hand clean off. The Emporium was covered in blood, floor to ceiling."

"Let's see if we can find those stinkers."

A dozen paces from the doctor's office, they halted when the door at the top of the stairs opened and three men led by a behemoth half as wide as he was tall stepped out. His right arm hung in a sling. Even in the dim light, his features, drained of blood, projected a façade so white he could have passed for a ghost. He swayed as if about to topple. Seizing the rail, he steadied himself, and descended the stairs, which trembled under his weight. Behind him came his companions, smaller versions cut from the same mold.

Once they reached the boardwalk, Flynn stepped into the light that emanated from the saloon across the street. The stinkers stopped shoulder to shoulder, alert for trouble.

The big man glowered through narrowed lids.

Flynn curled his thumbs in his gun belt to show he offered no threat. "You had a run-in with a breed."

Bull took a step forward. "You know the abomination who did this?"

"Before you get riled, you should understand we have no love for him."

"What's the breed's name?"

"If something was to happen to him, that's his hard luck. We would shed no tears. If you boys are thinking of going after him, I could make it easier."

"Flynn —" Dermot said.

Flynn continued without acknowledging his brother. "You can beat him to where he's going." He paused for the offer to sink in. He'd learned long ago most buffalo hunters lacked basic intelligence. They had only to load a rifle, shoot with reasonable accuracy, and skin a carcass.

"Let's hear it," Bull said.

"His name is Waco Joseph Callahan. He ain't in town. If he's headed home, he's headed south. He'll pass along the eastern edge of the Llano Estacado. There's a trading post on the Red River — Dobson's. He'll stop there to pick up supplies."

"Was the girl with him?" Bull asked.

"I know nothing of a girl. You've got your information. Do with it what you will. You bring me proof he's dead, I'll sweeten the deal with a twenty-dollar gold piece for each of you. You'll find me at the Bar 4 C. Ask anybody in North Texas. They'll point the way."

Flynn backed a step before he marched off into the darkness, Dermot at his heels. They stood before the Emporium before Flynn said, "Get it off your chest."

Dermot removed his Stetson and passed

his fingers around the inside band. Sweat beaded his forehead. "If the Captain finds out, he'll kill us for sure."

"You won't say nothing, I won't say nothing. Those stinkers sure ain't gonna say nothing."

"If he finds out — ?"

"It will be best for him if he lets it be. I've had enough of Waco. I've had enough of the Captain."

Dermot opened his mouth, Flynn cut him off. "For God's sake, your guts are spilling out of your mouth. What's done is done. Now go on. Find a whore. Get yourself a piece of tail."

Dermot pushed his way through the swinging doors.

Hidden in shadows, Flynn waited outside the Emporium and peered through the front window from where he viewed the whole interior. Past midnight, Zinman raked in his coins and carried them to the cashier, where he exchanged his winnings for paper that he stuffed into a money belt. He strolled out and headed up Front Street toward his haberdashery. Keeping ahead of him, Flynn arrived at the rear of the store and slipped into the shadows.

None too steady, Zinman rounded the corner of the building and set foot on the stairs leading to his living quarters above the store. Flynn came up behind and swung the .44, the barrel landing with a solid thud. The storekeeper dropped to a knee. Flynn brought the gun barrel down again. Metal cracked bone.

He rolled the man on his back, pulled open his waistcoat and untied the money belt. As he stuffed the pouch in his coat pocket, his gaze came in contact with the storekeeper, who stared up wide-eyed. Flynn jumped back, his thumb cocking his pistol, the sight lining up on the man's forehead. Zinman remained still, unresponsive, sightless.

Flynn ran.

Without realizing how he arrived there, he found himself behind the Bison Sporting Palace among the cribs, four individual structures with a bed the only furniture in each. From one came the grunts of a man mounting a woman. Here Flynn emptied the belt of the paper money and three ten-dollar gold pieces. He ignored the half-dimes and two-bit coins and threw the pouch in the brush.

His hands shook, and he told himself to calm down. He'd made a nice bundle, and he didn't have to share it with anybody, including Dermot. As for the storekeeper, the bastard wasn't laughing now. Nobody made a fool of Flynn Callahan. Nobody.

He strolled into the Emporium, where me and the boys were still celebrating. He bought us a round of drinks, which at the time I thought odd. Flynn was the dour sort who bought drinks only for himself.

"Lift 'em, boys." He held his glass aloft. "Tonight, I'm ridin' high."

CHAPTER FIFTEEN

Under a cloud-darkened sky, Waco and the girl crossed the Arkansas, a wide, shallow river with a sandy bottom. In early spring, the channel ran deep for short periods. This late in the summer, the water flowed well beneath the bellies of their mounts. Once on the opposite shore, they headed west. Waco kept up the pace until dawn, when he drew up beside a stream and allowed the horses to drink. Legion had arrived ahead of them, lapping water. The wolf dog glanced over his shoulder as if to say, "What kept you?"

Waco dismounted. The girl, despite the encumbrance of the tattered dress, sprang from the saddle. She knelt upstream, splashing water over her face and running her fingers through her hair, clearing it of tangles. As she wiped her hands on her dress, he realized for the first time she was more than attractive, a great deal more. Her clear skin glistened in the early light, and she projected a freshness he thought impossible under the circumstances. She must have suffered a hard day after which they had ridden all night, yet she showed not the least wear.

He removed the shirt and pants from his saddlebags and passed them to her.

"What am I to do with these?" she asked.

"Put them on. They will be more comfortable to ride in."

While she changed, he kept his focus on the trail behind, the Sharps cradled in his arms. She tapped him on the shoulder to signal she had finished. The dress lay at her feet, a discarded piece of trash. Her new clothes hung loose on her frame. She stood five two or three, which forced her to roll up the shirtsleeves and pant legs, the latter exposing a pair of moccasins that bespoke a sturdy craftmanship. She caught him staring at her footwear. "My mother taught me to make my own moccasins. Chewing the leather has made my teeth strong."

They ate hardtack, washing it down with water. Neither he nor the girl spoke while they ate. Once Waco finished his biscuit, he wiped his mouth with a sleeve and fixed his attention on her. "What do they call you?"

"The missionary couple christened me

Rachel. I prefer my Cheyenne name —
Meome'ehne. It means Morning Star."

"A fitting name, a good name."

"You?"

"Whites call me Waco, the people of the
Llano Estacado call me Brother Wolf."

With a nod, she glanced at the wolf dog.
"Because of him."

"He is more brother than my real broth-
ers." He had trouble taking his eyes off her.
He concentrated on his boots. "Where can
I take you?"

"Take me?" Her features darkened. She
had left a shirt button undone, and her
hand crept to the opening.

He realized at once he misstated his
purpose. "I am sure you wish to return to
your people. You are Cheyenne, are you
not?"

"Northern Cheyenne. I come from a place
whites call "Montana."

"That will be a long ride."

"A useless ride. Soldiers killed my mother,
my father, my brothers. I was a child, and
an officer gave me to a missionary family.
They taught me English. They sought to
civilize me."

"And they sold you?"

"The Reverend Josiah Jones's wife, Pru-
dence, believed her husband grew too fond

of me. One night, he came to my bed. As I said, I have strong teeth. I bit off his ear. That's when they sold me."

"So much for civilizing."

She stiffened. "You make fun of me."

"You make me proud of my blood. I am part Comanche."

"Are you not also part white?"

"My white father has taught me to ignore the color of skin and see what lies in a person's heart. My mother honors our heritage."

More than a mile away, a glint of sunlight off metal flashed a warning. Waco would brook no chances. They needed to move. Before he uttered his doubts, Morning Star read his expression and leapt aboard the pinto. They traveled south.

By four that afternoon, the horses dragged their hooves, raising dust, and he and the girl dismounted to walk beside the animals. Waco worried he pushed the girl too hard, yet whenever his eyes lighted on her, she appeared sturdy and determined. They crossed a buffalo wallow surrounded by a dozen stunted trees, their branches offering protection from the heat. A ribbon-thin creek ran through them. They allowed the horses to drink. Afterward the animals grazed on prairie grass. Waco didn't bother to hobble them. Diablo would stay close, the mare would stick with Diablo.

Waco and the girl chewed jerky, the juice providing renewed strength. After a twenty-minute respite, they mounted and rode on. Clouds pregnant with rain rolled in from the north. They came to a rise on which sat an abandoned sod house, one wall and part of the roof in rubble.

Lightning flashed, thunder rumbled. They guided the horses under the remaining roof. Waco placed both mounts as far back in the ruins as possible.

The storm arrived with a thunderclap followed by wind that drove the rain slantwise. They found a dry corner. With Legion between him and the girl, Waco threw a blanket around them, and the three shared each other's heat. Whenever thunder shook the ground, Legion whined and pushed himself tighter against his human companions. Morning Star stroked the wolf dog. He accepted her caresses as she whispered in her Cheyenne tongue, which he could not have understood. He did understand her kindness. He laid his head in her lap.

Waco and the girl leaned against a wall and slept. In the early morning before first light, a thunderclap woke them. They had fallen into each other, her head on his shoulder. Embarrassed, Waco climbed to his feet. He pulled a handful of oats from his saddlebags, which he offered to Diablo. He gave the mare an equal share.

"We must remain here for a while longer," he said.

"Do you not fear those who pursue us?"

"If they are on our trail, they must also wait out the storm."

Morning Star narrowed her lids as she scrutinized him. "Do you expect me to become your woman?"

"Considering what has happened to you, that is a reasonable assumption, though untrue."

"I am a woman. What else can I expect?"

"If that were my intent — which it is not — I would be a fool to force myself on you."

"Am I so ugly you would have nothing to do with me?"

He waved away her objections. "You pleasure the eyes. However, the weapon you conceal is a formidable shield."

"You know about it?"

"Since before we left Dodge."

From her shirt, she removed a homemade knife four or five inches in length that tapered to a point. She had fastened cloth to the handle. "I meant this for the one called Bull."

"He is a big man. It would be difficult to kill him with such a weapon."

"I would not have killed him." She returned the makeshift knife to its hiding place. "I would have taken his manhood."

"And he would have killed you."

"It would have been worth it to see his agony." She offered the observation in an offhanded manner. "You saved me. Now I am yours."

"You owe me nothing. You are free to go."

"You say that when you know I have nowhere to go. So, I ask you. Why did you take me from the hunters?"

"Three moons past, white men accosted my mother. They forfeited their lives. Had the buffalo hunters forced the issue, they would have forfeited theirs."

The rain died, and a patch of blue peered through dark clouds. Legion dashed outside and disappeared. Waco again fed the horses and watered them from a pond formed by the rain.

Once they climbed in the saddles, Waco laid back on the reins to keep Diablo from bolting. The girl laughed at his struggles. "Let him have his head. When he tires, we will catch up."

His hooves splattering water and mud, Diablo ran a mile before slowing. Waco turned him, and they jogged back. Diablo's chest expanded, his ears perked. He pranced.

Morning Star patted the neck of the mare. "He seeks to impress."

By noon they passed into country the storm skirted. From his saddle, Waco bagged two rabbits with the Sharps, the powerful weapon removing a head each time without damaging the body. They paused to build a fire with buffalo patties and dried grass. Once they ate, they tossed the bones aside and wiped the grease on their pants. They waited while the horses grazed. Legion returned, his belly full. He nudged the girl to stroke his neck and rolled his baleful eyes to Waco as if asking forgiveness.

"He seems to prefer your company," Waco said.

As she stroked the animal's nose, Legion edged closer.

Waco whistled. Diablo trotted over, the mare following.

At dusk, they caught the first scent of smoke, wood and sage and other smells he found difficult to separate and identify.

After sleeping on the open prairie, they arose in the dark. An hour after sunrise, they came upon the charred ruins of a ranch house. Their arrival disturbed a wake of buzzards that lifted into the air, their heavy wings raising dust over three men, one woman. Arrows protruded from bodies. The markings on the shafts said Cheyenne. Flies swarmed in clouds.

The corral fence lay broken and scattered, livestock gone. The prints of unshod ponies said seven to ten braves took part in the raid. Blood-spotted ground showed one or more attackers suffered wounds. Next to a body lay a single cap, the insignia of the Fifth Cavalry sown into the fabric. Far out, perhaps half a mile or more, a flash of sunlight glinted off metal.

"You saw?" said the girl.

"This is the second time they announced their presence. They have been with us since yesterday."

"I thought you had not noticed. Still, they were careless to allow us to see."

"They wanted us to know. They have given us permission to cross their land."

"The dead need burying."

"That is white man's thinking. You have lived too long among the proselytizers."

"Does not your white blood cry for you to bury them?"

"If we do, the Cheyenne will no longer welcome us. At any rate, the dead are dead.

I doubt they care."

"What of heaven and hell? Or the Great Beyond? Do you not believe they exist?"

He leaned forward and ran a palm along Diablo's neck. "In the Christian world, none of my friends would reach heaven. I would be without Diablo and Legion. What good is that kind of heaven? At least the Cheyenne and Comanche believe in an afterlife that does not exclude what is important."

The hoard of buzzing flies sounded more insistent, as if they feared the newcomers would interfere with their feast.

Waco fixed his attention on the horizon. "Let us move on before we wear out our welcome."

CHAPTER SIXTEEN

For the past year, Emile Dobson peed a dozen times a day, and when he filled the pot, he hauled the contents to the outhouse. That late August afternoon after a dump, he spotted three men approaching from the river, buffalo hunters by the look of their greasy clothes, their wide-brim hats, their heavy beards. Such miscreants had no reason to be this far south. The vast herds had vanished from the Panhandle years before, slaughtered or driven off.

Dobson sensed an unease in the way they held their rifles, thumbs hovering over the hammers. Two smaller riders flanked a bear of a man, his right arm in a sling, the hand wrapped in bloodstained cloth, his full beard bristling. All three carried six-shooters and skinning knives. They had exhausted their mounts. Lather covered their hides, their chests expanded and contracted in labored breathing, their heads hung low.

Over the years, Dobson had learned to follow his instincts. He still berated himself over the drifters who had accosted Blue Feather. On that occasion, he'd allowed the smell of money to blind his better judgment. He would not fall into that trap again.

He left the chamber pot outside to air out and hurried in the building. He kept the shotgun on the wall. These travelers might be peaceful customers seeking food and shelter. Ginger and Molly were in the store ahead of him, helping themselves to bacon and beans. They had laid out silverware and tin plates for three.

Dobson pulled open a drawer, snatched an 1849 Colt, a short-barrel revolver that held only five rounds. He stuffed it in his rear pocket. The weight provided instant reassurance.

Molly wrinkled her brow. "What's wrong, Emile?"

"Best if you girls retire to your crib for a while. Might be —"

Before he finished his thought, the door flew open. Sunlight flooded the room as the Goliath entered. A younger man followed, thin enough as to appear underfed. He cocked his Sharps, the barrel lining on Dobson.

"He's got a weapon in his pants, Bull, and

it ain't his pecker." The voice originated behind Dobson.

The third man had entered through the storeroom.

Bull strode forward. "Pass over that hog-leg. Be mighty careful. We are a right nervous bunch."

Dobson removed the pistol by the grip and held it out.

The youngster snatched the Colt and stuffed it in his belt, his gaze drifting to the women who huddled in the shadows. "Lookie what we got here."

"They'll keep, Pearly. First things first. Crawley, convince this gent he needs to listen."

Crawley slammed the stock of his Sharps between Dobson's shoulders. Dobson collapsed, his head bouncing off a shelf, splitting the inside of his cheek. Blood filled his mouth. A hand grabbed him by the shirt collar and hauled him to his feet.

Bull waved a .44 in his face. "I want to know one thing. Has Waco Callahan and the girl been through yet?"

Dobson kept a knife attached to his belt and covered by a shirt that hung loose. Most people never knew he carried it. His hand crept to the handle, and he eased the blade from its sheath.

Lowering his head, Dobson spit blood and mumbled words so low Crawley leaned in closer. "Say that again."

Dobson buried the blade in the man's thigh.

Crawley bellowed and dropped his rifle.

Bull jerked the trigger, and the boom of .44 rattled cans and bottles.

Ginger screamed.

The bullet struck the wall, missing the storekeeper altogether. Dobson leapt over the counter. Bull retreated before the crazed man and fired a second time. The storekeeper staggered, his features twisted, the knife raised. Bull fired a third, a fourth, a fifth time, the blasts thunderous in the confines of the store. Gunsmoke swirled around the men, engulfing them. As the smoke cleared, Dobson stared straight ahead, his eyes lacking focus, a glassy film spreading over them. Red stains merged until blood painted his entire shirt front.

"He ain't dead yet, Bull." A tone of disbelief infected Pearly's voice.

"Sure he is. He just ain't figured it out yet."

As if the words penetrated his consciousness, Dobson dropped to his knees before toppling face forward on the dirt floor.

Bull opened the rolling gate of the .44 and

passed the revolver to his younger brother, who replaced the spent shells. Bull studied the fallen man. "Tough little son-of-a-bitch. I'll give him that."

Pearly shifted his gaze to the women who clung to each other. "What about them?"

"The Good Lord provided them for our use. It would be sacrilegious to ignore such a gift." Bull shoved his pistol in its holster. "Business first. Go outside and stand guard. We'll take our pleasures once we give the breed his due."

"Why me?" Pearly whined, his voice high, nasal. "Why can't Crawley do it?"

"We've been over this a hundred times. The Good Book, Jeremiah, chapter three, verse four. 'My father, thou art the guide of my youth.' I am the oldest. It's like I am your Pa. Anyway, your brother's hurt."

Hobbling around the counter, Crawley gripped his thigh, blood running through his fingers. "He pig stuck me."

"Go on Pearly, keep a lookout." Bull lifted a finger, leveling it at the women. "Take care of Crawley."

Molly pushed Ginger behind her. "Do it your goddamn self."

Bull threw a backhand that sent her crashing to the floor. Ginger shrieked, and he hit her, too, a fist to the face that laid her spread eagle, her blond hair sprayed like a halo. As he hauled Molly to her feet, he twisted her arm. She heard a snap followed by pain that radiated from her fingers to her shoulder.

"Do it or I will put a bullet through your head."

Gritting her teeth, she rifled through a box of medical supplies. She snatched a strip of cloth and a bottle of carbolic. Crawley lowered his pants and long johns, both soaked with blood, and exposed a three-inch gash. She hoped he'd bleed to death. Yet she made a show of caring for him. If she didn't, Bull would kill her and Ginger, which was probably their fate even if she obeyed.

She removed the cork with her teeth, spit it out, and poured a fourth of the contents on the wound, the brown liquid mixing with the blood. Crawley screamed, the pain burning to the bone. He swung a wild backhand that Molly ducked under.

"It's to kill the infection." She dumped the rest of the bottle on the cut.

He gritted his teeth and glared at her. Despite the limited use of her left arm, she tied the cloth around his thigh, tightening it with her teeth and uninjured hand. He groaned. She glanced at his willy, hidden in his pubic hair, withdrawn, useless. He pulled up his long johns, then his pants, tightening the belt.

"Go on, git back with the other whore." Bull shoved her. She collided with the counter, her injured arm plowing into the edge. Her stomach churned, bile burned her throat. She swallowed it, determined not to let them see her agony. She staggered to Ginger, who stirred, returning to consciousness, her cheek swelling, her lip bleeding. With one hand, Molly dragged her friend under a table, their only protection the shadows.

From their position, Molly watched as Bull grabbed the dead Emile by the feet and dragged him into the storeroom, a path of blood soaking into the dirt floor. She wanted to cry. She held no illusions about the storekeeper. He provided a crib for their whoring and took a 20 percent cut of their take. Yet he never beat them, never cheated them, and never allowed clients to mistreat them, which was more than she could say for others who rented her out. He kept them stocked in food, ensured their shared crib was comfortable, administered to them when they were sick. She already missed him and his occasional nocturnal visits, never to Ginger, and he paid like any other customer. Since she began whoring more than a decade before, he'd treated her better than any man she had ever known. Now she must deal with men who showed no compunction in murdering women, for she was convinced they would leave no witnesses.

Pearly stuck his head in. "Two riders coming. I think it's them."

Bull retrieved his brother's Sharps, passing it to him. "You in any condition for shootin'?"

Crawley snickered as he took the weapon. "You know I always hit what I'm aiming for. A little scratch like this ain't gonna matter."

Crawley limped to the door, Bull on his heels.

Once they exited, Molly leapt from their hiding place, crossed the room, and heaved the crosstie into the metal joints. She dashed into the storeroom and bolted the rear door, too. When she returned, she found Ginger leaning against a table, her bottom lip quivering, her gaze unfocused. "What are you doing? They'll kill us if we put up a fight."

"They will kill us anyway, honey." With her good hand, Molly lugged the twelve-pound shotgun from the wall. It took all her strength to lift and steady it on the counter. She cocked each barrel as she lined up the sights. "Now remove the bar. If they come back, we'll let them walk right in."

Ginger's blond hair had fallen over her brow, the bruise on her cheek had turned dark red. "I'm scared."

"Just do as I say" — Molly heard the shake in her own voice — "and maybe we get out alive."

Ginger reeled across the room and lifted the bar. Running back to Molly, she slumped below the counter, drew her knees to her chest, and sobbed.

From outside sounded the boom of the Sharps.

Crawley shouted in triumph. "I got the breed dead center. You know I never miss, Bull, no matter what."

CHAPTER SEVENTEEN

On the evening of the fifth day as the sun lay low on the horizon, Waco and Morning Star sighted Dobson's Trading Post. The dying light reflected off the river the color of blood. The stream ran lower than when he'd crossed it more than a month before. Now sand bars peeked from the middle of the stream that flowed with far less urgency. An odor of decay floated on the wind.

The trading post appeared still, unoccupied. No horses or wagons stood before the structure housing Ginger and Molly. A half-dozen horses, three still saddled, loitered in the corral, milling around, nervous. The smokehouse stood inactive, its fires extinguished.

A gunshot flashed in the twilight.

Waco leapt from the saddle in the instant a powerful force slammed into his left side and spun him like he was at the end of the line in a game of Crack the Whip. He collided with the girl, and together they spilled to the earth, the blow knocking the breath from him. For precious seconds, he could not breathe. Then, as if he had swum underwater for a mile and surfaced, he sucked air, filling his lungs. He pressed a palm against the wound. Warm blood flowed between his fingers. He verged on passing out. If that happened, he would never awake. His attackers would put a bullet in his head. A grassy mound lay less than two feet away, yet when he crawled forward, the pain wrapped around to his back and forward to his belly, paralyzing him.

Morning Star grabbed him under his arms and dragged him behind the mound.

Waco told himself to keep alert even as the world tilted on its axis. His sight blurred, light faded.

"Give me a weapon."

The words roused him.

Morning Star held out a hand.

Twenty feet away, Diablo pawed the dirt. The Sharps resided in the scabbard. If he called the devil horse and they heard, the ambushers would kill him. Waco passed his Bowie knife to Morning Star.

Her fingers curled the grip, coming to rest on his initials carved into the wood. "If I survive and you do not," she said, "I will keep this always to honor you. If you survive, and I do not, remember this of me — my heart was Cheyenne."

Without another word, she disappeared into brush.

Legion crouched in a tuft of grass, and with a suddenness that surprised the kid, the animal darted across the open space that separated them. Another shot rang out. Fur on the top of Legion's neck exploded. He tumbled headfirst, rising a cloud of dust. When it settled, Legion had crawled off to die, and a great hollowness settled over Waco's heart.

Summoning his last reserves, Waco drew his pistol, parted the waist-high grass, and with both hands, steadied the weapon against the ground. He drew back the hammer and waited.

Movement in the brush made him believe Morning Star had returned. Instead, Legion settled in a position near him.

Waco experienced a surge of joy. A tuft of hair was missing as well as a piece of skin, a superficial wound at worse. The wolf dog's eyes blazed. He started to rise, but Waco signaled his friend to stay put. "Let them come to us," he whispered. "Let them believe we're dead. Then we'll show 'em a thing or two."

Horses splashed across the river, his attackers unconcerned about the noise. They must have believed Waco dead or dying, and Morning Star, only a female, offered no threat.

Once they reached dry land, they dismounted, their boots thumping the earth.

"Keep to the river, Pearly. Make sure that Indian gal don't get by. We got business with her, too."

Waco recognized the voice — Bull, from whom he had taken Morning Star. How had the buffalo hunters gotten here before them?

The answer slapped him across the face like an open palm.

Flynn and Dermot.

Blood be damned. He would survive this ambush and settle with his brothers.

He didn't have to see the buffalo hunters. Because of his heightened senses, every sound was magnified tenfold, their breathing as loud as winter wind, their footfalls thunder.

"I hit him square, Bull," Crawley said.

Bull growled. "That ain't in question."

The hunters rounded a thicket, Crawley limping, Bull screened by the smaller man. They carried revolvers, ready for a close fight if need be. Bull carried his weapon in his left hand. His right, heavily bandaged, hung in a sling tied round his neck.

Keeping his injured leg straight, Crawley bent to run his fingers along the ground. "Blood. Plenty of it."

He straightened.

Waco fired. The impact of the slug drove Crawley into Bull. His strength fast depleting, the kid squeezed shot after shot until the hammer snapped on an empty chamber. Smoke obscured his targets.

A breeze wafted away the smoke.

Crawley lay crumpled on the ground. Bull swayed but remained upright, his right arm above the elbow spewing blood. He staggered forward, lifting the .44 with a quivering hand.

"You shot my dog," Waco said.

"Killed that devil dog like I'm gonna kill you." Bull cocked the pistol.

Waco laughed. "You can't kill Legion."

Legion sprang from the brush, and the impact sent him and Bull to the ground. The mighty jaws clamped on the arm holding the pistol, teeth crunching bone. Bull screamed. Legion sprang for the throat. From his angle, Waco could not see the damage his companion inflicted, but from the snarls, the screams, the blood shooting skyward, he had a clear idea. Bull jerked and pitched, and in a final heave, his struggles ceased. Only then did Legion release his hold and retreat three or four paces. Satisfied, he trotted to Waco, who stroked the animal's nose, covered in blood.

A single pistol shot, sharp and loud, echoed from the direction of the river.

Morning Star.

In panic, Waco slipped his elbows under him and pushed up. Pain dropped him, and the world spun away.

CHAPTER EIGHTEEN

The morning after Waco and the girl escaped Dodge, the Captain made ready for an appearance by the buffalo hunters. Instead, around nine, Marshal Earp marched into our camp. In the light he appeared thinner, his inner fire burning less brightly. He walked straight to the Captain, who despite his illness projected authority.

The marshal wore a coat that covered his pistol, his intent, I believe, to show us he presented no threat. "I understand the kid is your son."

"Did you come to arrest him?"

"No, sir, I did not. The way I see it, your boy righted a wrong. I came to inform you that the stinkers departed at daybreak. Maybe they know the boy is connected to you. Maybe not. Either way, best you be aware."

An hour later, two riders informed the Captain of their intention to head north for the Deadwood gold fields, though I suspected they possessed more gold in their teeth than they would dig from the ground. The Captain allowed Flynn to hire new punchers. When he brought them into camp, we recognized them as hardcases down on their luck and willing to take any job as long as it provided food. They called themselves Bogdan and Rojas.

Bogdan had the appearance of a saddle tramp, his clothes worn thin, his features hardened by wind and sun, an unkempt beard to disguise his features, shifty eyes, always on the lookout for trouble.

The other man, Rojas, decorated his gun belt with silver conchas. He stuffed his striped pant legs in his boots so he displayed the exotic reds and greens of tooled leather. Pearl buttons adorned his shirt, and the ends of his long, multicolored kerchief flowed over one shoulder. He topped this off with a wide-brimmed sombrero. He carefully groomed his handlebar mustache, and his blond hair cascaded from under his sombrero and down his back.

If I made Rojas sound like a dandy, I have created the wrong impression. Though he peered out at the world though half-closed lids, he radiated a coiled tenseness. The first time he walked into our camp, I suspected he was more dangerous than a diamondback ready to strike.

One of our riders, Muncie, who had worked down around the border, knew the man. "He goes by Rojas now, but south of the border he went by another moniker, though I can't remember it right this moment. His real name is Goodall. He's a Texican. Word is, he crossed the border barely ahead of the Texas Rangers and disappeared into the Mexican state of Coahuila. That was ten years ago. Maybe he figures Texas has forgotten he robbed a couple of stages and killed a few bystanders doing it."

Rojas wore a Mexican loop holster, a fast-draw rig. When I asked Muncie if Rojas was proficient with a pistol, he frowned. "He brags, but he can back it up. Once in Brownsville, I saw him face off against a gent who thought himself fast. Hell, the poor bastard barely cleared the holster before Rojas put one in his gullet. Fastest gun I ever seen. Believe me, nobody's faster."

The Captain might have questioned his son's judgment in hiring the two hardcases. If he did, he kept it to himself. Once they joined us, they did their share of the work but remained aloof, isolated. They wanted nothing to do with us, we wanted nothing

177

to do with them.

We spent the remainder of the day packing supplies for the ranch. Most of us suffered hangovers. If we remained longer in Dodge, we would have exhausted our coin and returned as broke as when we arrived. We grumbled the boss was hard-hearted, though in reality, we were glad to be away from the corruption of the town.

Flynn complained not at all, which we found odd, considering we thought him a champion bellyacher. That evening as we sat around the campfire, his father cast a probing eye on his son. "You're mighty quiet, Flynn. What's got your craw?"

"Just glad to be on the trail, Capt'n." He smiled, satisfied with himself. "Had a high time, made a little money, ready to see where it leads."

We guessed he was pleased to be without the company of his half brother.

On the third day out, the boss became so unsteady, listing right, listing left, a puncher rode on either side to steady him. At noon we transferred a third of the supplies from the chuck wagon to remuda mounts. As we tied the unfamiliar weight to their backs, they pawed the earth to show their displeasure. We placed blankets in the cleared space. His skin flushed with fever, the

Captain insisted he was no goddamned dude to ride in the chuck wagon.

When he attempted to throw a leg over his mustang, he collapsed, his grip on the saddle horn all that kept him upright. MacInnis and I settled him in the chuck wagon. Too weak to protest, he stared at the canvas top like a man mesmerized.

To the north, dark clouds appeared.

"If it ain't one thing, it's another." Flynn uttered an exasperated huff. "With the Captain ailing, I'm in charge."

None expressed an urge to challenge Flynn, including Dermot.

Flynn twisted his mouth into a smirk. "Let's move. If we pick up the pace, we can keep ahead of the storm."

MacInnis spit, a wad of tobacco juice raising dust. "If we do that, the chuck wagon will toss the Captain around like a sack of flour."

"He's got a touch of ague fever." Flynn leapt in the saddle with a jaunty agility. "He's tough. He'll ride it out."

Every rider there had suffered through a bout of ague fever, and we knew the Captain's illness was deeper, more pervasive.

Dermot trotted up beside his brother. "MacInnis is right. Slower is better."

"My decision, my rules. Now move it.

179

Stop grousing."

The black clouds rolled onward, lightning streaked the sky, thunder followed. We passed through grassland neither high nor low, only flat. Though we journeyed faster, pushed our mounts harder, the rain caught us an hour before nightfall. We hobbled our horses and created a makeshift corral out of lariats. Flynn climbed in beside the Captain. To see to the needs of his father, he claimed. We donned our slickers, pinned extra canvas to the chuck wagon to keep us dry when we climbed under. The wind blew, lifting the canvas and swirling rain in our faces. The cold sweeping down from Canada this early harkened a hard winter.

I figured only Flynn and the Captain slept that night. The downpour grew harsher, the lightning closer, the thunder louder. Soon water ankle deep crept under the wagon. We sat up and prayed this was not the second flood. If so, the chuck wagon made a poor ark.

Sometime near three, the rain slackened and ceased altogether. We removed our slickers, leaving the air to dry our clothes. We unhobbled the animals in the dark, mounted, traveled on. The movement awoke Flynn, who grumbled before climbing out to claim his own mount.

MacInnis bit off a chew of Liggett & Myers and slipped the plug back in his shirt pocket. "Good to see you got your beauty sleep, Flynn."

Flynn touched the scar that ran the length of his cheek. "You're fired, MacInnis. You got paid off in Dodge. Go on, get out of my sight."

MacInnis scratched his beard, which over the last six months had transformed from a heavy grizzle into pure white. He cast a hard stare at Flynn. "Is the Captain still breathing this morning?"

Flynn pushed his lips together, refusing to answer.

"When he's up and about, he can cut me loose, if that's his druthers." MacInnis faced forward. "You can give all the orders you want, Flynn, but that don't make you the Captain."

Flynn wheeled his mount and rode to the rear to be with Bogdan and Rojas.

Late on the fifth day, we came in sight of the Red River and Dobson's Trading Post. Off to the west, perhaps two hundred yards, buzzards lifted above the grass, their heavy wings raising a cloud of dust. When they understood we presented no threat, they settled back to their feast. Once on the other side, we ambled toward the trading post where we planned to stop for the evening, rest our stock and fix a hot meal.

MacInnis noticed first. "The smokehouse ain't smoking." He jerked his Winchester from its sheath and worked the lever. Others followed suit, fearing a roaming band of Comanches or Cheyenne had descended on Dobson, although he had shown kindness to both. He never sold hooch to the heathens, though they weren't above taking it by force. Drunk heathens were capable of anything.

The front door opened, and Ginger and Molly exited. Both sported bruised cheeks and split lips. Molly held her left arm against her breast.

Ginger dropped to her knees, sobs racking her body. Molly kneeled, placing her good arm around her companion. "It's over now, honey. These boys will keep us safe." Her voice cracked as she lifted her gaze. "You will, won't you? You won't let them get us?"

"What the hell happened?" MacInnis looked beyond them into the store. "Where's Emile?"

"Three buffalo hunters showed up yesterday. They killed Emile. They were going to kill Ginger and me, too, but —" Tears watered her eyes. "They ambushed your brother, Flynn. I think they killed him. One of them said as much." She pointed across the river. "There was plenty of shootin'. Somebody's dead, that's for sure."

I whirled my mount and flew for the Red, four of my compatriots trailing me. The Captain climbed out of the wagon and dragged himself aboard a horse. By the time I splashed midstream, he cantered beside me, his frail body ghostlike in its whiteness, his cheeks skeletal, his lips cracked from fever.

We headed straight for the area where the buzzards fed, all the time afraid of what we would find. If those Buffalo hunters had slain Waco, their days were numbered. I wouldn't be alone in my quest. MacInnis and four or five others would join me in the hunt. We loved the kid. He was the best of us, a man to ride the river with.

Once we arrived at the far bank of the Red, the Captain plunged ahead into the waist-high grass and brush. The buzzards again took flight, their black wings flapping, their mouths open and screaming obscenities.

Torn flesh and clothes littered the feeding ground, though enough remained for us to identify the bodies, the massive Bull Bryson and his brother Crawley. Though we searched for the youngest, Pearly, we found only boot prints along the riverbank, too small to be Waco's. We also uncovered traces of blood on a clump of brush.

Upstream, we discovered where a single horse entered the water. MacInnis, the finest tracker on the payroll, dismounted and examined them. "The bronc this fella rode was ten stone smaller than Diablo. The shoes have square ends where ours are more rounded. Whoever rode this way, it weren't Waco."

I gripped my Winchester all the more tightly. "Pearly."

"Where are Diablo and Legion?" The Captain ran a sleeve across his eyes. "Neither of them would desert my son, alive or dead."

Dermot had accompanied us, searching as diligently as any. When we found no further evidence of the events, a mood of pessimism weighed in. It was as if a supernatural spirit had whisked away Waco and his companions. As if to confirm our fears, lightning flashed in the distance, white streaks stretching from the darkening clouds to the horizon. Moments later, thunder rumbled for a full minute. A wall of rain raced from the northwest, obscuring the sun. It would reach us in a matter of minutes.

"What'll we do?" MacInnis asked.

The action had proven too exhausting for the Captain, who leaned over his saddle horn, gripping it, and coughed and coughed until blood flecked the back of his hands.

I relieved him of his reins. "Nothing more we can do here."

"What about them?" MacInnis nodded toward the stinkers.

"Let the buzzards finish their meal, though I hope it doesn't make 'em sick. We need to get the Captain inside before the storm hits and the river rises."

We forded the Red, and when we climbed the far bank, spotted a freshly dug mound with a cross planted at one end. Two of our punchers rested on shovels borrowed from the store. The rest of our outfit along with Molly and Ginger stood with bowed heads while Flynn read the 23rd Psalm, the traditional lament for those who passed. As we drew closer, Flynn's voice became clearer, and while he never stumbled over words, his presentation lacked conviction, as if he recited an unwanted school assignment. Once he muttered "Amen" and snapped the book shut, the others turned as a group and trudged toward the trading post where, eager for news, they met us.

As we helped the Captain dismount,

MacInnis related our findings. When he finished, disappointment was written on all their faces, even Flynn's. I suspect in his case, he hoped for a more definitive conclusion concerning Waco.

Molly pushed dark hair from her eyes. "Though he never availed himself of my services, Waco was about the nicest young feller I ever met. Always tipped his hat and said a kind word."

We unsaddled our broncs and cloistered them under a covered overhang. Five minutes after we entered the trading post, the heavens opened, rain pounding the roof, the building trembling under the wind, which made me believe God Himself was angry over Waco's death. A month after I came to work at the Bar 4 C, a tornado caught me on the open prairie, passing a quarter mile from where I watched it tear up the earth and send debris high into the dark sky. The roar that day sounded much like the roar on this day. I feared any moment the building would disintegrate, the whirling gyre sweeping us to our doom.

By noon, the wind subsided to a breeze, the rain slackened before ceasing altogether. The dark clouds had moved south, leaving behind a morass of mud. Our mounts, sensing a power at work greater than themselves, huddled close, their eyes wild, their nostrils flaring. The flanks of several showed teeth marks, as if they'd attempted to eat one another.

We moved among them, singing, stroking their necks. Once they settled, we saddled up and attached a team to the chuck wagon in which we again laid the Captain. He appeared more frail than ever, Waco's demise too much for him to endure. The storm had ended any chance of finding tracks and discovering the fate of his son and the girl.

We had three days' hard ride to the ranch. Flynn took the lead, sending Dermot ahead to scout. As long as Waco rode with us, we felt safe passing through Comanche country. Without him, we were a bunch of punchers for whom the Comanches held little respect.

Less than an hour out, Dermot came galloping back to rein in beside his brother. They spoke in hushed tones. Flynn halted the caravan, and they rode off, their horses' hooves kicking up geysers of mud.

They found Pearly where Dermot had left him sitting on a rock. He removed the stub of a smoke and flicked it away with his thumb and middle finger.

Dismounting, Flynn squatted before Pearly. A bright froth colored the young buffalo hunter's lips, a Bowie knife jammed in his belly. "You got them gold pieces? We took care of that breed."

"You sure?" asked Flynn.

"Crawley never misses." Pearly coughed and wiped his mouth with the back of his hand. He studied the red streak against the white skin. "Caught him in the breadbasket. I bet that bullet went clean through to Canada."

"If he's dead, how did you get the pig sticker?" With an index finger, Flynn tapped the handle of the knife.

The kid glanced down at the blade. "The Injun gal — she jumped me. I put a bullet in her." His brow knotted. "I think I did. Let's see now — yeah, I shot her — I think."

"And the breed — ?"

"Ain't a proper question. He's dead for sure."

Sweat broke out on Dermot's forehead. "Once the Captain hears his story, he'll kill us."

Pearly leaned forward, wincing. "Did you see Bull and Crawley? They should be here by now."

"They ain't coming." Flynn grabbed the knife, jerking it up and down, widening the wound before he pushed it deeper. Pearly emitted a grunt, his eyes wide with surprise and shock. With a flourish, Flynn pulled the blade free. A river of blood erupted from the wound and mixed with the red earth.

Dermot grabbed his brother's arm. "What the hell?"

The buffalo hunter toppled forward, his head striking the earth, his body rigid. He uttered a last gasp, and his muscles relaxed. His bowels and bladder released, and the stink of shit and urine engulfed them.

Flynn grinned. "Now we tell the story our way."

When the two brothers returned, Flynn tried his best to project a solemn demeanor. He guided his mount to the chuck wagon, where he dismounted. The Captain found the strength to lift his head. Flynn showed him the Bowie knife, bright with blood. He tapped the initials carved into the wood. "We took this off the buffalo hunter Pearly. Before he bled out, he told us they got Waco."

The Captain's brows came together. "Maybe he — he lied."

Flynn tossed the weapon beside his father, the blade clattering against the wood. "Dying men don't lie."

The Captain dropped his head on a rolled blanket that substituted for a pillow.

I can't speak for any of the others, though I suspect most must have experienced

Waco's loss much the same as I. We counted on Waco despite his taciturn personality. He brought order into our world. Only seventeen and far too early to meet his maker, he showed himself more of a man than any Bar 4 C rider, including Flynn and Dermot, pale imitations of their half brother. Flynn was untrustworthy, Dermot weak. Waco and the Captain represented the moral center of our universe. Now with Waco gone, and the Captain dying, a hollowness grew inside of me.

I had seen other men like the Captain, stricken with consumption, eaten up by devils until mere skin and bones. From the look of him, I reckoned the Captain might not make it another week. His will to live faded as Waco's demise became a reality. He needed hope.

"What you can't see, you can't prove," I said. "We have no proof Waco and the girl are dead or alive."

Flynn shot me an angry glance. I didn't care. Once the Captain passed, Flynn would fire me regardless of what I did or said.

The Captain's gaze met mine. A grateful smile turned the corners of his mouth.

I walked away. In half a dozen paces, Flynn caught me, grabbing my arm, spin-

190

ning me around. "I'm tired of you butting in."

With my thumb, I flicked off the hammer guard that secured my .44. "Lay hands on me again, I will kill you." I kept my voice low. Flynn retreated a step. He must have figured since I hung around with Waco, I picked up a few tricks.

"Waco's dead." He flashed a triumphant smile. "And with the Captain in the shape he's in, you're through here."

He stalked off.

MacInnis, who stood only a few steps away, felt the need to offer a comment. "Bastard."

"He's right about one thing. The Captain's hours are numbered. When he sheds this mortal coil, you and me are minus jobs."

"What about Waco? You really believe he's alive?"

I frowned. "I fear the odds favor Flynn's version."

"What do you suspect happened?"

"Animals got 'em maybe. Dragged them off into the brush. Maybe before Bull cashed in his chips, he threw the bodies in the river. If we followed the water, we might find them washed up on a sandbar."

MacInnis peered after Flynn. "How is it hombres like Flynn always wind up on top?"

Two days later near sundown, we made the Bar 4 C. Three other waddies and I carried the Captain into the house. Blue Feather had their sheets turned down, the pillows fluffed, the room aired. We sat the Captain on the bed and removed his boots. Under ordinary circumstances, he would have berated us for invading his privacy. This time, he offered no protest. There wasn't much left of him.

The boys and I departed. At the door, I glanced over my shoulder. I thought the Captain too weak to speak. He surprised me again when, as his wife reached down to unbutton his shirt, he whispered, "Te amo, mi amor."

I averted my eyes and followed my mates.

Most loitered in the bunkhouse. Flynn joined Dermot at the table. From six feet away I smelled the whiskey on Flynn's breath. He pulled a bottle from his pocket. As he drank, his complexion grew more red. "I've got a good mind to go tell that squaw about her breed meeting a fitting end. Tell her to move on."

He pushed himself up, swaying.

In two steps, I blocked his path.

With his index finger, he poked me in the chest. "Listen, you black son of a bitch —"

"Your father is dying. Blue Feather comforts him. You will not spoil it for them."

Dermot saved Flynn further embarrassment. "He's right, Brother. Let it be."

Flynn dropped beside Dermot. He scrunched his features, the scar wrinkling like a dried up worm.

Somewhere along four in the morning, we heard the death song. We rose, dressed, and hats in hands, gathered outside the ranch house. Despite my sentiments concerning heathens, Blue Feather's refrain repeated over and over drove a knife into my gut. The Captain was my boss, yet he represented far more than that — my teacher, my protector, my brother. I was thankful first light had yet to break the horizon. When I ran a sleeve over my face, none of the other punchers noticed.

I suppose Blue Feather understood civilized people needed a Christian service, though she might have preferred an Indian ceremony. We buried him on a knoll a quarter mile from the house, the shade of a cottonwood providing comfort from the boiling sun. We took turns digging. When we finished, we lowered him into his resting place. Blue Feather had wrapped him in white linen. With the heat so fierce and the body stiffening, we wanted him in the ground before he smelled.

The punchers asked me to speak. I intended to recite the 23rd Psalm, which I knew by heart. When my gaze alighted on Blue Feather, I rejected a Bible reading. Instead, I said, "The Captain was a man foursquare. With him, we rode the river, and we are better men for having done it. Now he has gone to where no traveler returns, and it is a better place because he is there. We will not see his like again."

A sprinkling of "Amens" ended my sermon.

At that point, Flynn staggered graveside. As we shoveled in the dirt, he glared at Blue Feather. "Time for you to vacate my house, Squaw." He lifted a shaking finger, leveling it at me. "You, too. Move on down the trail."

MacInnis spit. Tobacco juice splattered the mud and spotted Flynn's boots. "I guess I'll mosey along, too."

Once in the corral, MacInnis and I saddled up. Blue Feather, close to forty, leapt aboard a pinto, intent on riding it bareback. Despite her age, she retained a trim figure. She lacked classical beauty as white people defined it, her hair too black, her skin too brown, her cheekbones too high. To me, these qualities bestowed on her an exotic appeal. I doubted many women her age were as handsome or desirable. All of this without a touch of lip rouge or face powder.

We opened the gate. Before we traveled ten paces, Flynn blocked our path, Rojas and Bogdan, the hardcases he hired in Dodge, on either side.

Flynn placed his fists on his hips. "That pinto is our stock."

MacInnis must have suspected trouble because he held his Winchester across his saddle horn, the hammer already cocked. Removing my hat, I sat it in my lap. In doing so, I covered my pistol. I made a pretense of running my fingers around the inside sweatband.

"Blue Feather came here with a horse, she's leaving with one." When I slapped my hat back on, I held my .44. Neither Flynn nor the hardcases liked that. I cocked my weapon to show those boys we meant business.

Dermot hurried forward and seized Flynn's wrist. "Leave her be. She deserves the pinto."

As we trotted past the men, I turned to watch. I believed Flynn not above back shooting, even in front of witnesses. We traveled fifty yards before I faced front.

"Did the Captain tell you about your son, Blue Feather?" I asked.

In all the years I had known her, I doubt I

heard her speak more than a hundred words. Now she looked at me in a manner that said I was deluded. "Waco is not dead. I know. In here." She touched her breast.

I saw no use arguing the point. Let her hold out hope as long as possible. She would have years to mourn his passing.

"Where can we take you, Blue Feather?" I asked.

"To Lone Wanderer."

"The Comanche are always on the move. How will we find them?"

"They find us."

Neither MacInnis nor I looked forward to riding the Llano Estacado. After the devastating defeat at Adobe Walls and the subsequent invasion by the U.S. Army, Quanah Parker and his band of Comanches traded their freedom for reservation life in the Oklahoma Territory. Those who remained in the Llano Estacado were the wildest of the wild. Stories abounded that they roasted their enemies and ate babies. While I discounted the most extreme as ridiculous, we all had heard stories of the ferocity of Lone Wanderer and his son Straight Lance. True, they left the Bar 4 C alone because of the Captain and his family, but the world had changed. Perhaps Blue Feather's presence insured safe passage for MacInnis and me, though the possibility existed that before the next Sabbath, our scalps would end up on lodgepoles. No one could predict the actions of heathens. For the first time since a boy, I uttered a silent prayer.

CHAPTER NINETEEN

From the moment we left the Bar 4 C, I sensed we were followed. At first, I believed it was the hardcases, Rojas and Bogdan. Late the next evening as we approached the Llano Estacado, I knew for certain it wasn't them. They lacked the courage to follow us into the land of the renegade Quahadis.

On our third day, we stopped at noon. Blue Feather built a fire, piling on brush so that once she lit it, smoke curled toward the sky. Earlier, MacInnis shot a prairie hen, and we roasted it over the open blaze. As we ate, we tossed the bones in a pile. Once we finished, Blue Feather dug a hole with her knife, scooped in the remains and thanked the bird for providing a meal. She stood, and wiping her hands on her skirt, asked for our sidearms.

Though nothing out of the ordinary presented itself, I trusted her judgment. So did MacInnis. We handed over our revolvers.

Ghostlike, six Quahadis rose out of the earth as if God himself molded them from the clay. They had crept within ten feet of us, and I never sensed their presence. All except one gripped bows notched with arrows. The other carried a pre–Civil War breech-loading carbine, so old the varnish of the stock had worn away. If their arsenal appeared less than intimidating, their demeanor supposed otherwise. Though they were thin to the point of emaciated, their skull-like countenances reflected a barbarism for which I was ill prepared. Their war paint was enough to frighten even the staunchest Indian fighter. I feared MacInnis and I had forfeited our lives.

Lone Wanderer led them. I had last seen him in the camp of Quanah Parker four years before, yet he surprised me, not that he led this band but rather that time and circumstances had ravaged his appearance. His wrinkles had deepened, his body grown thinner. He spoke with Blue Feather for several long-drawn-out minutes. During that time, the other braves gathered round. While they pointed their weapons at the ground, their expressions said if we offered the slightest provocation, MacInnis and I would wind up as pin cushions. Once the palaver concluded, Blue Feather informed us the Quahadis would escort us to their encampment. Until then, she would keep possession of our six-shooters. The Indians thought so little of our abilities to inflict damage, they left our Winchesters in our scabbards and our hunting knives in our belts.

Five to seven miles away, a mesa cut a slice out of the horizon. In between us and the mesa lay acrid plains broken by a few undulations which if I were to label hills would be an exaggeration. We traveled over two hours before we arrived at the mesa and ascended a brush-filled, rocky mountain-side. Soon, the trail narrowed into a ledge wide enough for a single rider. The Indian ponies were as sure-footed as mountain goats, while MacInnis's mount and mine slipped and slid, threatening to send us tumbling off a thirty-foot drop to the rocks below. MacInnis and I considered ourselves accomplished riders, yet neither possessed the ability of the warriors of the Llano Esta-cado. Even Blue Feather, who had lived for years among civilized people, maintained a steady balance despite the fact she, too, rode a shod horse. I was proficient with a six-shooter, fast and accurate to a point. In all other skills, these scrawny men could better me at every turn.

We reached the end of the trail atop the mesa. A guard with an unobstructed view down the mountain offered plenty of warning if an enemy approached. The narrowness of the path ensured that, if an army attempted to penetrate their defenses, it would sustain grievous losses. I understood little about military strategy, but even a man as inexperienced as I understood the logic of their fortifications. Problems lay in keeping the tribe supplied with food and water.

Eleven tipis constructed from ragged buffalo hides made up their encampment. The Quahadis could dismantle these dwellings in a matter of minutes, which suited their nomadic life. A dozen women and girls, no healthier than the men, scrutinized our arrival, concentrating on Blue Feather, who displayed a roundness of breasts and hips none could match. Their reactions, stoic as always, revealed nothing of their genuine feelings. I suspected our well-fed, nourished bodies provoked some envy.

A corral of brush and boulders set apart from the living area boarded twenty ponies, some branded, most once-wild mustangs. Among their number stood a magnificent stallion fifteen hands high, dark as midnight on a starless night. My spirits soared. It was the devil horse, Diablo. The pinto was there, also, the animal Waco gave the girl the night they escaped Dodge.

Lone Wanderer halted our caravan before a tipi. Blue Feather leapt from the saddle. With a wave, she bid us follow. She tossed aside the flap and entered.

Waco Joseph Callahan lay wrapped in blankets. Beside him perched the Indian girl, Morning Star, now dressed in Quahadi fashion, her face clean, her hair free of tangles, her cut lip healed. I doubt most white people would have considered her beautiful. They would have argued her eyes held too much slant, her cheekbones rested too high, her black hair hung too straight. Perhaps in the past I accepted the same values. Now I recognized the absurdity of my prejudices. Neither Blue Feather nor Morning Star claimed the classic beauty defined by white Americans. What the hell did they understand anyway? They never saw what I saw.

Blue Feather knelt beside her son and stroked his forehead. He offered a tired smile.

MacInnis and I sat cross-legged at his feet, a woman at either hand. At his head rested the wolf dog, Legion, his gaze focused on his friend. The animal projected a sense of anxiety, as if he feared for Waco's future, which did not stretch my credulity. Waco's cheeks had shrunken, and his eyes retreated into his skull. His darker pigmentation failed to disguise his paleness.

Waco never asked his mother the reason for her presence. He must have known. I was certain the Quahadis spied on the ranch. They would have heard Blue Feather's death song for the Captain and have watched the burial. They witnessed our leave-taking and followed us.

"When we found no trace of you at Dobson's, we figured you both dead," I said.

In a halting voice, Waco related their escape from the ambush at Dobson's Trading Post.

CHAPTER TWENTY

Morning Star crouched in the brush ten paces from the river and spied on Pearly, the youngest of the three buffalo hunters, backlit against a quarter moon.

A series of gunshots rang out in quick succession. Pearly stopped and stared in the gunfire's direction. She sprang from the bushes and plunged the Bowie knife in his belly. When she tried to jerk it free, she discovered it wedged too deeply. With a wild swing, Pearly clipped her on the head and sent her stumbling back. At point-blank range, he fired. The boom of the .44 sounded as if it originated in her head. Yet he missed, not even grazing her. She dove into the brush.

Pearly stumbled along the river's edge as he sent three more wild shots in her direction, each of which crackled undergrowth. He slipped in the mud, dropping to all fours. Picking himself up, he staggered on, his hands gripping his belly. Morning Star waited until he had disappeared twenty yards downstream before she leapt to her feet and sprinted for Waco. She clawed inside her shirt for the makeshift knife.

The scene she encountered was far different from the one she expected. Crawley lay on his side, four black holes decorating his shirt, his dead pupils reflecting moonlight. A few yards farther, Bull lay on his back. In his left hand, he still clutched his pistol, but the wrist bent at a right angle, jagged bone sticking straight through bloody flesh. Yet, he still lived. Each breath pumped blood from a ragged gash across his throat.

Kneeling, Morning Star drove the homemade blade into his groin, penetrating penis and testicles. He grunted, and blood discolored his pants. The fresh injury added pain without ending his misery. He would linger, the longer the better.

The wolf dog whined, calling her attention to Waco. She hurried to him and tried to lift him. Her fingers came in contact with his back where the bullet exited, opening a hole the size of her fist. She needed to stop the flow of blood, which soaked the ground beneath him. She scooped up red mud, packing it against his wound, pressing until it solidified. She snatched the skinning knife from Bull's belt and cut away Waco's shirt, tying the strips together, creating a bandage to circle his middle.

What was she to do now? The youngest buffalo hunter lived. If they attempted to cross the river, he might ambush them. She gathered Diablo and the pinto, leading them back to Waco. I doubt Morning Star weighed more than 110 pounds and stood less than five three. Yet she lifted Waco into the saddle. He slumped forward, ready to topple. She held him upright while she secured him with his lariat.

She led the horses two hundred paces, covering their tracks with tumbleweeds. Only then did she mount the pinto. Grasping the reins of Diablo, she headed west into the darkness toward the Llano Estacado. She hoped she could keep Waco alive until the Quahadis found them. Of them, she knew nothing other than the stories Brother Wolf told her.

They rode the entire night. When the sun peeked over the horizon, Morning Star halted. She untied the lariat and laid Waco on the ground. Unsaddling the horses, she removed the blankets and covered him. For the next ten minutes, she gathered brush for a fire, adding clumps of green grass to create extra smoke. Plumes soon rose into the clear morning air, announcing their presence. If no one came, if the Quahadis missed the signal, Waco would die. An icy hand gripped her heart.

But fate took a hand.

With a growl, Legion announced their presence. She caressed the wolf dog, avoiding the spot above his shoulder blades where a bullet had nicked him and a scab had formed.

Five horsemen galloped toward them. They arrived in a cloud of dust, and their leader, who bore scars on his chest, leapt from his pony. He placed a palm over his friend's heart, which stopped the moment the hand came into contact with flesh.

The girl snatched Waco to her breast, squeezing as if to merge her body with his. He gasped, and his heart beat in rhythm to hers.

CHAPTER TWENTY-ONE

"I traveled to the land of the dead and returned," Waco told us.

"What was it like?" I asked.

"I wandered alone in darkness. Far ahead a light shone. I walked toward it, and it grew closer. If I had reached it" — he rested his hand on Morning Star's — "perhaps even Morning Star might have been unable to call me back."

"Were you frightened?" I regretted my question the moment I uttered it. "No, not you."

"Am I not human?" Waco's features hardened. "For days, I feared I would die before I had my revenge."

"Revenge?"

"My brothers sent the buffalo hunters to kill me. They hastened the Captain's passing. They exiled my mother."

MacInnis scratched his beard, which grew whiter each day. "You ain't in shape to do much of anything."

"Flynn fired MacInnis and me," I said. "The hardcases he hired follow his orders. Sooner or later, he'll replace all the old riders with those of his choice. If you make it known you are alive, they will shoot you on sight."

"Each day I grow stronger. In the spring, I will be ready." Waco regarded me with an intensity I can only describe as mesmerizing. "I am the dead. I am a ghost. You cannot kill a ghost."

MacInnis and I stepped outside, followed by Morning Star. Appraising her in full daylight, I wondered where she discovered the strength to save Waco. She was only a slip of a thing, yet she had driven off the buffalo hunter, Pearly. She administered a coup de grâce to Bull. After that, she managed to put Waco aboard Diablo and find help. Hers was a remarkable feat that would have thwarted many a full-grown man.

Yet, I feared her efforts were in vain. I had seen dead men who looked healthier than Waco. MacInnis and I viewed his wound, scabbing over, raw around the edges, leaking fluid, and we concluded he would not last the week.

The girl addressed our concerns from a different perspective. "There were days I believed he welcomed death. Since then, his heart has grown strong. He desires to live."

Straight Lance found us outside Waco's tipi. He offered safe passage out of the Llano Estacado or we could share the fortunes of the Quahadis for as long as we wished. He considered us honorable men because we had brought Blue Feather back to her people and because we treasured our friendship with Brother Wolf.

"As long as Waco — Brother Wolf — remains, so do I." I glanced at MacInnis.

His old eyes wandered around the village, which, once you got past the tipis and corral, was a dusty mesa devoid of life except for lizards and rattlesnakes. "Sure," he said. "I'll stick as long as I ain't a bother to nobody."

Straight Lance crossed his arms over his scarred chest. "If white men come, will you fight with us?"

Like all his kind, his countenance remained emotionless, noncommittal. If I saw anything in that face, it might have been a touch of surprise that we threw in our lots with a ragtag tribe of renegade Indians.

"If they come, I stand with Brother Wolf," I said.

"Them are my sentiments, too," MacInnis said.

Ten minutes later, Straight Lance returned our revolvers.

As prognosticators, MacInnis and I proved happily inaccurate. Waco not only clung to life but each day grew stronger as he promised. Morning Star was as responsible as Blue Feather for his recovery. She slept in the same tipi with Waco and his mother. Blue Feather provided herbs and potions she had practiced on Bar 4 C riders, curing everything from gunshot wounds to boils and bellyaches. The girl didn't know the same remedies as Blue Feather, but she burned with a fire she imparted to Waco, an insistence on living, a grasp of the future, a battle to survive against all odds. Those qualities saved them at Dobson's Trading Post and worked for Waco now.

About this time, the Quahadis, fascinated over Waco's death and resurrection, gave their mesa the name Mesa del Fantasma Viviente, Mesa of the Living Ghost. Today, if you look on a map, you won't find the name. Most who called it such are gone, but I remember. When I think of those days, now more than twenty years past, my heart sings. I was at once young enough and old enough to know I was living the great adventure of my life. I had no idea where or how it would end, perhaps in my death, yet for as long as I did live, I would have stories to warm my nights. I would have shared my life with people who I loved and respected. A man can't ask for more.

By my second week on that mesa, our meat ran low. Soon winter would be upon us, when the world atop that rock would get cold and inhospitable. Without fresh meat, living conditions would become unbearable. To keep up his strength, Waco needed meat, and my belly grumbled at the most inopportune moments.

Straight Lance formed several hunting parties, including one comprised of Motsai and Yapa, both boys who had yet to see fourteen summers, scrawny kids who rode with a grace that belied their ages, in sync with every move, every sway, every footfall of their ponies. Straight Lance asked me to accompany them. They spoke a smattering of English, and I had picked up a few words of Comanche, so together we made known our needs. What we were unable to say aloud, we communicated with hand signs.

That first day, we ranged far from our home, twenty miles or more, camping that night beside a creek, which the dry spell had reduced to a stream no wider than the palm of my hand. A few yards downstream, the creek widened into a pool large enough to water the horses. Once the sun dipped below the horizon, we slept, waking the next morning before sunrise. Five minutes after we broke camp, we came upon a prairie antelope. In my lap, I cradled my Winchester, a shell in the chamber. Sensing us, the creature lifted its head. I raised my weapon and fired. The slug struck the animal in the head, taking its legs out from under it.

I had doubts about the boys. I suspected Straight Lance sent Motsai and Yapa along to give them a bit of experience. Their weapons appeared less than impressive, their bows constructed from branches of chokecherry or ash. The barbed arrowheads were quartzite, honed to a knife-edge sharpness. Yet on the whole, their weapons lacked the power and distance of my Winchester.

An hour later, they verified my assumptions were rooted in prejudice. My companions spotted another antelope a quarter mile downwind. When I failed to distinguish it from the landscape, they pointed it out to me. They dismounted and crept forward until within fifteen feet of the animal. Concealed in the grass, they launched arrows, which struck at the same instant. Caught in the middle of feeding, the buck sprang up and dashed a dozen paces before

213

it realized it was dead.

Later that day, each kid brought down a prairie hen, Yapa as the bird took flight, an impressive feat of marksmanship that put to shame my limited skills with a rifle.

We spent another night on the trail and rose early again, eager to return home. By then, we had crossed into land claimed by the Bar 4 C, though no official documents gave possession to the Callahan family. If we varied a mile, we could refill our water pouches at a well the Captain built years before that serviced the ranch and that he encouraged the Quahadis to use.

We filled our leather pouches and allowed the horses to drink. I slung my water pouch over the saddle horn and went off to relieve myself. Once finished, as I buttoned my pants, I heard the hoofbeats and pushed aside brush. Two riders, their pistols drawn, galloped toward us. I snatched my Winchester and worked the lever.

Motsai and Yapa dropped behind the trough as a bullet whined over their heads. The punchers reined up a dozen feet away in a cloud of dust. I recognized Bogdan, whom Flynn hired in Dodge.

I emerged from the brush, my weapon leveled.

"What the hell?" Bogdan twitched his

nose as if my smell offended him. "You're the nigger the boss fired."

Tied to his belt, he carried a fresh scalp, tangled black hair covered in blood and flies.

"On a hunting expedition?" I asked.

"The boss is paying twenty dollars in gold for every Comanche scalp. Me and Murdock, here, aim to get more now. Yours will do as well as any." He snapped off a shot, his horse shying the very moment he fired. The bullet cut a path by my ear.

Acting out of instinct, I squeezed the trigger, and the boom of my Winchester startled me. The impact lifted Bogdan clear of the saddle and threw him backward.

Before Murdock reacted, two arrows punctured his chest. He toppled to the ground. Both horses, frightened by the noise and blood, bolted back for the Bar 4 C.

I approached the downed men. Murdock stared up at the sky, his sightless eyes full of surprise.

Though gutshot, Bogdan lived. Blood poured from his belly, the pallor of his skin a chalky white. His nose twitched again, and I understood it was nothing more than a nervous habit.

As I kneeled beside him, he pointed to his boots. "Take 'em off for me."

"You call me 'nigger,' and then you ask a favor."

"Please — I promised —"

"Damn you to hell." Laying my rifle aside, I pulled and jerked until his right boot slipped free. I gripped the left when Bogdan emitted a last sigh and his head tilted away from me.

I wanted to feel bad, but instead I was angry at myself. This man deserved what I had given him, and I acted the fool in trying to accommodate his last wish.

For all we knew, others heard the shot. When I signaled the boys to mount up, they offered no objection. They, too, realized our vulnerability if more armed riders appeared.

We rode due west in the opposite direction from our mesa, then cut across rocky ground where we left no tracks before entering a creek so shallow it looked as if the horses walked on water. When we exited, I roped a tumbleweed and dragged it along behind, erasing any evidence of our passing.

Near sundown, we climbed the shadow-filled trail and entered the village where the women relieved us of the antelopes and hens. When I dismounted at the tipi that MacInnis and I shared, Blue Feather was waiting. Without asking, she unsaddled my mount and carried the rig inside where she dropped it beside my bedroll.

Waco pushed aside the flap and entered, Legion at his heels. The kid appeared robust, his cheeks flushed, his step confident. "I hear you had trouble."

Once I explained, Waco uttered a disgusted grunt. "So, Flynn put a bounty on our scalps. And you say this Bogdan had one?"

"It was fresh. A couple of hours old at most."

"The owner of that scalp must have belonged to Quanah Parker's band. Whoever it was, he wasn't one of ours."

A tightness gripped my chest. "I've never killed anyone before. I've never even shot at anyone."

"You feel bad about it?"

"Given the circumstances, I'd do it again. Still, a part of me wishes it hadn't happened."

"Never hesitate," Waco said. "If you do, you'll be the one lying in the dirt."

CHAPTER TWENTY-TWO

September passed, and we drifted into late October. The winter gales from Canada arrived early, sweeping across the Mesa del Fantasma Viviente, threatening to collapse our tipis with each gust. But the Quahadis made their constructions to bend, not break. We hunkered inside to keep warm. We had no protection against hunger.

On four separate occasions, braves rode out hunting, each time encountering gunmen from the Bar 4 C who drove them back empty-handed into the Llano Estacado. No one died, although a brave caught a bullet in the arm. The day of that incident, Waco pushed aside the flap of our tent and sat cross-legged on the floor facing McInnis and me.

"We cannot survive the winter without food." He laid a hand on the Sharps that rested in his lap. "Flynn and Dermot have more cattle than they need. I think we should claim a part of my inheritance."

"A raiding party?" I said.

"I will not let my people starve."

I thought it odd he referred to the Quahadis as "my people." He dressed in his old shirt and pants, his only Indian regalia his moccasins and the feather in his hatband. The six-shooter added to the impression that while he was of mixed blood, he was civilized rather than a heathen, although I no longer saw the Quahadis as such. They were people, no better or worse than the rest of us. Often, I chided myself for taking so long to reach such an obvious conclusion.

Before dawn, Waco, MacInnis, Straight Lance, and I descended the trail. Even before we exited the village, I feared our journey would push Waco beyond his endurance. Yet, he sat astride Diablo with a confidence that announced his return to health. Right behind trotted Legion, whose coat glistened. Daily the beast vanished near sunset, always returning with a full belly. Of those who lived on the mesa, Legion was the best fed.

We headed straight for the Bar 4 C range, our plan simple. We would locate a herd and cut out twenty head. We hoped the foul weather forced the riders to shelter indoors,

219

though in hindsight, we should have known Flynn understood he was most vulnerable during such a cold spell. As we approached the edge of the Llano Estacado, we spotted five horsemen a mile or more away. They were traveling the border between Comanche country and the ranch. I doubted they were looking for strays. They were hunting Quahadis.

Straight Lance steered us through gullies, around hills, among cottonwood groves. If he experienced the least bit of doubt, he never showed it. I trusted him as I did Waco.

Another time, we spotted the dust of a dozen riders. We dismounted and hid behind brush. The riders passed, and I caught a glimpse of them. As I surmised, Flynn fired the old hands. I judged the new hands a rough lot like Rojas and Bogdan, hired guns first, punchers second. For them, riding herd was a nuisance. They desired action.

Late in the afternoon, we arrived at Canyon de Mort, so called because years before, a group of ten miners seeking yellow dust prospected there. To protect their territory, the miners killed a brave and his son. In retaliation, the Comanche raided their camp. They left the bodies where they fell and hung the scalps on branches so anyone who passed would see. That ended the hunt for gold in the Panhandle, although if truth be told, there was none to begin with.

We secluded ourselves in a cave large enough to include our horses and ourselves. To cover the entrance, we uprooted brush, filling the opening until we covered it. If a person looked closely, he might have spied an isolated tangled root or broken branch, but it appeared to be a solitary wall of vegetation, the entrance a mere shadow.

Legion had disappeared. Now he squeezed through the brush to lie beside Waco. He had a belly full of prairie hen. We knew this because a single feather clung to the wolf dog's hindquarters. Waco plucked the feather and stuffed it in his shirt pocket. I thought this odd, unless he was keeping a souvenir of the night's proceedings.

In the half light, I studied him, amazed that he had regained most of his weight, his face its fullness. The wound, the size of a dime where the bullet entered, the size of two silver dollars where it exited, had lost much of its inflammation, although front and back scarred an ugly reddish pink. Fewer than three months had passed since the encounter with the buffalo hunters, and though we had ridden fifteen miles, he appeared as fresh as when we began.

He caught me observing him. "Buck up, old friend. They have stirred a hornets' nest. The world is about to get a great deal more interesting."

He delivered the last line with a lightness that belied our situation. I am not saying Waco was humorless. On the contrary, he understood humor better than most. His was of an uncommon sort, dry wit opposed to low comedy that the average cow puncher practiced. If you consider he grew up alone without playmates, if you recall Flynn and Dermot looked to do him harm at every turn, if you consider his Indian blood that made him see life as a continuous struggle, then you can understand his reticence.

Take his words, "The world is about to get a great deal more interesting." An understatement full of irony. Is irony not also a form of humor?

We spoke no more until the sun dropped below the horizon. When the shadows closed in, we emerged into the night. Broken clouds hid most of the stars, though a quarter moon rose in the east providing a sliver of light. The wind picked up, the raw chill intensified, and our breath showed white against the black night. I always believed my eyesight superior, but Straight Lance led us along trails made by squirrels, so faint only he could see them.

Emerging from Canyon de Mort, we descended into a valley fifty or sixty feet deep and a half-mile wide, which protected cattle from the elements. We separated twenty head from over a hundred. Keeping them in a tight group, we drove them up the incline until we cleared the rise where, without a word, Straight Lance and Waco disappeared.

Neither MacInnis nor I offered a word of protest or questioned their reasons. We could find the mesa by the stars. Still, with them gone, I imagined a Bar 4 C gunman behind every rock, every scrub. I held no illusions concerning our fates should Flynn's men catch us. They would find the nearest cottonwood and stretch our necks.

Minutes after Waco and Straight Lance departed, we rounded a clump of brush, and sure enough, three mounted men, Winchesters drawn, waited for us. While darkness hid their features, the quarter moon provided enough light for us to see the barrels of their rifles. They sat on their mounts, silhouettes against the blackness. I considered reaching for my pistol. Fortunately, my better judgment won out, and I remained motionless.

The cattle stopped, trapped between the

men in front, MacInnis and me in the rear.

"Well, lookie here." The fellow in the middle snickered. "We're going to have a good time tonight."

"Toss those rifles."

Waco's voice sounded if it originated from above and possessed an ethereal quality like a disembodied spirit, a ghost if you will. His tone raised the hairs on the back of my neck. If it frightened me, it must have scared the bejesus out of the gunmen.

One emitted a nervous laugh as he glanced over his shoulder. He could have seen nothing except shadows. "A shot will bring a dozen riders."

"They will arrive too late to do you any good."

With their attention diverted, MacInnis and I drew our pistols, cocking them, the click of the hammers distinct in the crisp air.

"The question is, are you willing to die for another man's cattle?" Waco said.

"I ain't." One gunman tossed away his rifle, which acted as a signal for the other two who followed suit.

"Now climb down, unbuckle your gun belts, let them drop."

We used lariats to bind the men hand and foot, their kerchiefs to gag them. Waco squatted behind the three hardcases. When he spoke, his words held the same ominous tone as before. "If you get loose in the next hour, you'll be tempted to raise an alarm. If you do, I will come back and slit your throats."

He reached in his shirt pocket and removed the prairie hen feather, its whiteness bright in the light of the quarter moon. He slipped it in the hatband of a puncher with such a light touch, I doubt the man realized what Waco had done.

To the south, gunfire erupted, sharp pops in the night air.

Waco gathered up the rifles and pistols. "Time to be on our way. We will have no more trouble tonight."

The sporadic gunfire continued, moving south away from us, and later a glow flickered on the horizon.

For the rest of the night, we drove the cattle over hard rock surfaces and up creek beds. Waco knew all the tricks to cover our tracks. Because of such a convoluted route, we didn't arrive at the mesa until first light streaked the clouds. We drove the cattle into a makeshift corral on the far side of the village. Morning Star held open the gate. When the last cow entered, she closed it, securing it with rawhide strips.

"Where's Straight Lance?" I asked.

"He created the diversion," Waco said. "By now, they understand he is like the wind. It touches your skin, but you never see it."

Half an hour later, Straight Lance arrived. A coat of dust covered him and his mount. Considering the beast led most of the Bar 4 C on a merry chase, the pony exhibited a freshness that denied the circumstances. It pranced as if acknowledging his accomplishments. Straight Lance leapt to the ground with a jauntiness that said he enjoyed the nighttime frolic. Blood spotted his face and hands.

"We saw a fire," said Waco.

"I set flames to dry grass. The riders scattered like frightened children."

"Anything else?"

"I found the three you left bound."

"Did you kill them?" I asked.

"They will remember Straight Lance."

He sliced the mouth of one, plucked out an eye of another, sliced off an ear of the last.

"You ruined them," I said.

"If that is all it takes to ruin a man, he is too weak to matter," Waco said. "A man faces adversity his whole life. The way he handles it shows who he is." The faintest of smiles crossed his lips. "Though I dare say, those three will skedaddle at first chance."

CHAPTER TWENTY-THREE

Dermot counted out ninety dollars in gold pieces and spread them on the counter. When Ginger reached for the coins, he laid his hand over hers.

She offered a smile. "I ain't in that business anymore."

Since Dobson's death, Ginger and Molly ran the trading post, and in doing so, put aside their whoring. Although they promised to import girls as soon as opportunity permitted, those wanting female companionship traveled another day to Sparrowville, a tent emporium that sold rotgut and overcharged for a gap-toothed brunette and a skinny squaw.

"Aw, Ginger, I ain't looking for a quick poke and a quicker goodbye."

The storeroom door opened, and Molly stepped through carrying a stack of long johns. "There will be none of that now. You know our rules, Dermot."

Dermot's cheeks burned. "This ain't what you think, Miss Molly. I'm courtin', all proper-like."

Molly dropped the underwear on the counter. "That brother of yours is a son-of-a-bitch."

He slid his hand from Ginger's and stood straight. "I ain't Flynn." Dermot infused his voice with righteous indignation. "I'll grant you, there are things I've done I'm not proud of. I got my faults. But I try to do my best."

"Your brother is one too many Callahans for my taste."

"How about Waco? You liked him, didn't you?"

"Him I trusted, but I never saw much love between you two."

Dermot focused on Molly, his eyebrows coming together. "I regret he is gone. You won't believe me, but I wish he was here so I could make amends."

Molly set her fists on her hips and glared at him. "Easy words now that you and Flynn have the Bar 4 C to yourselves."

"I can see I'm not changing your mind, Miss Molly." Dermot tipped his hat. "Miss Ginger. I'll say good day and be on my way."

"Come back when you need more supplies or have a better story," Molly said.

Ginger's features collapsed in disappointment, but she made no overt move to stop Dermot.

Dragging his feet, he stepped into the morning sunlight. Enos waited in the wagon, the lines intertwined with his fingers. He was the only one from the old crowd Flynn kept on the payroll. Though he served with the Captain in Mexico, no one, including Flynn, expected him to fight for his pay. He carried an extra fifty pounds or more, most around his middle. He cooked for twenty punchers, and while some grumbled that the meat was overcooked or the bread lumpy or the coffee burnt, those who complained the loudest cleaned their plates.

Dermot mounted his bay. Enos flicked the lines. The wagon, weighed with supplies, groaned as if protesting its load, but it rolled forward, the tracks leaving a visible impression in the red earth. Four other riders fanned out behind. This was still Comanche country.

Dermot glanced back once to see Ginger in the doorway, her golden hair lifted by the wind. He cursed himself for a fool. A dozen times, he'd paid for her favors, so now she quit selling, he wanted her more than ever. He faced forward, gritting his teeth.

Near noon on the third day, they pulled

up before the house. Flynn stood on the porch and his expression said trouble. "What's wrong?" Dermot asked.

For most of the morning, Flynn had watched riders wander in, all accounted for except three from the west range. The stories were all the same. None slept during the night. Instead, they pursued a phantom they never saw, yet who set fire to dry grass and sent them scurrying. Now smoke drifted over the ranch house, and the ash filled the air.

As Flynn finished his story, a ranch hand hurried over. "Looks like Mort, Bud, Castor riding in."

Dermot followed his brother to the corral where the men drew rein, each clutching the horn to keep from falling, each covered in blood. Others helped them from the saddles and sat them against the corral fence. Because of their similar facial features — squinty eyes, little mouths, bushy eyebrows — rumors persisted they were the Thomas brothers, who once rode with Sam Bass, although they called themselves "Smith."

A bloody kerchief covered Mort's mouth, another the eye socket of Bud. Castor pressed his kerchief against the area where the right ear should have been.

231

"What the hell happened?" Flynn asked.

"Three men — jumped us —" In a halting monologue, Castor told of the theft of the cattle and the aftermath. Of the three he was the oldest, half past thirty, his raised knuckles revealing his stiffening joints, the veins stretched against the skin. "We was there a long time trying to get free. Then this Injun comes along. He cuts us up, then he cuts us loose."

Flynn plucked a feather from Castor's hatband. "What's this? Some kind of joke?"

Castor looked to Dermot. "What's he talking about?"

"It was in your hatband." Flynn crushed the feather and tossed it to the wind. "It didn't get blown there."

"The fellow who came up behind us —" Castor took a deep breath trying to ease his pain. "He must have put it there."

"What did he look like?"

"It was too dark. He was behind me."

"And those in front? Did you see them?"

"One had a white beard. The other was —" Castor's paleness contrasted with the red-stained cloth he held against his ear. His voice sounded more strained with each word. "He was dark skinned."

Flynn touched his scar, which, over the years, had expanded, rising out of his beard like a red snake. When stressed or when things went badly, he fingered it as if he found comfort in its existence.

He signaled Baxter, who'd hired on a month earlier. While no posters circulated on him, the man admitted to spending five years in Huntsville, although he never explained the circumstances. He carried a wide body with the beginnings of a gut pressing over his belt. Gray streaked his week-old stubble and handlebar mustache.

Dermot followed them into the house. In his office, Flynn unlocked the bottom drawer of his rolltop desk and opened a tin box from which he pulled six twenty-dollar gold pieces, passing them to the gunman. He closed the box, crammed with paper money and gold coins, and slipped it back in the drawer.

"What's this for, Boss? You want me to kill somebody?"

Flynn flipped through papers in the pigeonholes until he found a map, which he opened and spread over the desk. With a finger, he tapped an area near Victoria, Texas. "This is Matagorda County. There's a ranch there, the Bow and Arrow, owned by John Moore. The last I heard, a tracker named Nantan worked for him. I've been told he's the best in the state."

Baxter wrinkled his nose. "I don't cotton to redskins."

"Tell him I've got a one-time job for him. Four hundred dollars. While you're at it, find twenty more guns willing to work for my wages."

"What's in it for me?"

"A two-hundred-dollar bonus plus your pay."

Baxter shook the coins. "This ain't much. I probably won't be back till spring."

"The sooner you bring me Nantan, the sooner you collect your bonus."

With a laugh, Baxter shoved the money in his pants pocket.

"He's part Mex, part Apache," said Flynn. "Whatever you do, don't call him a breed or feed him liquor. Word is he was drinking in a saloon in San Antonio when some son of a bitch did both. By the time Nantan walked out, four men were dead."

Once the front door closed, Dermot said, "What are you planning?"

"I had my suspicions all along about who gunned down Bogdan and Murdock. It was MacInnis and that darkie." He slammed an open palm on the map, sending papers flying. "They joined with the goddamned Comanches."

"So?"

234

"In the spring, I'm going to hunt down and kill every Comanche on the Llano Estacado. There can't be that many, not with Quanah Parker and his bunch gone. We'll get 'em all. Wipe 'em from the face of the earth."

Dermot removed his hat, exposing a forehead damp with sweat. "Women and children, too?"

"They're vermin, all of them. Scum." Flynn's cheeks glowed red, the veins on his nose pulsated. He grabbed a bottle and a glass and poured himself two fingers. He downed the fiery liquid in a single swallow.

Over the next month, Flynn's drinking increased so that by noon he slurred his words and stumbled over his own feet. The lines around his eyes and mouth grew deeper until late in the evenings they became so exaggerated they appeared drawn on.

During the final week of 1876, snow flurries and sleet cast the days into continual tones of white, and an Arctic gale threatened to carry away the earth itself, confining all the hands to the bunkhouse. As a result, Dermot spent more and more time cloistered in the house.

One morning Flynn leapt out of bed, and still in his long johns, charged into the study. His hair was matted, his skin pallid, his eyes bloodshot. "They're stealing us blind. By spring, we won't have a damned longhorn left. By God, I'll make them pay for this. Every single one of them."

He poured himself four fingers of whiskey. Over the past months, he had grown thinner, the flesh in his neck sinking to expose a sharp Adam's apple, which jumped with each swallow. His face fell in on itself, making the scar even more prominent. He banged the glass on the table and fled the room.

Confined as he was, Dermot had discovered some solace in reading. The day before, he had begun *Henry V.* Though he didn't understand every word, he followed the course of the story. Now he laid the volume aside and considered the future.

With the additional gunmen, Flynn would possess a small army. The Llano Estacado harbored at most thirty-five renegade Comanches, the majority of whom were women and children. The Indians might muster a dozen warriors. Against forty well-armed and well-mounted riders, how long could a ragtail bunch of savages hold out? Flynn would eradicate them with ease.

The Bar 4 C had encountered no trouble from the Comanches until Flynn exiled

Blue Feather. Now he and his brother suffered the comeuppance of their miscalculation. A war with the Quahadis loomed in the spring. People were going to die. Maybe a lot of people.

Dermot soon realized Flynn feared more than a few renegade Indians. While Dermot read more and more, moving from Shakespeare to Dickens's *Great Expectations,* Flynn lacked any compensating activities. He drank, he mumbled to himself, he planned. He'd lost fifteen or twenty pounds over the winter, and he walked with a perpetual stoop. Before noon, reeking of whiskey, he stumbled into the study, ripped the book from Dermot's grasp, and tossed it on the floor. He thrust his open palm forward, exposing a crumpled feather of a prairie hen. He swayed, unsteady on his feet. "Waco's Bowie knife is gone. Right off my desk. This was in its place. Did you do this? Is this some kind of sick joke?"

"Why would I do that?" Dermot leaned over and retrieved the book.

Swaying, Flynn clutched a chair. He gripped a bottle from the table and poured himself four fingers of whiskey. Raising the glass, he stared off beyond the walls of the house. "Unless — unless Waco is alive. I've had my suspicions all along." He whirled to face Dermot, liquor splashing over the rim. "The third man — the bastard who drew down on Castor and the others. It was Waco. It had to be him."

"That's crazy talk."

"We never saw his body. He's alive, I tell you, and once Baxter gets here with Nantan and more men, I'll hunt down the son of a bitch and finish the job."

In early March, when the snows melted and the winds died, the punchers once again rode the range. On the second day, four riders reined in before the ranch house, dust rolling over the porch. A rowdy who called himself Tucker carried an Indian across his saddle. Tucker was smiling, his brown beard bristling. Grabbing the Indian by the hair, he threw him to the ground where he lay face down, the expanding and contracting of his chest the only evidence he lived.

Dermot stepped off the porch, kneeled, and laid a hand on a bony shoulder. The dry skin resembled tanned leather rather than flesh. The years had exacted their toll. His wrinkles were deep canyons eroded by wind and sun. His lids fluttered, and he exposed dark, ancient eyes. He spoke in a guttural tongue, and Dermot caught a tone of resignation.

Tucker wiped his palm on his shirt. "We

caught this Comanche over by Silver Creek."

"After we get through with him, he ain't going to rustle no more of my cattle." Flynn stepped off the porch and removed the lariat from Tucker's saddle.

"He's not Comanche." Dermot stepped off the porch and gripped his brother's arm. "He's Cheyenne. I've heard enough of their lingo to know the difference."

Flynn jerked his arm free. "They're all alike."

"You miss my drift. He left his tribe because he was a burden. By their custom, he's already dead."

With his foot, Flynn rolled the Indian on his back. "Then we'll finish the job." Flynn uncurled the lariat, made a knot and slipped the noose around the Indian's neck.

"He can't hurt us," Dermot said. "Let him be."

"We'll take him to the barn. Stretch his neck there."

"You're drunk."

"And I'd act different if I was sober?"

As Flynn dragged the Indian across the yard, the Cheyenne lost consciousness. Flynn tossed the lariat over the hoist and tied the lariat to Tucker's saddle horn. Tucker hauled the Indian until he dangled

239

ten feet from the ground. The man jerked and flailed. He was so dehydrated and starved that when his bladder and bowels emptied, only a half dollar–sized spot soiled his breechcloth.

Flynn left him swinging. When a breeze picked up at noon, the body swayed as if filled with feathers. At sunset, a puncher cut him down. The arms and legs snapped as they hit the hard-packed earth, bones breaking skin, their whiteness aglow in the dying sunlight. A rider dragged him to a far field where the scavengers would feast on the remains.

That night, Flynn drank his dinner until his head dropped on the table.

Dermot pushed his chair back, stepped to his brother, and removed keys from a breast pocket. For a full minute, he waited to make sure his brother slept. Satisfied, he entered the study, unlocked the bottom drawer of the desk, and took out the iron box from which he drew bills and gold pieces, over six thousand dollars. He pocketed all but five hundred. Flynn still had access to over ten thousand in a Dallas bank.

Afterward, Dermot went to his room and collected his saddlebags, already filled with extra clothes and cartridges. In the study, he sat at the rolltop desk and wrote out a note:

You have bought my share of the Bar 4 C for $5500. I want nothing more.
It's all yours now.

Your brother,
Dermot Callahan

As he crossed to the barn, the punchers lounged in the bunkhouse laughing and congratulating themselves on disposing of the redskin. He saddled Billy, his favorite bay, leading him out the back a hundred yards before he mounted.

He rode through the next day. Before sunset, he made a dry camp in an arroyo ringed with brush. For most of the night, he huddled in his blankets, his .44 tucked against his breast, his thumb on the hammer. At most, he slept four hours. Long before first light, he woke, saddled up, and rode on, always alert, for death lurked in the shadows.

At sundown he sighted Dobson's Trading Post, a pony waiting the hitching post. As he drew closer, he recognized a saddle with the initials MAC chiseled into the horn. Off in the corral a dozen horses milled around raising dust so they were mere outlines in the dying light.

He tied his own mount next the other and, throwing his saddlebags over his shoulder, walked to the trading post. Inside, a single kerosene lamp lit the enclosed space. Darkness darker than the night hugged the corners. Molly waited behind the counter, Ginger beside her. Ginger's wrinkled brow was a warning.

"I know you're here, MacInnis. I ain't looking for trouble." Dermot swallowed, his Adam's apple jumping. "Are you going to kill me the way you did Bogdan and Murdock?"

MacInnis stepped from the shadows, his pistol leveled, the hammer drawn. "Son, I ain't never killed a man. I'd prefer to finish my days able to make the same claim."

The man's stern countenance and bushy white beard reminded Dermot of Old Testament prophets pictured in the family Bible.

"Look, I'm dead tired," Dermot said. "Other than a few hours sleep, I've been riding since I left the ranch."

"Where are your men?"

"I'm alone."

"Alone?" MacInnis narrowed his eyes. "That's a mighty dangerous proposition. I never knew you to be so full of daring. Where's Flynn?"

"He and I parted company."

"I find that hard to believe."

"I'm too tired to care. Do what you need to do, but I'll not debate my motives. I came here for something, but it has nothing to do with you."

Men like Bogdan and Murdock would have put a bullet in Dermot's belly without the least remorse, but MacInnis, despite his cantankerous nature, was a person of conscience. Dermot laid the saddlebags on the counter, careful to press his palms flat against the oak surface.

MacInnis holstered his pistol. "I guess you read me pretty well, son. I hope I made the right choice."

"I spoke true when I said I came with a reason that has nothing to do with you. But what are you doing here?"

"Picking up a few supplies. No harm in that."

"If I was you, Mac, I'd skedaddle. Before you get your dander up, that ain't a threat, and it ain't me doing Flynn's work."

"Then what is it?"

"Flynn has sent for a tracker named Nantan. He's going after anyone he thinks rustled his cattle. White or Indian, it don't matter. He intends to wipe out the Comanches, all of them, women and children

243

included." He regarded Ginger. "I'm leaving for good and asking you to come with me, Ginger. We can start afresh far from here. Now Molly, you've made it clear what you think of Flynn and me, but from now on, I'm cutting my own trail."

Molly crossed her arms over her chest, her lips pressed together. "What are your intentions? You get down the road and find you're tired of her. What then?"

"I aim to marry her."

"Marry me?" Ginger lifted a hand to her throat and glanced at Molly. "He wants to marry me."

"First preacher we come to, honey."

Ginger turned her mournful eyes on Dermot. "But you know what I was."

"You're kind and good and you never lifted coin that wasn't owed you. Once we leave here, we never speak of it again."

The door flew open, and Rojas entered, his blond hair flowing down his back. He wore a Mexican loop holster, a fast-draw rig. He always bragged, but Dermot had seen him pit his skills against other gunmen. True, they shot at stationary targets, but Rojas was far faster and more accurate than any of them. He could drop MacInnis and him before either cleared their holsters. His sky-blue eyes appeared half closed as if he were ready for a nap. "Your brother says you must return." He smiled, but it lacked humor or compassion. "You took something of his."

"I took what is mine, and I will not go back." His voice quaked, and he feared Molly and Ginger and MacInnis heard the panic in his voice.

Rojas rolled his shoulders, simulating a shrug. "So be it." He cast his lazy eyes on MacInnis. "Are you taking his side in this, old man?"

MacInnis spewed tobacco juice that rimmed the edge of a spittoon. "You think you're in charge here, but you ain't."

The gunman raised a questioning eyebrow. "You think God is on your side?"

This induced a laugh from MacInnis. "That's one way of putting it."

"Touch your gun, and you die." The voice came from the right — or from the left — or from above, its deep bass firm, decisive, each word pronounced with clarity. Shadows haunted every corner, hiding the shelves, the merchandise, the speaker. The words echoed, hollow and emotionless, without form, without substance.

The smile vanished from Rojas as he stared into the blackness. "Where are you, my friend? Let me see you."

"I am everywhere."

The disembodied words came from all directions at once.

"I am the dead. I am a ghost."

Frozen, Rojas made no move for his .44. MacInnis stepped forward and slid the weapon from Rojas's holster and stuck it in his own belt.

"Move on." The ghost intoned the words rather than spoke them.

Rojas smiled. "Perhaps someday, we will meet again on more equal footing."

"Pray we don't."

In an effort to appear casual, Rojas stuck his thumbs in his belt and strolled out of the door. They waited until they heard hooves galloping west. A two-legged shadow flitted out the door followed by a four-legged one, both more apparitions than solid bodies.

Wide-eyed, Dermot removed his hat and ran his fingers through his hair. "Was that — ?"

"Could be," MacInnis said.

Dermot reached under his shirt and pulled out a Bowie knife in a leather sheath, the initials WJC carved into the handle. He offered it to MacInnis. "When you see the kid again, pass this along. It belongs with him. And for God's sake, you and anyone con-

246

nected to the Comanches, get the hell out of the country. Flynn's got a goddamned army on the way."

CHAPTER TWENTY-FOUR

From the window, Flynn watched Rojas ride up to the ranch house, his mount bedraggled, its head hanging, its body quivering. It favored its right foreleg. Flynn strode to the porch. Rojas leaned forward in the saddle, his elbow propped on the horn. The gunman was missing his .44.

"Dermot take away your shooter?" Flynn scratched his beard as he studied Rojas. "If so, I have newfound respect for him."

Rojas dismounted, and reins in hand, faced Flynn. "As you suggested, I found him at Dobson's. I would have brought him back, alive maybe, dead maybe. One way or another."

"What stopped you?"

"A voice."

"A voice?"

"It came from the shadows, but it was everywhere at once." Rojas spoke in a soft

248

tone, close to a whisper. "He said he was a ghost."

"And what of my brother?"

"By now he has ridden on."

"Along with my fifty-five hundred dollars." Flynn uttered a disgusted grunt. "I'd say you pretty well botched the job. So what now? Are you planning to cut and run?"

"Oh, no, amigo. You misunderstand. It was no ghost. Only a man. He had me at a disadvantage. If we meet again, I will kill him. No man is faster than I, no man a better shot. This is not bragging. I only state fact."

"I hired you for your pistol. Now you don't even have one." Flynn turned away but paused in the doorway. "Get another rig from the storehouse. You lose it or you ruin another horse, you're fired, regardless of your reputation."

Flynn headed straight for the liquor cabinet where he poured himself four fingers of whiskey. As he sipped the liquor, he stared out the window. Clouds covered most of the sky. Lightning speckled the dark undersides like fireflies, followed by distant thunder. He figured it for a dry storm, the kind that often plagued the Texas Panhandle, full of sound and fury signifying nothing.

He flinched as if dodging a punch. Full of sound and fury signifying nothing. That expression wasn't his, yet it surfaced unbidden, unwanted.

Waco had spoken those words to him.

He fingered the scar that rose like a goddamned mountain ridge.

Why did he think of his half brother now? Did he equate Rojas's ghost to Waco? The kid was dead. Maybe he doubted for a while, especially when alcohol fueled his brain, but in the sober light of day, he reasoned that the idea was foolish. Waco died on the banks of the Red River, and scavengers carried away the body. Otherwise, he would have shown up long before now.

Tomorrow he would ride out to the north range. By now, Rojas had told his story to the crew. If Flynn holed up behind four walls, his riders would view it as fear. Anyway, he knew the identity of the invisible voice — that colored bastard he'd kicked off the place. He and MacInnis rustled stock together, and once Flynn caught up with them, they'd hang together.

As for Dermot — sooner or later, his brother would pay for his betrayal. For the time being, though, Flynn needed to concentrate on wiping out the last of the renegade Comanches.

Before sunup, he saddled his pony. When his crew emerged from the bunkhouse, he sat aboard his mount, waiting impatiently for his men to saddle their own mounts.

Once they reached the north range, Flynn left his crew to do the tally and branding of new calves. With Rojas as his companion, he headed toward the Llano Estacado with no more than a vague need to see what lay in that direction.

They kept to the open so they could see trouble coming. A mile or so before the gradual slope that signaled the beginning of Comanche country, they came across an Indian. The tracks told the story. The pony had stepped on a Diamondback. The rattler lashed out. The pony reared, throwing the rider. Both horse and snake were dead.

From his features, the Indian appeared no older than eleven or twelve, although Flynn had trouble distinguishing ages of heathens. The kid's features were gaunt, skeletal. Bone from the boy's wrist had broken through skin, blood spotting the ground like red rain. He lay face down, unconscious. Buzzards circled high overhead.

A Comanche. No doubt here. The blanket thrown across the pony's backside displayed a pattern consistent with their work, although his tribe mattered not a whit to Flynn. They were all dirty, foul-smelling creatures, less than human, no better than a coyote you'd shoot on sight.

Flynn dismounted and slipped his lariat from his saddle.

CHAPTER TWENTY-FIVE

MacInnis and I spent that winter with the Comanches huddled on top of the mesa. Almost daily, the wind whipped down from Canada. In late December, the snow arrived. The beef Waco brought to the village saved the inhabitants from starving. The Quahadis supplemented the meat with herbs and roots, and, as long as we stayed in the tipis swathed in moldering buffalo hides, we remained comfortable, although I must admit my conversations with MacInnis grew stale if not downright wearisome.

To no one's surprise except perhaps their own, Waco and Morning Star discovered they hungered for each other. Every time they passed, each eyed the other like a piece of sugar candy. I am unsure who said the first word. My two bits would be on the girl because the kid had absolutely no understanding of women, even though the fairer sex thought him quite a catch. Both Molly and Ginger had kind words for him, and I never heard a saloon gal in Dodge deny him a place in her bed, but he knew precious little when it came to serious courtin'.

Waco learned fast. His tipi lay right next to ours. Once Morning Star moved in with him, their moans and groans often kept me awake late into the nights and early mornings. MacInnis had no trouble. He drifted off the moment his head touched soft fur, his snoring adding to the cacophony. When the racket became too loud, I wrapped myself in a robe and wandered out on the mesa. The biting wind cleared the sky of clouds, exposing millions of stars that stretched from horizon to horizon. I had never taken the opportunity to see the grandeur above, to grasp the smallness of man, to understand my own insignificance.

One evening as I sat there trying to figure out my role in this vastness, I discovered Blue Feather beside me. I had no recollection of her arrival, and her presence unnerved me. Not only because she appeared out of nowhere, but because I had little idea why she chose to visit me. We spoke not one word but stared off into the sparkling ceiling for perhaps an hour. When I glanced over, she had gone, once again without disturbing me.

The next night, I returned to that same spot. She showed again, seating herself at arm's length, both of us facing south toward the Bar 4 C. I could not help but wonder if she longed for her old life with the Captain. After about fifteen minutes, I gathered enough courage to speak. "I am grateful for your company."

If she reacted in any way, I could not tell. She neither accepted nor rejected my sentiment, although she came the next night and the next and the next, until it became a routine part of the day. I dreaded the day it would end. She would grow tired of the quiet, grow tired of me. I was no Comanche brave, only an aging colored man without prospects who, when the spring arrived, would probably move on.

Then, on a night when clouds obscured the sky, when biting winds stung our faces, when we stared into the gathering darkness, she spoke at last. "Together, we have more heat than if we are apart."

I opened my robe, she opened hers, we came together. And by damn, we created a furnace inside our mantle. Every fifteen minutes, I had to stick my head out to catch a breath of fresh air to keep from suffocating.

The next morning, I moved my few possessions into Blue Feather's tent, and at night, when Morning Star and Waco frolicked, I minded not one fig.

CHAPTER TWENTY-SIX

In late March, when the thaws eased our suffering, Waco and MacInnis set off for Dobson's Trading Post to renew supplies. When they returned, they called together the men of the village to let us know what they had discovered.

Waco sat between Lone Wanderer and Straight Lance, the wind lifting their long, dark hair. With the eagle feather in his hatband, Waco looked as much an Indian as either of those who flanked him. We had seen little sun that winter. During the harshest months, the Quahadis coated themselves with a crushed powder from seeds of prairie sunflowers, which produced a yellow-brownish sheen that acted as a barrier against inclement weather. It prevented the skin from drying up, the lips from cracking. Blue Feather applied the concoction on me. It did little to change my color, already a solid brown, but it deepened the skin tone of Waco so he appeared a hundred percent Comanche. His change manifested itself in more than appearance. The moment the kid took Morning Star as his wife, Waco Joseph Callahan turned pure heathen. He became Brother Wolf.

Yet neither MacInnis nor I feared the people of the Mesa del Fantasma Viviente. Even MacInnis, a white man, they accepted as readily as they accepted me. I do not wish to imply the Quahadis were better than any other people. They were human beings with flaws and foibles the same as any, yet they saw beyond color. In the white man's world, I forever suffered the fate of the outsider, fit to eat in the kitchen, never the dining room. In the world of the Quahadis, I shared equally in all their daily activities.

I would have died for those people. Despite — or possibly because of — her silences, Blue Feather brought me more contentment than I thought possible. For that alone, I owed these people everything.

"Flynn will have a well-heeled army at his disposal and a tracker of repute in Nantan," Waco said to the group.

"So what are to do?" asked MacInnis.

"We will make sure they see a single entrance leads to the summit. They will block our path and try to ascend."

258

"If they block our only way out —" Mac-Innis caught himself. "There's another way off the mesa, ain't there?"

"A foot path," Waco said. "Wide enough for a man, no more. We will make good use of it."

We began our preparations by piling rocks above the trail that from below resembled a wall. At another spot lower down, we piled brown-dried chaparral fifteen feet high on both sides of the slope. MacInnis and Waco had brought two cans of coal oil that they poured over the brush.

Waco flashed a rare smile. "They will come when they think we are asleep. They believe Indians are afraid to fight in the dark."

"You mean it's not true?" I said.

"It is a tale told by those who know nothing of the Quahadis."

An hour past noon, an ancient warrior, Ten Bears, whose wrinkled and scarred face suggested an embattled past, found Waco as he talked with Straight Lance. The moment he stepped within their boundaries, they cast their attention on him. "My grandson Running Deer rode out yesterday. He has not returned." The old man held himself erect, proud. "He is the last of my blood."

"In which direction did he ride?" Straight

Lance asked.

"West toward the Canyon of the Cave."

"And why did he go?"

"Because he is a child who needs to prove himself a man." Ten Bears dropped his gaze as if seeking sanctuary within the earth. "I have failed my grandson."

Straight Lance laid a hand on a bony shoulder. "Like the eagle, a boy must learn to fly on his own."

"I will go," Waco said. "Running Deer may have drifted too far to the south. If that is the case, I have a better chance of bringing him back."

"It was foolish for the boy to go alone." Straight Lance looked southward into the haze rising out of the valley floor. "You should not be so foolish."

"I will take one of my companions. A pair of punchers will draw less attention than you or any of your braves."

"We are not afraid." Straight Lance kept his voice level, without rancor.

"I suggest this only because it may be the best method of bringing the boy home."

Straight Lance crossed his arms over his chest. "I give you until the sun rises in two days. If you have not returned by then, my warriors and I will seek you out."

Waco found me in my tipi with Blue

Feather. I had spent the morning watching her chew leather in preparation of making a pair of moccasins for me. The soles of my boots were wearing thin. I admired the manner in which she masticated that cowhide until it was as soft and pliable as cotton. Before Blue Feather, I would have thought watching a woman chew cow leather all morning would bore me to death, but this small act, mundane as it was, only made her more beautiful in my eyes. No one had ever done such a thing for me, including my mother, who each day receded further into the dark recesses of memory.

I say this because when Waco asked me to accompany him to find Running Deer, he asked me to leave my paradise. Happy, content, I nevertheless understood if I expected a piece of paradise, I had to fight for the privilege. I could not refuse.

The weather had turned again, a cold front moving down from Canada. We bundled up in our coats, leaving the buffalo hides behind. Together we passed the pile of rocks we built for defense before we descended through the wall of chaparral that towered over the narrow trail. We traveled west toward the Canyon of the Cave, riding in a zigzag pattern, hoping this might make us less visible and also increase our odds of crossing the boy's trail. As the sun dipped below the horizon, Waco spotted the tracks of an unshod pony. He dismounted, and kneeling, ran his fingers around the outside of the print as if his touch would tell him how long ago the rider had passed.

Shadows closed in as overcast skies darkened the landscape. The conditions failed to slow Waco. He sensed Running Deer's direction as much as he read the signs. An hour after the darkness fell, Legion growled. Waco reined in Diablo. Drawing his .44, he dismounted.

I fell in behind. Although Waco gave no signal or command, Legion disappeared in the chaparral. I knew Waco saw me as a friend, yet, after Blue Feather and Morning Star, his most important relationships were not with human beings but with the devil horse and the wolf dog — magnificent creatures to be sure, but Waco connected with them on a level that bordered on the supernatural. Even his Comanche blood could not account for this mixing of souls and minds. A mystical cord bonded them, a gift from God or the Great Spirit or whatever you wish to call it, a gift bestowed upon Waco alone.

On that dark prairie surrounded by brush, I saw or heard nothing except my own ragged breathing. Then, as if the darkness intensified my senses, I caught a whiff of burning buffalo patties mixed with dead grass. Soon a flickering glow shone through the thicket. We crept up on the campsite. At ten paces, we split up, Waco to the left, I to the right.

Two Bar 4 C riders had climbed into their bedrolls, scooting as near as possible to the fire. Nestled in the shadows near their mounts lay a limp body, the hands and feet bound so tightly the rope dug in, cutting off circulation. Bone poked through the right wrist.

Ready to send both men straight to hell, my finger curled around the trigger. Before I could act, Waco glided into the clearing, moving like the breeze, soundless, without form. Coming to the first man, Waco cracked the man's skull with the barrel of his pistol so hard I swear he splintered bone. Alerted, the second rider rolled over in his blankets and reached for his pistol.

Legion dashed from the dark, his teeth bared, a snarling monster. The man froze. I relieved him of his sidearm. With my boot, I rolled him over so that he stared into the black muzzle of my Winchester.

I recognized him as Gaddis, who Flynn had hired a week before he ran me off the

Bar 4 C, although I doubt we had spoken ten words to each other. Gaddis tried to disguise his age behind a full beard, yet I judged him to be a year younger than Waco. A feral kid, his eyes darted this direction and that, and he twisted his mouth into a perpetual sneer — tactics, I suspect, he employed to survive among a crew of toughs older than he.

Waco severed the bonds of Running Deer before carrying the unconscious boy within the borders of the firelight. Cuts and burns disfigured his upper body. In the middle of his chest someone had branded him with a Bar 4 C iron. A rope burn circled his neck where they dragged him along the ground. He breathed in gasps. Kneeling, I felt for a pulse, so faint it barely registered.

My anger boiled over. Sweeping up my rifle, I slammed the stock into Gaddis, the impact splitting him from hairline to eyebrow. He hit the ground, arms and legs splayed. I drew my knife, prepared to gut him from nave to chops.

Waco gripped my wrist. "He is not yours to kill."

We tied up the unconscious riders, gagging them with their own kerchiefs. We tied them belly down over their saddles. Waco mounted Diablo, and I lifted Running Deer to him. Before I mounted my steed, I kicked the embers into the dry chaparral. A blaze erupted.

The growing fire lit Waco, dancing shadows chiseling his features. "Now you think like a Quahadi."

We rode north, the flames spread south.

At daybreak, we ascended the mesa, passing through the chaparral barrier and under the hanging rocks, a Comanche-style Sword of Damocles. Crossing over the crest, we found the village waiting. Straight Lance relieved Waco of the boy, carrying him off to the grandfather's tipi. Other braves ripped the riders from their horses. Gaddis had regained consciousness, his twisted features articulating his fear. The other rider, who Waco had crowned with his pistol, lay inert where they dropped him. The warriors pounded stakes into the ground, each taller than an average man. To these, they secured Gaddis and his partner with wet rawhide. As the rawhide dried, it would tighten, cutting into their flesh.

Gathered outside the grandfather's tipi, we waited through the morning as the women plied their cures. Along about ten, the wind whipping the mesa, stinging our faces with dust, Ten Bears began his song of death, and we turned to those responsible.

Women worked to revive the unconscious puncher, a wiry man with skeletal features and an unhealthy pallor. They forced liquid down his throat before coating his lips with a foul-smelling balm.

A squaw removed the gag from Gaddis, who coughed until his throat cleared enough to speak. "It weren't me. It were that Rojas. He did all the cutting and burning. Yeats there" — he shifted his gaze to his partner tied to the other stake — "he did it, too. Not me. I swear it. I swear it on my mother's grave."

Tears ran down his cheeks.

"Enough lies," said Waco.

Gaddis strained against his bonds, forcing the rawhide to dig deeper. "I didn't do it. Rojas did. Rojas."

"And Flynn?" asked Waco.

"He watched. Rojas did most of it. Not me. Not me."

"And where are Rojas and Flynn?"

"They went back to the ranch." His tone deepened, each word a strain. "We were supposed to bring the Injun kid the next morning. They were going to string him up. Not me. I was gonna to let the kid go. I swear it." Gaddis pleaded with eyes that swelled with tears. "You won't let them do this to me." He shifted his attention to me, but since I lacked the proper pigmentation, he concentrated on MacInnis. "You're a white man. Make 'em stop!"

MacInnis scratched the underside of his silver beard and gazed at Gaddis with disgust. "If you believe in the Maker, you best pray. Not for life. You've thrown that away. Pray you die well. I suspect you won't. That'll give these righteous people and me some satisfaction."

Ten Bears, his dirge ended, emerged from his tipi. He crossed the open space to stand beside Waco, who held out his Bowie Knife. "They belong to you. I ask only that you take the young one as near to death as you wish. Preserve enough of his spirit to deliver a message."

Ten Bears began by cutting a circular path along Yeat's hairline, blood flowing down his face in waves. Half-conscious, Yeats screamed, arching his body to dislodge the blade, which succeeded only in making the cuts more jagged. The grandfather clutched the thinning hair, pulling while he cut.

Yeats turned rigid, his eyes bulged. "I can't breathe."

His muscles turned flaccid, his bowels and bladder surrendered, the stink pervasive.

Ten Bears threw up his hands in disgust. "His cowardly spirit has flown." He placed his palm over Gaddis's heart. "This one beats strong."

For the next three hours, Ten Bears sliced jagged rectangles in Gaddis's chest. Each time he cut, he pulled, the skin separating with an audible rip. Whenever Gaddis passed out, the women revived him. When alert, Gaddis screamed so loudly they must have heard him all the way to the Bar 4 C. After Ten Bears skinned most of the flesh from Gaddis's chest, he removed the gunman's boots. With measured exactitude, he sliced through flesh and tendons until the blade scraped bone. At last, with the precision of a surgeon, the old man removed the eyelids.

I owed it to my companions to see this spectacle to its conclusion, though it sickened me. Steely-eyed, MacInnis never flinched, not once, and every Quahadi, including women and children, watched in rapt attention. When he grew too tired to continue, Ten Bears passed the knife to Waco. "He is yours to do what you want." He dragged himself to his tipi and disappeared inside.

Straight Lance cut free the body of Yeats. He dragged it to the edge of the cliff and tossed it into the ravine, where it would lay hidden from all except predators. By morning, little would remain.

Waco freed Gaddis. With my help, we got him aboard his horse and tied him in the saddle. We fastened a stick to his back to keep him straight. When evening shadows stretched across the mesa, Waco led Gaddis and his mount down the trail. Gaddis remained in a stupor, neither conscious nor unconscious, somewhere in between, his mind shutting down because of the pain. For the entire ride, the odor of burnt prairie hung heavy in the night air.

Near sunrise, Waco drew within view of the ranch house. He leaned over and jammed an eagle feather into Gaddis's hatband. With a slap on the horse's rump, Waco sent the animal scurrying toward the corral.

He wheeled Diablo, and along with Legion, headed back for the Llano Estacado.

CHAPTER TWENTY-SEVEN

"The brush just exploded." Platt wrinkled his brow, darkened with soot. "We were a quarter of a mile away when the fire broke out. That's when we spotted the horse. Biggest damn bronc you've ever seen, twenty hands high. Steam shooting out its nose."

Flynn sat looking out the front window as the young puncher reported what he'd seen. The fire had died out when it reached Aspen Creek, but a breeze drove smoke across the corrals with such thickness the barn existed as a hazy outline. Ash swirled like snow within the smoke.

"What about the rider?" Flynn asked.

Platt curled the brim of his hat. "He didn't look real. I tell you, Boss, if I didn't know better, I'd swear all this talk of a ghost ain't so far off the truth."

His arms folded across his chest, Rojas leaned against the door jamb. "There is no ghost. Only one who claims he is a ghost."

"Yes, sir, you're probably right." Platt aimed his words at Rojas although he refused to make eye contact. "Still, by the time we got to the spot where you left Gaddis and Yeats with the Injun kid, they was all gone, not a trace of 'em."

"So what are you saying?" Flynn asked.

"I'll guess I'll be moving on."

"You've got a week before payday. I ain't paying for work that ain't done."

Platt looked down at his boots as he considered his options. "I guess I can last till then."

Rojas opened the door to allow Platt to exit, but the puncher stopped at the threshold. "There's a rider out by the corral. He don't look like one of ours."

Smoky haze turned animal and man into ghostly figures. The rider sat astride a pony that pawed the ground, but an outline of a feather in the hatband caught Flynn's attention. Springing from the chair, he rushed for the door, pushing aside Platt. They approached cautiously, not wanting to spook horse and rider. Despite the coolness of the morning, sweat beaded Flynn's forehead.

His hat pulled low over his eyes, the mounted man wore no shirt, although a red cloth covered his chest —

Slowly the realization dawned that it

271

wasn't a red cloth. Some devil had ripped the skin from the body, ragged pieces of flesh hanging like thread and swaying in the breeze.

Rojas grasped the reins, holding the mustang in place. "It is Gaddis. Get him down. He lives."

From his belt, Platt pulled a knife and severed the bonds holding the rider to the stick that kept him straight. Gaddis slid from of the saddle, and Platt lowered him to the ground. Gaddis moved his lips, his voice so weak only Platt heard. With a last gasp, Gaddis stiffened before his muscles gave way and his head rolled to one side.

"What did he say?" Flynn asked.

"I barely heard him. I ain't sure." Platt rubbed his palms on his shirt, smearing blood across the cloth. He stood, holding his hands away from his sides.

Heat rose to Flynn's face. "What did he say?"

"I don't know. Not for sure." Platt lifted his eyes to Flynn. "I think — maybe he said 'devil.' " He backed off a step, placing distance between him and the dead man. "Maybe I'm wrong about sticking around. Maybe it is time to move on."

"If you run, they all run." Rojas caressed the butt of his .44. Smiling, he clapped Platt on the shoulder. "We cannot have that, amigo. You will stay. You will say nothing."

Platt jammed both hands under his armpits. "Yeah. Sure."

Flynn's crew had wandered over from the barn or the corral or the bunkhouse. They gathered round, a half dozen staring at the body, the other half dozen trying their best not to stare.

A voice rose in consternation.

"Those heathens skinned him alive," a puncher said.

Another said, "His eyes! Look what they did to his eyes!"

"Where's Yeats? What happened to Yeats?"

"Maybe it's best we don't know."

During the silence that followed, Flynn feared that his men, seeing the damage done to Gaddis, would, like Platt, see flight as the best option. Instead, Rojas saved the moment. "We need to wipe out the Comanche devils. Make sure this does not happen again."

The cries for vengeance came in a rush.

"Dirty, stinkin' savages!"

"Vermin!"

"They don't deserve to live!"

"Kill 'em all!"

"Every last one of 'em!"

Satisfied, Flynn offered a nod of approval

and walked back to the house. He reseated himself at the window and watched four men carry Gaddis out to the north pasture. Smoke continued to roll in, turning the gravediggers into gray outlines, phantom figures who worked in a silent world.

His hands shook, not from fear but from anger. This feather meant to fray his nerves, to put him on edge, to keep him from thinking straight. They underestimated Flynn Callahan if they thought such a cheap trick would frighten him. Soon the renegade Comanches would feel his wrath. This thing with Gaddis fired up his men, who were ready to charge into the Llano Estacado. As soon as the reinforcements arrived —

That very evening, Baxter returned with Nantan accompanied by another dozen guns.

Flynn strolled out on the porch, where Rojas was having a smoke.

Rojas removed the roll-your-own and tossed the stub into the yard. "Your army has arrived, amigo."

Dust covered the newcomers' clothes and exposed skins. Except for Nantan, Baxter had hired only white riders, hardcases every one, whose descriptions probably adorned wanted posters. They ranged in size from short to tall, wide to lanky, but shared common characteristics. They sported beards or handlebar mustaches, even the youngest among them. They carried revolvers strapped low, knives in their belts.

Four, including Nantan, wore sombreros, those wide-brim Mexican hats favored by punchers in the South. The hat dwarfed Nantan. He stood less than five two or three in moccasins, clean-shaven, lighter skin because of his mixed blood, yet darker than the other riders. His weathered wrinkles told a story of a life lived in the open under the sun. He wore a leather shirt and breeches stained with grease and blood. He carried a tomahawk and knife in his belt but no sidearm. His cradled a Winchester, model 1866 known as "Yellow Boy" for the bright engraved-metal finish. Even as they waited, Nantan pulled an oil-stained cloth from his belt, passing it over the twenty-four-inch barrel, removing the trail dust. "I track. I will not fight for you. I will not kill for you."

Baxter leaned forward, an elbow on the saddle horn. "Maybe the redskin has a yellow streak." He laughed.

Nantan swung the rifle in an arc. The barrel caught Baxter across the face, the blow propelling the gunman off the rear of his mount. His back and head struck the ground with such force bones cracked. Nantan slid from the saddle. Baxter lifted his head and tried to focus. He clawed for his .44. Nantan pressed his foot on the man's wrist, pinning it to the ground, and removed the tomahawk from his belt.

His eyes wide with fear and shock, Baxter watched the tomahawk descend, closing his eyes the exact moment the blade struck his skull. The angle was so straight, the blade so sharp, the cut so precise, the blow emitted a muted sound, as if the weapon struck a slab of meat rather than flesh and bone.

Grunts of surprise and shock sprang from the riders, but no one reached for his pistol or offered a stronger protest. Even though the incident stunned Flynn, he too only watched. He had heard rumors of the halfbreed's dangerous mixture of coldness and volatility. Here he had seen it firsthand and realized, if anything, the stories understated his ferocity.

Placing his heel on Baxter's chest, the Apache ripped the tomahawk free and turned his gaze on the other riders before focusing on Flynn. Blood flecked his face and hands. He waved his tomahawk in the direction of Baxter. "Do you question Nantan as this one did?"

Flynn tried to keep his voice steady, unaffected, but to his ears it sounded strained. "I hired you to track. I expect nothing else."

Rojas lifted an eyebrow. "You just killed Baxter, yet you will not fight for us."

"No man insults Nantan."

Rojas grunted a laugh that held no humor, and he said to Flynn, "The number of dead grows already, amigo."

"From now on, those who get dead are Comanches" — Flynn slammed a fist into an open palm — "and anyone with 'em."

CHAPTER TWENTY-EIGHT

Our scout, Yapa, rode into camp at mid-afternoon. Although he had seen only thirteen summers, the entire village called him a warrior because of his actions with his friend Motsai when they accompanied me the day we encountered Bogdan and Murdock. We listened while he addressed Lone Wanderer. Reinforcements had arrived at the Bar 4 C, which meant, once they completed their preparations, they would move on the Mesa del Fantasma Viviente.

Lone Wanderer ordered us to put our plans into effect. First, we needed to get the women and children off the mesa. This included two expectant women, Morning Star, who was beginning to show, and Fair Winds, whose belly said the baby had dropped. Five boys and six girls, all under the ages of ten, and eleven other women made up the remainder. Of these women, Old Grandmother was so ancient she remembered when the Spanish claimed Texas. Blind in one eye, the other covered with a fine white coating, she would slow the immigrants' pace to a turtle's crawl. Blue Feather and the warrior boy, Motsai, would lead them out of the Llano Estacado and into Oklahoma Territory, where they would join Quanah Parker and his people under the protection of the U.S. Army.

As the group came together, Waco lifted Morning Star aboard her pony. She glowed with expectant motherhood.

"No matter what you hear, I will find you," Waco told her. "If they think they can kill Brother Wolf, they are mistaken."

She leaned over, her hand caressing his cheek. "Even when you are a tottering old man, our children will say, Here is a warrior among warriors."

Before or since, I have never seen a couple more in love, and their parting, as the Bard said, was sweet sorrow, but in stark contrast to Shakespeare's lovers, these two faced a tangible danger not of their making. Every time one of us left the mesa, we risked an encounter with death. Now an army, which possessed countless advantages, threatened our homeland. We had only one advantage. They believed they had surprise on their side. We needed to be able to take the fight to our enemy. In order to do so, we needed the women and children safe.

While Waco whispered his farewell to Morning Star, I performed the same task with Blue Feather.

"Take care of yourself, my husband." Her voice held more tenderness than I expected.

We had no official marriage service that would stand up in a white world, but we were husband and wife. I loved her with the same intensity as Waco loved Morning Star. Although we shared a tipi, I had little idea of her feelings for me, other than she enjoyed our frolics among the buffalo hides. She exhibited few outward endearments. I put it down to the Captain, with whom she had shared her life for eighteen years. When I took stock of myself, I came in a poor second. For the rest of my life, I would battle a ghost, but that didn't prevent me from loving her.

The caravan descended the trail, passing first under the rock wall we had built and through the chaparral trellis soaked in coal oil. Whining, Legion fidgeted beside his master as if pleading with Waco to run after Morning Star and bring her back.

For close to two hours, Waco wandered around the mesa, inspecting the wall or the escape route or whatever else he could find to keep his mind occupied. I don't believe I had ever seen him so nervous. When I suggested he go after them to see them safely away, Waco jumped astride Diablo and galloped down the mesa, Legion on his trail.

The moment he vanished out on the prairie, I wondered if I should have made such a suggestion. A lone rider presented an inviting target.

CHAPTER TWENTY-NINE

Once he reached the open plain, Waco kept his eyes to the south, sure if he encountered trouble, it would originate from that direction. He followed the dust that lingered in the air. Half an hour later, Diablo carried him within hailing distance of the caravan.

Waco followed for over an hour until satisfied they had gotten away. He took a last look at the women and children before he whirled Diablo and began a circle that would carry him halfway to the Bar 4 C, confident that if he ran into riders, he could outdistance pursuit. He checked his .44 to ensure a round filled every chamber. Satisfied, he replaced the pistol and withdrew his Sharps. So armed, he felt confident that, if trouble found him, he could meet it on equal footing.

He soon discovered he had sorely overestimated his abilities.

Ten miles below the south fork of the Red

River, he caught the scent of rising dust.

Reining in, he remained still, expecting a bullet.

Legion growled and looked over his shoulder. "Easy, old son."

With slight pressure, Waco shifted the reins, and Diablo rotated so they faced his adversary.

A wiry man perhaps five two or three crouched twenty feet away, a Winchester pointed in Waco's general direction. His brown face showed no expression. Nantan could have shot him from ambush, yet he hadn't, and this gave Waco hope.

"Your people call you Brother Wolf." Nantan spoke without an accent. "The whites believe you are dead."

"I passed into the land of the dead, but I returned."

"Any man tells me such a story, I say he lies." Nantan stared long and hard at Waco before he spoke again. "You do not lie. I see it in your face."

"My breath stilled, my heart stopped. My woman pulled me back after I crossed over. She would not let the spirits keep me."

Nantan lowered his weapon. "Your brother has paid me to lead him to your stronghold. You have purposely left tracks so my ancient eyes do not miss them. I thank you for your concern. Once I take him and his men there, I leave. He knows this."

Waco slid from the saddle so he and Nantan faced each other on equal footing. "What brought you here?"

"He paid me much money."

"An honest answer."

"I do only what I am paid to do. I owe him nothing more."

"What are Flynn's plans?"

Nantan's mouth tightened. "I will not betray my employer further. I am surprised you asked."

"That was unworthy of me. My only excuse is that my white blood asserted itself."

"Your scout informed you of all you need to know."

"You saw him?"

"He was a boy. If he lives, his skills will improve. You are few if you must send a child to spy."

"Flynn must suspect our numbers."

"He suspects, but he underestimates you. I have seen the wall you built and the brush you piled along the trail. All very clever. Yet, I doubt you will win this war. Their strength is too great."

"Perhaps we can make winning too costly."

"Let us hope."

They had nothing left to say, and they both knew their meeting had ended.

"Vaya con Dios, Brother Wolf."

Nantan disappeared in the brush.

Legion pressed himself against Waco's leg. Waco squatted, throwing an arm over the wolf dog. Feeling ignored, Diablo wandered over, and Waco rubbed the animal's nose.

He mounted and rode on, his rifle cocked, although his faith in his abilities was tarnished. Like the young scout to whom Nantan referred, Waco hoped he lived long enough for his skills to improve.

CHAPTER THIRTY

With Waco gone, that left nine of us to defend the mesa.

Lone Wanderer remained in charge, organizing our defenses. Alert as ever, he directed us to shore up the rock wall, to familiarize ourselves with the escape route, to prepare our weapons. Despite his youthful enthusiasm, he was well past his dancing days. Old battle scars and injuries slowed him, especially in the morning before his joints loosened. While his physical abilities troubled me, neither I nor anyone doubted his courage. I doubted the courage of only one person. If I had loved Blue Feather any less, I might have bolted for the safety of civilization. A man never knows the way he will react in battle until the time arrives. After a bit of philosophic meditation, I reached the conclusion that civilized white society offered me little. Of all the white men I knew, I trusted only two, and the

Captain had passed on. The other, MacInnis, sat with me as we cleaned weapons.

We had captured enough rifles and six-shooters for each brave to carry a firearm along with his other weapons. In preparation, MacInnis and I broke down the armaments, cleaned and reassembled them. As he finished the last pistol, his lips formed an equivocal smile. "When I am gone, there will be few to mourn me. Yet, if you ask if I regret my months here on the mesa, I'd tell you they was about the best days of my life."

"Considering we might be dead by this time tomorrow, I find that an odd thing to say."

"I always seen Injuns as a nuisance, like bad weather you had to endure. I never thought much of them as people. Living with them has taught me they're no worse than many, better than most. I sure as hell trust these Quahadis more than any white men I've known except for the Capt'n." He laughed as he studied me though deepening shadows. "It's funny, but once you get to know a fella, the color of his skin don't matter, son."

That was the first and last time a white man called me "son." He didn't mean it in a literal sense but as an endearment, about as much as a man could give another while

287

still considering himself upright and decent.

Embarrassed, I ran a sleeve across my eyes. "The world's a funny place all right."

"Yeah, that it is. That it is."

Around midnight, Waco returned, leaving Diablo with the other ponies at the bottom of the mesa, and climbed the escape trail with Legion. The next morning as I stood at the makeshift wall overlooking the trail, he found me. Throughout the night, my nervousness grew. What if Flynn's men discovered our mounts? When I expressed such an idea, Waco shook his head. "Even a tracker like Nantan would have to stumble on the place. It's too well hidden. If they did find it, we'll hear gunshots. If that happens, we will fall back on another plan."

"We have a fall-back plan?"

"We will find one if we need it." He looked off to the east where the haze obscured the horizon. "Flynn has paid men to fight for him. We fight for our homeland." He turned his gaze on me with a determination I perceived in only one other human being. "They do not understand the devastation they are about to unleash."

From that moment of his youth when he tamed the devil horse, I trusted Waco as much as I trusted the Captain, two men cast from the same mold. Each believed in truth, justice, friendship, yet each could be hard and calculating. I had written my fears in the sand, and with a pass of his boot, Waco wiped away the markings, making me whole, instilling me with bravery.

Past three, our scout Yapa rode into camp. Drawing rein before Lone Wanderer, he leapt from his pony and pointed south. "They come."

"How many?" asked Lone Wanderer.

"Twice the number of my toes and fingers."

MacInnis spit a thin stream of tobacco juice. "Them are four-to-one odds."

Waco laid a hand on the older man's shoulder. "I see your point. They bring too few."

At dusk, as I overlooked the trail, Lone Wanderer came to stand beside me, although I smelled him before I saw him, a mixture of prairie grass and wood smoke, an odor that clung to all the Quahadis. Before joining their encampment, I had found it unsettling, but over the course of my stay, I grew to regard it as comforting. He was a man of the earth, of the vast grasslands, canyons, and rivers that made up the Llano Estacado.

Far out on the plains below, rising dust signaled the arrival of Flynn and his army.

Lone Wanderer's face was full of creases. His misshapen knuckles showed signs of stiffening joints, yet he gripped a Winchester in both hands, his countenance exposing an angry resentment. "They do not hide their approach. They do not fear us. They believe we are women."

"They are about to learn different," I said.

As the sun dropped in the west, Flynn and his army gathered at the head of the trail. They didn't come right away. They waited until two in the morning.

CHAPTER THIRTY-ONE

Clutching his Winchester, Flynn strode out to face his men, already mounted and waiting for his appearance. The roan he picked from the remuda waited, too, the reins held by a rider. He took the reins, threw a leg over the saddle, and led the group of forty-four north toward the Llano Estacado. He had sent Nantan ahead to uncover the Quahadi stronghold. More likely a pigsty inhabited by a few dozen dirty, untamed animals. Leaderless except for two ignorant punchers, they would offer little resistance. His men, armed with repeating rifles, would sweep away the ragtail bunch of underfed, outgunned savages in minutes. Then his range would be secure forever.

They camped that night on the banks of the south fork of the Red River. It would take another half-day's ride to reach the Llano Estacado. Soon after the evening sun dropped below the horizon, Nantan arrived.

The tracker peered through narrow lids, which disguised all too well his thoughts. A fellow never knew what to expect from the little bastard.

As Nantan approached, Flynn laid aside his hardtack and beans and stood. He enjoyed looking down on the Indian. "Well?"

"The tracks led me to their stronghold." Nantan crossed his arms over his chest. "Other tracks lead east. Women and children."

"How far ahead are they?"

"Three, four hours. But they are of no consequence."

Flynn called over Rojas and three riders whose names Flynn had forgotten. "The Comanches sent their women and children away. In the morning, go after them."

"And?" Rojas asked.

"Kill 'em all."

"I said they are of no consequence." Nantan's expression hardened. "The warriors are those you must worry about. They know you are coming."

"How many? A half dozen? Ten at most. We've got enough firepower. Once we take care of them, this territory will be safe for white men."

Flynn turned his attention to Rojas. "If

you expect to be paid, bring me proof."

"What proof, amigo?"

"Scalps. A ten-dollar gold piece for each scalp." Flynn chuckled. "Maybe I'll nail them to my bedroom wall."

Nantan waited until Rojas left before he spoke again. "You will pay me the rest of my money now. I will lead you to them, but as I have said, I will not fight."

Don't have the stomach for it.

The words almost slipped out, but Flynn caught himself. He remembered Baxter and the swiftness with which Nantan dealt with him. "I don't carry that kind of cash around with me. I'm good for it. You already got $200."

The Indian held out a palm. "Pay me or find Comanche on your own."

"Now just a second —" Flynn stared into the hard-set features of the tracker and understood he either paid up or Nantan would leave him and his army stranded. Digging into his pockets, Flynn pulled out six twenty-dollar gold pieces and two ten-dollar gold pieces. "That's all I got on me."

With his fingers, Nantan plucked the coins. "You still owe me fifty dollars. When this is over and if you are alive, send me the fifty dollars. General delivery. San Antonio.

Or I will come and collect, if that is your wish."

Once Flynn climbed in his bedroll, he struggled to discover a comfortable position. He wanted to pistol-whip Nantan. Was every half-breed as stubborn?

On the verge of drifting off, he conjured up a vision of Dermot, whom he missed far more than he believed possible. With Dermot's desertion, he trusted no one. And his brother knew too much. If he ever spilled his guts —

He tossed and turned until dawn, at which time he roused his men. They had coffee and hardtack for breakfast.

As he flung away the dregs of his coffee, Flynn motioned to Rojas. "Nantan says we are close. You go now. Hunt down those squaws and kids."

Moments later, Rojas and his companions spurred their ponies east, dust rising in their wake.

Despite the head start of the squaws and children, Flynn calculated Rojas would overtake them sometime late the next day, long before they reached the safety of Quanah Parker and his band. They moved only as fast as the slowest among them. The pregnant women, the old ones, the children would hold them back. Nantan objected to killing kids, but if you took care of the nits, they wouldn't grow into lice.

His fingers traced the scar that ran from his right eye to his jaw. His eye drooped, and lately the world darkened around the edges. Even his thoughts had turned black. If he were bound for hell, so be it. Only the here and now counted.

He and his men traveled most of the morning before crossing into the Llano Estacado. As the sun moved toward midday, they came in sight of a mesa where Nantan pointed out a trail that led up the side of the cliff. A thin ribbon of smoke drifted from the top. Up on the ridge, stick figures looked down on them. By sunrise they would be dead, and Flynn rejoiced in his coming victory. The Quahadis — for that matter, all Indians — weren't human beings but somewhere between human and animal. Savages held back civilization, prohibited rightful people from reaching their destinies. No longer, not in his corner of the world.

Within a quarter mile of the mesa, Nantan wheeled his mount and headed south without a goodbye or adios. Flynn experienced a momentary sense of disquiet at the loss of the tracker. Perhaps he should have offered him more money, insisted he stay and fight. Nantan saw signs others missed.

He understood the Indian mind.

A sudden urge rushed over him to send riders after the tracker, but when he looked at the departing dust, he knew such a move useless. The Indian would kill whoever he sent. He cursed Nantan, and he cursed himself for a fool. He didn't need the advice of a savage.

As he watched from more than a mile's distance, his former guide turned east and disappeared in a forest of chaparral.

Once darkness enfolded the landscape, Flynn toyed with the idea of leading the charge, playing the hero. Afterward, his legend would be greater than Waco's, but the first up might also be first dead. Three of his crew were callow boys, all under twenty, eager to prove their manhood. When Flynn offered fifty-dollar gold pieces for the first ones to reach the mesa top, they talked themselves into charging into the breech. They would find their glory and prove their worth.

Their courage grew when Flynn assured them they had little to fear from the enemy. "Sure, the Comanche are crafty devils, but they have no more than half a dozen fighting men. Everybody knows they can't stand up to a head-on charge by white men. Never could. Guts and a .44. That's all it'll take."

Platt, one of the riders, pointed at the horse trail. "If we go up single file, they can pick us off with ease." A thin man with an unkempt beard, he spoke in a Southern accent that said Georgia or Alabama.

"We go at night," Flynn said. "The clouds will cover us. They'll never know we're there until we're in the midst of 'em. I've told you boys a hundred times, Injuns won't fight at night. They're afraid if they die in the dark, their God won't be able to find them. With the first shot, they'll take off running like scared jackrabbits. There's no cover up there. We'll send those redskins straight to hell in fifteen minutes."

The boys drew straws to see who would lead, and that honor fell to a kid named Bobby, a scarecrow with a prominent Adam's apple and pimples. Once he drew the longest straw and realized he won, he puffed out his chest and thumped it, but early that morning as they began their ascent, he dragged his boots, sending pebbles rolling down the slope, raising dust. Flynn followed behind the first six, his pistol gripped so tightly his knuckles hurt. Each man carried a revolver. Once on the mesa, pistols would be more useful than rifles for close-in fighting.

Shadows cloistered them. Heavy clouds

blocked out the moon and stars, aiding their cover. Except for the mosquitoes buzzing in their ears, the night had turned quiet. Even the cicadas concluded their unique singing. Far off across the plains, the yapping of a pack of coyotes ceased.

CHAPTER THIRTY-TWO

We waited in the dark, too nervous to sleep, our ears alert, our rifles ready. Clouds moved from the north, providing additional cover for the invaders. Waco and I peered into the black abyss. The Quahadis had set small traps of loose rock that would break free with the touch of a horse's hoof or a boot, sending them rolling down the mountain, giving us warning.

"If Flynn comes, will you kill him?" I asked.

I could not see my companion's face, his voice a disembodied spirit. "I have given it much thought. I only know I will not let him kill me."

"Cain killed his brother. His name is cursed."

"And Joseph's brothers sold him into slavery. These are Bible stories, the white man's Bible. They mean nothing to me." We sat silent for some time, and he must have sensed my unease. "What matters is this moment I share here with you, my brother. In the years to come, we will show our scars, tell our stories, and those who hear will regret they were not here with us at the battle of Mesa del Fantasma Viviente."

"I fear history will not be kind."

"Yes, even if we win, we are on the losing side."

Though he had turned eighteen the previous September, Waco understood much more of the world's machinations than I. He understood winners wrote history. Who speaks for the Persians at Thermopolis? Who pleads the cause of Hannibal and Carthage? Who defends the Moors? Three years past, the second battle of Adobe Walls occurred. For four days, less than thirty buffalo hunters held off over five hundred Comanches, which led to the end of Quanah Parker's domination of the Llano Estacado. All the previous Comanche victories were forgotten because of that loss.

The approaching battle would never erase the memory of Adobe Walls, but if we inflicted a little payback on a group of Indian hating bastards, then our efforts possessed meaning. History would recognize our struggle as just.

I deluded myself. The white world would

never acknowledge an Indian cause as just. An intrinsic distrust of skin color forever blinded them to the truth. Sure, a few white men like MacInnis and the Captain used the heart to judge a person's worth. I felt lucky that in my lifetime I had known two such men. Why do I not put Waco with them? Because he was no longer a white man, if he'd ever been one, though like his father, he judged a man by his moral character.

Pebbles tumbled down the slope.

Waco cocked the hammer of his Sharps. "They will come single file on foot. We will kill many, but eventually they will break through. When that happens, stay close to me."

"You don't have to worry. I can find my way."

"Once the shooting starts, all will be confusion."

I wanted to appear brave in the kid's eyes, but more protest would only make me look foolish. "I'll stick close."

Another avalanche of pebbles alerted us to their progress.

I crouched lower behind a rock where I waited. My hands shook, and I feared my courage would desert me.

Three warriors lined up behind the wall

of rocks. The Quahadis had positioned thick tree branches at an angle to act as levers. By exerting upward pressure on the branches, the rocks, heavy, formidable, would tumble on those below. A part of me wished to warn our foes in hope of turning them back, a silly thought, which I quickly discarded. They must pay.

Despite the cool breeze, sweat dripped into my eyes. I passed a sleeve to clear my sight. Boots crunched pebbles, sending them scurrying down the slope. A puncher dashed from the shadows, pistol drawn.

Waco fired, the blast like a thunderbolt in my head.

Two other warriors lighted arrows and launched them at the brush and chaparral soaked with coal oil. The barrier exploded into flames, illuminating the trail and the men on it.

CHAPTER THIRTY-THREE

Up ahead, Bobby reached the plateau. A shot rang out, heavy and deafening. The impact of the slug lifted the boy off his feet and tossed him into the kid behind. Together they toppled off the trail and disappeared into the chasm. Flynn pressed against the mountain at the same moment the brush behind him burst into flames, making his men and him easy targets.

The mountain groaned. As he peered up, his sight played tricks on him. The wall appeared to lean outward, pausing as if trying to make up its mind. It disintegrated, and hundreds of rocks and boulders plunged toward them. Men screamed. A stone half the size of an ordinary man careened into Flynn and carried him over the lip of the trail. Beneath him, the ground sloped for twenty yards before ending in a precipitous drop. As he plunged down the incline, he scratched and clawed for a handhold, any handhold, and his knee slammed into a stationary boulder larger than a horse, bringing him to an abrupt and agonizing halt. Around him, bodies and boulders flew off into black space, which the light from the inferno failed to penetrate.

Fire shot a hundred feet into the air, lighting the mountainside where three men still clung. The Comanches opened up with Winchesters. More men tumbled past him into the abyss.

Surrounded by rocks, Flynn lay hidden from the Comanches.

On the other side of the blaze, his remaining crew discharged round after round, their bullets flying wildly overhead.

He had underestimated the Comanche preparedness, mistook savagery for ignorance. He should have known better. Quanah Parker held the U.S. Army at bay for fifteen years until they overwhelmed the Quahadis by sheer numbers. For years Flynn believed it was Parker's white blood that made him an excellent tactician, but he realized now the Comanche were cunning and determined fighters.

The brush collapsed on itself before tumbling down the slope, shooting embers into the sky. Within minutes, the night returned darker than before. Dust and smoke drifted over him, creating a fog.

With the trail passable, a dozen men rushed forward, their pistols barking. He gripped a rock and tried to pull himself up. The movement sent shock waves rumbling through his body. He screamed and grabbed his leg, his fingers contacting jagged bone. He passed out.

CHAPTER THIRTY-FOUR

The interceding flames grew so intense we could not see those beyond the firewall, nor could they have seen us. Regardless, our enemies' bullets whistled over our heads. Our warriors had far less ammunition to waste, and they silenced their weapons.

Waco inserted another cartridge in his Sharps. "The fire will die soon, and they will come. We leave now."

Even as he spoke, part of the chaparral collapsed, the fiery brush cascading down the mountain.

We ran, the warriors leading, MacInnis and I following. Waco brought up the rear, Legion at his heels. Smoke and dust drifted across the mesa further obscuring the landscape already bathed in shadows. Behind us rose the curses of our pursuers. A Winchester spoke four times, followed by a flurry of pistol shots.

Glancing over my shoulder, I tripped on a

boulder and went sprawling, knocking the wind from me. Choking, gasping, I got to my feet, disoriented. I had lost my rifle. Without landmarks, I had little idea in which direction my companions fled. If I wandered off, I might encounter the invaders. If I stayed, they would find me. A calmness settled over me. I reached for my pistol. I would take a few with me. If I were lucky, one might be Flynn.

A ghost emerged out of the haze, an eagle feather in his hatband. He held out my Winchester. "Come. Hurry."

CHAPTER THIRTY-FIVE

When Flynn regained consciousness, two of his riders had traversed the incline, each seizing him under an arm, lifted him. He almost passed out again, but he forced himself to remain alert. They hefted him to the trail and, with others in the lead, forged ahead.

Reaching the tabletop, Flynn expected the Indians to make a last stand. Instead, only a lone warrior, covered in paint, whites and reds blending together, waited amidst the smoky haze. He was past fifty if a day, his face full of crevices, and his eyes shone with an unsettling hatred. Jamming his Winchester into his shoulder, he opened fire. With each blast, a man dropped.

Flynn's men opened up, their pistols flashing in the night. The Indian wheeled and stumbled away until his legs crumpled, the rifle spilling from his grasp.

But the ancient Comanche had exacted a

toll. Three of Flynn's men lay dead, the fourth dying, a hole in his chest bubbling black blood.

When Flynn counted his force on the mesa, he had eight men including himself. With so few, he feared a Comanche charge would overwhelm them. He gritted his teeth as he tried to figure out his next move. With every breath, every movement, pain exploded in his leg and stormed its way up to his belly and neck and head.

They sat Flynn with his back against a boulder. Only with the greatest effort did he keep from passing out. The right side of his face burned as if scorched by a red-hot branding iron. He touched his scar, beneath which a flap of skin hung like torn paper, which made him want to weep at the injustice of it all. Waco and that damned horse destroyed his good looks, and now these damn Comanches intended to finish him off. A chill swept over him, and his stomach churned, bile burning his throat.

Cries for help issued from the ravine. One man there still lived. When the moans rose to a scream, Flynn shouted, "Somebody shut him up!"

Not one volunteered, even when Flynn offered a fifty-dollar gold piece. Every man among them feared a Comanche trap. When the moans faded to a whimper and gradually to nothing, the men cast guilty glances at one another.

Once the night quieted and the Comanches failed to attack, Platt and two other men stepped off into the haze of smoke and dust. While they were gone, another rider descended the trail and brought up the cook Enos, the only holdover from the old crew. He refused to carry a sidearm or to fight, but the job of resident medic fell on his shoulders. During the War with Mexico, he assisted army doctors. No one else among them possessed his experience.

Using dried grass and sticks, two men had built a fire. Squatting beside Flynn, Enos cut apart the pants leg. "That's a bad break, Boss. We need to set that leg." He pointed to the ripped cheek. "Your face needs sewing up, too."

Before Flynn could reply, a voice hailed from the shadows. "We're coming in. For God's sake, hold your fire."

The three men, led by Platt, stepped into the circle of firelight.

His body tense, Platt rested the heel of his hand on his holstered .44. "They was here, but they're gone."

Flynn winced, not from physical pain, but from his own stupidity. The Comanche had outwitted him.

"We uncovered a footpath on the other side," Platt said. "They had their horses waitin' at the bottom. They was ready for us."

With blinding insight, Flynn understood the Indians' next move. Even as he shouted a warning, a flurry of gunshots echoed through the night.

CHAPTER THIRTY-SIX

Waco led, I stayed close. Raised voices sounded farther away. Our pursuers feared the darkness. We reached the path and began our descent. A break occurred in the clouds, the half-moon shining through. Once below the plateau, visibility improved, and we had enough light that I walked the path without help.

The warriors were mounted, MacInnis among them. Waco leapt aboard Diablo, and I climbed on my pony. Already my joints had grown stiff, my pants rubbed against skinned knees, my heart beat furiously, all of which pointed to the fact that, like Lone Wanderer, my dancing days were also past.

I took notice of those around me. "Where's Lone Wanderer? We must wait for him."

Waco's brow furrowed, his brows arched. "He chose to delay our enemies. An honorable decision. A warrior's decision."

Our band of nine, instead of ten, rode into the night, circling the mesa. Fifteen minutes later, we came upon the Bar 4 C riders clustered at the head of the trail, looking upward, unaware of our approach. The darkness covered us. Even the clouds once more blotted out the moon, but a rider had taken himself out in the brush to shit. He emerged as we came upon him buttoning his pants. Seeing us, he clawed for his pistol.

Legion sprang for his throat, the impact sending both tumbling. The gun discharged, a bullet whining off into the darkness.

The gunshot alerted our adversaries. They ran for cover, firing in our direction, their pistols flashing in the night. We scattered and returned fire. Another of their number dropped, grasping his belly. The rest retreated up the trail, firing back, the curve of the mountain providing us protection. Bullets smacked the earth or stirred brush, but none of our warriors suffered an injury.

Because our own gunfire blinded us, Straight Lance called a halt to the shooting. By the time our night sight returned, the last of the gunmen had vanished, although their voices resonated from up the trail. I had counted twelve or thirteen, minus the two left behind.

They had left their mounts hobbled

nearby. We cut the ties and spooked the horses, which broke into a run, heading south toward the ranch.

At least twenty well-armed men now huddled on the tabletop. If they had not already discovered our backdoor exit, they soon would. Our band consisted of six braves plus Waco, MacInnis, and me, which, when daylight came, tipped the odds in the favor of our enemies. We had to move or risk entrapment in a two-pronged attack.

Straight Lance pointed west. "We will lead them toward Palo Duro Canyon. If they follow, they are dead men."

The vastness of Palo Duro Canyon insured that only an army with scouts could root out the Quahadis. Second in size to the Grand Canyon, the area contained so many twists and turns, so many caves and washes, those unfamiliar with the territory might wander forever trying to find their way out.

Straight Lance leaned across the saddle and laid a hand on Waco's shoulder. "And you, my brother?"

"I go for my wife," Waco said.

"I've been separated from Blue Feather too long," I said.

"And what of you, my friend?" Waco asked MacInnis.

The older man scratched his beard. "This

has been an exciting time, but I'm getting a little long in the tooth for such shenanigans. I have a younger brother somewhere near San Antonio. I'm thinking I might like to see him one more time." The half-moon broke through the clouds, lighting enough of MacInnis's face so his wrinkles appeared deeper, more entrenched. He addressed his next remark to Straight Lance. "It was a real honor. I thank you."

The Indian replied with a grunt. I had heard it before from the Quahadis, as if in that moment when emotion threatened to surface, they used that wordless utterance as a tactic to deflect it. He wheeled his pony and galloped off with his warriors.

"You are welcome to accompany us," Waco said.

"Thank you, son. I rightly appreciate that." He slapped his knee. "These old joints are at the breaking point. Maybe I should have had stayed with Lone Wanderer. That would have been a fittin' way to cash in my chips."

With a wave, he headed south, where the shadows swallowed him.

I never saw him again. Three years later when I passed through San Antonio, I asked after him, but no one knew of him or his brother. When I think of those days working at the Bar 4 C and later with the Quahadis on the Mesa del Fantasma Viviente, I treasure those days my old friend and I shared on top of that mesa. We shared numerous hardships, and there were few people I trusted more. Funny thing, though. That was the first I knew he had a brother.

Waco and I struck out east, passing first through a hard surface of rocks. After a mile or so, as we crossed into sandy ground, Waco roped a tumbleweed, dragging it behind to cover our tracks. After another mile, the tumbleweed disintegrated, and Waco coiled his lariat.

We rode until sunup, when we stopped to relieve ourselves and eat hardtack and beans. The first breezes arrived smelling of sea air, though the Gulf lay five hundred miles southeast. Nighttime black painted the underbellies of accompanying clouds.

If I were superstitious, I would have seen this as a grim omen.

CHAPTER THIRTY-SEVEN

Late on the second day after leaving the sanctuary of the Mesa del Fantasma Viviente, Blue Feather spotted four horsemen pushing their mounts, a speck of dust far out rounding the southern end of the Caprock Escarpment.

The boy Motsai who accompanied them called himself a warrior, though he had yet to reach his full growth, his only weapon a bow and a quiver of arrows. Blue Feather did not doubt his courage, only his ability. Most of the women possessed a skinning knife, she an ancient Navy Colt that held only five rounds. Their pursuers would be armed with repeating rifles. They would be far better adept with the white man's weapons than she with her puny pistol.

A glance at Morning Star told Blue Feather she sighted the riders, too.

As last light streaked the sky, Blue Feather ordered Motsai to veer north, where she had spotted a tree-lined gully. By then everyone knew the situation. Blue Feather told them to dismount. She intended to take the horses and lead the white men away from their band. She tried controlling thirteen mounts, but her hands were too small to hold all the reins.

Morning Star, Blue Feather, and Motsai each took control of three horses, leaving the others behind. They rode through the night, exhausting themselves. As the sun lit the eastern sky, they discovered the trackers had closed the gap, perhaps an hour behind, perhaps less, but as she hoped, all four followed them. Now she must lose them.

To the south, black clouds formed, lightning streaking their dark underbellies. Her spirits lifted. If they could maintain the distance, if their ponies didn't give out, if they caught the rain —

She gradually turned south so they didn't give their pursuers an angle. The wind picked up, dust pricking their exposed skins and frightening the ponies. Morning Star lost her grip, the three horses bolting north, away from the approaching storm. Motsai's horses reared, snorted, kicked. Unable to control them, he tossed their reins to the wind, and they darted after their companions.

They entered dunes, the sand blasting them. Lightning struck, setting off a ball of fire that rolled down a slope. The pony of Morning Star reared up and fell backward, the girl landing first, her mount crashing on top of her with its full weight. The animal bounded up after its companions, disappearing into the darkening prairie.

Releasing the last of the horses, Blue Feather leapt from her mount and dropped beside Morning Star. A deep rattle in the girl's chest sounded above the roaring wind.

A shot flung Motsai from his pony.

A rider crested the dune. He worked the lever of his Winchester, ejecting a shell and inserting a fresh round. As he leveled his weapon, the site lining up on Blue Feather, another gunshot sounded far away like cracking ice. The Bar 4 C rider slumped forward and tumbled from his sorrel. Another shot rang out, another, another.

Blue Feather used both hands to cock her pistol.

A voice called out. "If you are alive, do not shoot. I have come to help."

An old man rode over the top of the dune, a rifle cradled in one arm, his other held aloft to show he meant no harm. He dismounted. The wind buffeted him as if to carry away his frail body. Canyon crevices covered his face, liver spots his hands.

Blue Feather lowered her weapon and glanced over her shoulder at Motsai. The bloody hole in his chest told her she could do nothing for him.

The old man leapt from the saddle, and cradling Morning Star, carried her to his pony.

"We must find shelter." With an ease that surprised Blue Feather, he climbed aboard his mount, the girl held in his arms. His pony cooperated by remaining as still as a rock.

The man was not Comanche. Though she saw no reason for his sudden appearance, he had saved Morning Star and her. The one who had killed Motsai lay dead himself, his face buried in the sand. A second Bar 4 C rider with half his head blown off sprawled less than ten feet away. These were professional gunmen, yet this man, smaller in stature than Blue Feather, had killed both. Far out on the prairie, the other two gunmen, mere specks against the landscape, fled west.

All the horses had bolted except for the old man's. He freed his foot from the stirrup and motioned for Blue Feather to grab hold of it. With a click of his tongue, he ordered the pony forward. It trotted at a pace, which caused her to break into a run. She was strong with good lungs, but the past few days had drained her. After a mile, her side radiated pain around to her back. She offered no complaint, kept the same steady pace, but the old man understood her distress. "Only a few steps more."

He halted beside a rise where a lip in a hill provided a natural roof. Once he placed Morning Star under the protective cover, he waited for Blue Feather to settle before he tied the reins to his wrist and crawled in with them.

The rain arrived in a rush, the landscape disappearing under a wall of water.

Their savior had brought a blanket, which he spread over Morning Star.

"What do they call you?" Blue Feather asked.

"Nantan."

Blue Feather gripped the hilt of her knife. "You track for Flynn."

He peered through mere slits, yet he projected a sadness she had seldom seen in a human being. She had the distinct impression that if she plunged the knife in his heart, he would make no move to prevent her.

"The devil hired me to track the Quahadis." A quiver infected Nantan's voice.

"From the first, I told him I would not fight for him. My job, only to find the Quahadis. Once I did, I came after those he sent to murder your people." He lowered his gaze to Morning Star. "I arrived too late for her, for the boy."

He wore a wool poncho that he slid this over his head and laid across Morning Star. Despite his wiry muscles, skin hung from the undersides of his arms. "For too long, I have served the whites in pursuit of Kiowa or Arapaho or Comanche. Never again."

"Yet you led Flynn to the Mesa del Fantasma Viviente."

Water swirled in under the overhang, darkening his shirt and breeches. He rocked on his haunches. Water poured off his chin. "I saw the fortifications, the traps. By now, Flynn has suffered the wrath of the Quahadis."

The storm raged for an hour. Lightning streaked the clouds followed by thunder so often, so close, the blasts overlapped, shaking the earth beneath them. Morning Star remained lost in her darkness. The rattle in her chest grew louder. She coughed, blood flecking her lips. With her sleeve, Blue Feather wiped away the blood. Morning Star burned with fever. At dawn, the gale slackened and she opened her eyes.

Blue Feather rested a hand on the girl's forehead, pushing hair from her face. "Your time is near, my daughter."

"Tell him" — her voice failed to rise above a whisper — "in my heart, I died Quahadi."

After her spirit departed, they prepared her body Comanche style. With the help of Nantan, they bent the knees to her chest, the legs flexed upon the thighs. They bowed her head, secured her limbs with a section of a lariat. They wrapped her in the blanket, which they corded as well. Together they lifted the body aboard his pony. Blue Feather mounted behind Morning Star to hold her in place. Reins in hand, Nantan led them. Blue Feather chanted the death song.

At noon they came to a ravine so deep shadows obscured the bottom. From below came the sound of water rushing over rocks. A path led down into the darkness. They descended, moving from a hot humid climate into the coolness of a false night until they reached a plateau still far from the bottom. Here Blue Feather dismounted. Together they laid the body on the moist ground. Nantan uncovered a flat rock that he used to scoop out the earth. When the hole reached the proper depth, they placed the body in a sitting position, shoveled in the dirt, and covered the fresh mound with the flat rock to keep her safe from predators.

Nantan held out the reins to his mount. "I know it is your practice to kill a pony so the dead has a ride to the Great Beyond. Give her mine."

Blue Feather looked up from the grave. "Morning Star is young. Her legs are fresh. She can find her way." She ran her fingers across the natural gravestone. "We have much to do, my daughter. We have need of your pony for the sake of others."

Nantan led them out of the ravine. Once they emerged from the gorge, they rode double.

As the shadows lengthened, they spotted two riders headed toward them. Her heart sank.

The Bar 4 C riders had returned.

CHAPTER THIRTY-EIGHT

We ignored the gathering clouds and rode through the night, eager to reunite with our wives. The storm arrived after daybreak. We donned our slickers, tightened the drawstrings of our hats. Still, we were ill prepared for the ferocity of the rain, the tornado-like winds, the thunder that shook the ground. Forty yards to the south, lightning struck a tree, setting it ablaze for a full minute before the deluge extinguished it.

Spooked by the thunder, Legion leapt up and Waco caught him, holding him across his saddle. The wolf dog buried his head in the crook of Waco's arm. Diablo carried the extra weight as if Legion were no heavier than a bag of potatoes.

The storm delivered a blessing. If those who descended the mesa came after us, the wind and rain covered our tracks. Even hounds couldn't follow a trail under these conditions.

At midmorning, we passed two other rid-ers headed in the opposite direction and separated from us by less than a hundred yards. The one who trailed behind leaned forward and gripped his stomach as if suf-fering a bellyache. Obscured by the rain, they appeared ghost-like, mere outlines in the distance. We didn't hail them. We had no time for small talk.

My mount tired, his sides heaving, and we found a grove of weeping willows where, despite the danger from lightning, we crouched among thick branches that shielded us from the full force of the tem-pest. With our reins tied to our ankles, we lowered our heads and pulled up the collars of our slickers, determined to wait out the storm. Our mounts found forage at their feet and pools of water from which to drink.

By midafternoon, the rain slackened to a steady downpour, and by the time we mounted and traveled on, it ceased. The sun emerged from behind the clouds, warming the world. Legion regained his courage and loped beside Diablo. An hour later, we spot-ted our people, pale apparitions among swirling mist. For a fleeting moment, I believed they were the restless dead returned to haunt the prairie. To them, we must have appeared as spectral horsemen coming to carry them to the Great Beyond.

All my life, I heard lies of the stoic Indians incapable of emotion or love or remorse. I had learned the truth. Perhaps they were more reticent to show their emotions than the average white person, but their feelings did not differ from those of the rest of us. For days, these people had labored under a terrible strain. As we approached, they huddled together, believing their fate sealed. When they recognized Diablo and then Waco and me, the tenseness in their bodies dissolved, and their eyes alighted with hope.

Neither Morning Star nor Blue Feather was among them.

They had only one horse. Aboard sat Old Grandmother, her shoulders stooped, a rain-soaked blanket around her shoulders, her gnarled hands gripping the pony's mane. Upon our arrival, several women tried to speak, but Old Grandmother cut them off. "Four men pursued us. Your women and the boy Yapa left a false trail. We hid in a ravine until water rose to our knees." Close to blind, the old woman had perfected other senses. Lifting a finger, she pointed southeast. "There was shooting."

Perhaps Waco or I should have stayed with the group, but neither had the courage for such a selfless act. Together we rode in the direction Old Grandmother pointed. The bulk of the storm had moved north over the Kansas plains, yet more clouds gathered, signaling more trouble ahead. We cared nothing about the future. We cared only about Morning Star and Blue Feather. Fear lodged in our hearts.

Near dusk, as the sun peeked through broken clouds, a pair riding double crested a rise. Seeing us, the rider lifted his rifle. Even from a quarter of a mile, I recognized his companion, Blue Feather. I lifted my hat and waved. She spoke words, the man lowered his weapon.

I failed to recognize the man. As if divining my ignorance, Waco said, "Nantan."

We reined before them. I leapt clear of my saddle and, circling my hands around her waist, lowered Blue Feather beside me. I held back from embracing her, knowing such affection embarrassed her. She peered at her son with such hesitancy, such sadness, both Waco and I understood the tragedy that lay in unspoken words.

Waco pressed his lips together, his attention fixed on Nantan. At that point, I believed he was ready to kill the diminutive tracker, yet Nantan made no move to flee or protect himself.

Blue Feather said, "The blame is not his."

328

"Then whose?"

"I arrived too late for the boy, for your wife. For that, I offer no excuses." Nantan turned his gaze westward. "Your brother sent Rojas and others."

"Others?"

"Two are dead, a third is wounded here." Nantan touched his belly. "He fled with Rojas, but he will not last long."

"We passed them in the storm," I said. "It must have been them."

"Then they are headed for the Bar 4 C." Waco clenched his jaw. "I will find them there."

"No," I said. "*We* will find them there."

Blue Feather gripped my arm, her nails digging in that fleshly area above the elbow enough to cause me to wince.

"You will not go without me." She turned her dark, fiery gaze on her son. "It is my right, too."

Nantan grunted. "Two men and a woman against how many?"

"Twenty or so, I suppose," Waco said.

"You make a pitiful army." Nantan smiled. At least, the corners of his mouth did an upturn, which I took for a smile. "I shall join you. That tips the odds in our favor."

We had a job before we turned our sights to Flynn and his hired guns. Women and children needed our help.

When we returned to them, Old Grandmother sensed the ones missing.

"Morning Star? Motsai?" Without waiting for an answer, she began the death song.

I cast a glance at Waco. For the first time in my memory, perhaps the first time since he was a baby, his eyes teared. I looked away, embarrassed, having intruded on a such a private moment.

Even before Old Grandmother finished her requiem, three Quahadi warriors emerged from the mist, although calling them warriors stretches the truth. I say this because they wore neither war paint nor their more traditional dress but white man's clothes. Their hair hung from under their hats. All three carried bows and arrows but no firearms. Their leader, Quanah Parker himself, held a deer carcass draped over his pony.

Dead tired, Waco and I had ridden all night, and Waco struggled under the additional burden of losing Morning Star. Yet, our people still needed help.

Quanah sent a warrior for wagons to transport his people. He ordered the other brave to build a fire. The immediate prairie was devoid of trees. While the buffalo had disappeared years earlier, they left behind buffalo apples that dotted the prairie. With the assistance of the older children, they soon collected enough for a roaring blaze. Quanah carved up the deer and roasted strips.

As the meat cooked, my stomach grumbled. Neither Waco nor I had eaten for close to a day. We fed the children and the women first. By the time Quanah Parker cut away strips of meat and handed them to me, my stomach growled louder than an angry Legion. That deer meat was as tasty a meal as I'd ever eaten. Juice ran through my beard, and I didn't bother to wipe it away. All the while, Blue Feather sat at my side. Her presence lifted my spirits, and I wanted to tell her so but I refrained from any show of emotion. She continued to grieve for Morning Star and for her son, and I had no right to intrude.

Once we finished, Waco related the story of the battle atop the mesa, the attempt of Straight Lance and his band to draw the attackers into Palo Duro Canyon, and finally the death of Morning Star. Finished, he stared into the fire, the embers still alive, sparks lifting into the air. "Flynn and those with him will pay for what they have done."

"Vengeance will not return your woman."

Quanah wiped his greasy fingers on his pants. "But it will prove most satisfying."

CHAPTER THIRTY-NINE

Enos held out a bottle of whiskey. "A feller got this out of your saddlebags, Boss."

Flynn snatched the bottle and drank without taking a breath. The liquor hit his empty stomach with such force he was drunk before the bottle slipped from his hand. Flynn awoke when four men seized him and held him down. Enos grabbed the leg Flynn had broken during the battle, pulling it straight until the bone snapped into place. With a scream, Flynn passed out again. He came to after Enos had sewn the flesh together, spread sulfur over the wound, bandaged it. He applied a splint, sticks on either side of the leg secured with a lariat from ankle to thigh. As the cook sewed Flynn's face, Flynn lay awake through the ordeal, groaning each time the needle pierced his flesh.

They stayed on the mesa for three days, living off meager rations. Of the original forty-five men, only twenty-three men remained upright, and a dozen of those appeared ready to hit the trail for parts unknown. They had one dead Comanche older than Methuselah to show for their efforts, and he had dropped four of Flynn's men.

Among their causalities, they found fifteen dead and three were missing, their bodies probably rotting in the gully below the mesa. Four others would not make it through the first night, one charred over his chest and face, the others broken inside.

For those three days, Flynn drifted in and out. The horses had scattered when the Comanches attacked the pickets at the bottom of the mesa. His riders recaptured three and headed for the ranch to bring more mounts. When they returned, they discovered it was impossible to get a horse up the trail because part of it had collapsed when the Quahadis sent the rock wall crashing down.

Enos directed the men to fashion a litter from horse blankets and rifles. Struggling down the escape route taken by the Quahadis, keeping close to the cliff side, they carried Flynn to the bottom where they loaded him in a wagon, the bed piled with blankets to cushion the ride. They traveled two days, the ride jarring every time a wheel dipped into a depression or lifted over a rock.

Although his riders remained ready for a surprise attack, they saw nary an Indian. Flynn's spirits lifted. Once the Quahadi men discovered the women and children were dead, they would have nothing left to fight for. Their spirits broken, they would be easy prey.

A hundred yards from the ranch house, a rider said, "Rojas."

Flynn pulled himself up and peered over the edge of the wagon. The gunman leaned against the hitching rail, his arms crossed over his chest, a smoke dangling from his lips.

When the wagon drew up, Rojas tossed the butt to the wind and strolled to Flynn.

"Well?" Flynn looked around the area including the bunkhouse but saw no evidence of those who accompanied Rojas. "A bunch of squaws and their brats got the best of you?"

"It was your man. Nantan."

"Nantan?"

"Perhaps you did not pay him enough. Perhaps he does not like you. Whatever the reason —" Rojas peered through half-opened slits, which projected an attitude of disinterest.

"You couldn't handle one old man?"

"How do you handle the wind? Impossible. He was Nantan. He was the wind. Two died on the spot, the other on the way here." Rojas cast his eyes on the riders who accompanied Flynn. "It appears your efforts did not go according to plan either, amigo."

Flynn waved to those standing around the wagon. "Get me inside."

Four men carried him in the house and laid him in his bed. He ordered one to bring him a bottle and afterward told them all to get out. Alone, he popped the cork and drank. The whiskey burned all the way down, but for the moment, it eased the agonizing pain. He drank until he emptied half the contents. He laid the bottle on a side table and tried to sleep. Instead, the world spun. He had eaten nothing in the past twenty-four hours.

Once the sun dropped and shadows invaded the room, he dozed off and on. As long as he stayed still, the whiskey did its work.

In the night, a pistol shot, loud and crisp, woke him. When he heard no others, he believed he must have dreamed it.

At six in the morning, Rojas brought him a tray of scrambled eggs, beef, and a pot of coffee. He maneuvered himself into a sitting position, and the gunman laid the tray in his lap. Flynn thought it odd Rojas showed such kindness.

Flynn took a bite of eggs, a sip of coffee.

Rojas pulled a chair beside the bed and seated himself. "You know, amigo, your injury will not heal fast. I am afraid you will not be able to oversee things as you would like."

"Are you angling for the foreman's job?" A listlessness in his arms made him feel as if the cup weighed twenty pounds. He laid it on the tray.

"Foreman?" Rojas waved away the suggestion. "The way I see it, you need a partner. You need someone to make sure the work gets done, to keep the men in line."

"And that's you?"

"Already we have experienced desertions. Two before I knew they were gone. Another last night. With him, I put a stop to it."

"How many do we have left?"

"Thirteen including myself."

Flynn frowned. "Thirteen?"

"I know what you are thinking. You are thinking 'thirteen' is an unlucky number. For us it is adequate to run the Bar 4 C. If we need more, we hire more." He slapped the leather holster that housed his .44. "I will hold it together — for us."

Flynn dropped his gaze to the weapon. "Are you as good as you claim?"

"If you could ask the poor devil who pushed me last night, he would tell you. He had a reputation. He thought he was faster than Rojas. He barely cleared the holster when I put one in his heart. No one is faster than Rojas, no one a better shot."

"You're asking a lot."

"If I ride away now, by morning, you will have only what they give you in hell." Rojas stood and walked to the door where he paused. "I will return in an hour for the food tray and your answer."

"You're fiddle-footed. You're not the kind to settle down. Why now?"

"It is a business deal. Nothing more. When I was in Mexico, I saw many fine ranches and the grandees who owned them. Now such a chance is offered to me. I would be a fool to ignore such an opportunity."

Once Rojas left the room, Flynn burned with anger. The nerve of the bastard! Yet the more Flynn deliberated, the more he realized choices didn't exist. He picked at his food. By the time Rojas returned, he had consumed only a few bites although he drained the coffeepot. Rojas arched an eyebrow, his lips curling into an expression of smugness. He knew as well as Flynn that Flynn had no choice.

"A sixty-forty split," Flynn said. "Sixty for me. I keep controlling interest."

Rojas pushed his lips together as he considered the offer. "I am not greedy. It is a reasonable offer. I do insist on one thing, amigo. We put it in writing. Right this minute." Again, he tapped his holster. "I will not take it kindly if you back out on our agreement."

CHAPTER FORTY

We stayed a week with Quanah Parker while we gathered strength. Most of his people lived in permanent sod houses, although a few still preferred tipis. We feared Colonel Mackenzie, now the Indian agent rather than an adversary, might discover us hidden among his wards. None of us wanted that. Later, stories emerged concerning the corruption of Indian agents, but Colonel Mackenzie proved the exception. Once the army relocated Quanah Parker's band to Oklahoma Territory, Mackenzie showed himself a trustworthy friend. Often, he visited the chief in his home, and on several occasions, entertained Quanah and his wife. He may have defeated the Quahadis, but he respected them and their ways.

Regardless of the close relationship between the two men, our little band preferred anonymity. Nantan and Blue Feather fit right in with the Quahadis, but a colored fellow like me parading around among them would have caused suspicion. During the day, I spent most of my time hidden in a tipi or if I wandered outside, making sure I avoided army men, which wasn't all that difficult. I doubted Mackenzie had more than a half-dozen recruits at his disposal. I feared more for Waco. If the army spotted him, they would have thrown him in the stockade, not because of his skin tone, which closely resembled that of the Quahadis, but rather the permanent scowl that lined his features. Twice when white troopers stopped to question Quahadis, I restrained him from attacking them.

"The army is not your enemy," I said. "Your enemy is at the Bar 4 C."

Every day near sunset, he took himself two miles west where he practiced with his six-shooter. I accompanied him once. He had discovered a dry riverbed that ran between cliffs fifty or sixty feet in height. The red sandstone, brilliant in the last light of day, muffled the shots. Twenty feet away, he set up rocks the size of a man's fist. Each time the pistol cleared the holster, each time it spoke, a rock exploded. After he reloaded, he tossed a half-dozen pebbles in the air, blasting each before it hit the ground. I wondered where he got the money to buy shells. As it turned out, Quanah Parker had a stock of hidden weapons and ammunition, which he opened to Waco.

As much as I admired Waco's speed and accuracy, I worried for him. "From the tales I've heard, Rojas is a gunman of repute. He is said to have killed over a dozen men. Some claim he's the fastest gun in Texas."

Waco waved off my concerns. "He may be all you say. It does not matter. If I fail, I fail."

"Then what's the point?"

"We must try. Otherwise, fear and doubt rule our lives."

In that week with Quanah Parker, I discovered the Apache tracker Nantan to be knowledgeable in areas that surprised me. He was much better read than I expected, much better than I.

"White man's books interest me. They think in odd ways." He removed his tattered hat, faded to a dull green. He ran a hand over his bald head. "When I am under the sky, whether night or day, I wear my hat. White men think it strange. If they read their own books, they would understand."

I admitted I, too, didn't understand.

"I am an enigma, even to one whose skin color is closer to mine than the whites. That is good. I enjoy being an enigma." He enjoyed poking fun at my ignorance. His eyes shone with humor. "Have you heard of Aeschylus? He lived many years ago across the Great Water." He slapped his hat back on his head. "Like me, he lacked hair on top. One morning, he sat in an open meadow, his mind on the hereafter rather than the present. An eagle swept down from the sky and snatched up a turtle. The way the bird broke the shell was by dropping its prey on a rock. That day, the eagle mistook Aeschylus's head for a rock."

He was the only Indian I ever met who knew about ancient Greek playwrights. This is not to imply Comanches or Apaches or any Indian tribe lacked intelligence. Their insights into their environment, their recognition of the foibles of people, their determination to succeed by their standards often astonished me. The standards by which white people judged the Comanche, and all Indian tribes for that matter, bore little reality to the world in which they lived. They saw little value in books or reading but they set great store in understanding the connection between man and nature.

Nantan proved the exception as far as book learning was concerned. When I asked where he gained his education, he related the story of a white army officer who taught him the basics of reading and writing. "I already spoke English. The rest was easy."

He also played chess. He carried a fold-up set with him wherever he went, often engaging in games against himself. When I told him I knew the rules, he insisted we play. "Chess helps you understand your adversary."

He understood me far better than I him. We played every morning. In our first game, he checkmated me in five moves. After that, I played with far more caution, far more thought, but he won every time.

During one of our sessions, I asked Nantan why he felt compelled to accompany us, a bold step on my part since I preferred to keep my mouth shut, a safer option for a colored man. Because I had come to trust Nantan, I found the courage to broach the subject. To his credit, he took no offense.

"Too long, I followed the dictates of white men." He sat straight. Shorter and thinner than Blue Feather, he exuded a certain wildness. He may have worn white man's clothing, but his demeanor, his stern countenance, said he had chosen the path of the Apache. He had committed to the path of his ancestors, ready to rain destruction on those he despised. "Your Mister Flynn deserves what is about to befall him."

"The last time I saw him, I pulled down on him," I said. "In hindsight, I see I should have plugged him."

"To look back and say I should have done this or that is foolish. If we attend to the now, tomorrow takes care of itself."

In the afternoons, Blue Feather and I shared a meal before retiring to our tipi, provided by Quanah, where we engaged in serious bouts of physical activity and took our midday nap. Later, we met with Waco and Nantan to discuss our plans. Although we debated various possibilities, we always returned to Nantan's plan. "We go in. We kill them all."

Quanah Parker would have supplied men, but we agreed not to ask. It might undo all he had worked for since his surrender. In one way, Quanah did help. Both Waco and I opted for additional sidearms from Quanah's hidden cache of weapons, Blue Feather a double-load shotgun with twin eighteen-inch barrels.

Nantan tapped the metal finish of his Winchester and the tomahawk in his belt. "These speak for me."

The night before we left, I had trouble sleeping. My restlessness kept Blue Feather awake, so I slipped on my boots and wandered into the warm night. Clouds gathered on the western horizon, lightning streaking their underbellies. Early summer brought storms to the prairies. In the evenings, you saw them from afar as I did that night, playing out or changing direction long before they arrived. Other times they charged straight on as if intent on causing as much havoc as possible.

I sensed Waco's presence before he took a place beside me. Of all the men I had known, only the Captain and he possessed a quality that few could claim, a rocklike steadfastness to stay the course and to get others to follow. Morning Star once claimed that in those days after Waco suffered the wound from the buffalo hunters, when she struggled to keep him alive, he longed for death.

"I was at peace," he said of those few seconds his spirit departed the earth.

Whatever the case, he no longer sought death, although it continued to be his constant companion for the rest of his life.

Lightning lit the horizon. A breeze carried the smell of rain.

"It looks like a big storm," I said.

"We will weather it," he said.

When I returned to our tipi, Blue Feather lay on our blanket, waiting for me, an outline in the dark interior. I dropped beside her, our bodies touching, her heat radiating through our clothes. "You are concerned, my husband," she said.

I rolled on my side so I faced her, though her features were a dark mask as were mine. "We have been together for only a short time, but this has been the best part of my life."

"And if one of us does not survive?"

She asked the question I most dreaded, one to which I had given much thought. "If that happens, the other lives for both. Memories will see us through."

We lay together without speaking, our breathing the only sounds between us. The thought of a world without her or Waco was too much to bear, and I feared if I spoke, my voice would betray me. Silence was its own curse. I dreaded the possibility of leaving here without her understanding. "I have never loved a woman before," I said.

Her hand found my face, caressing it. "Do you know why I chose you?"

I had no idea and told her so.

"When the Captain knew death approached" — her voice was a whisper in the night — "he told me to look for a man who would sacrifice himself for me. You were that one."

"MacInnis was willing to die for you, too."

She laughed, which she so seldom did, a lilting laugh of a young girl rather than a mature woman. "A good man but too old."

She pressed her body against mine.

CHAPTER FORTY-ONE

During that week we spent recuperating and planning, Straight Lance's band wandered in one at a time so as not to draw attention. Once the Quahadis had reached Palo Duro Canyon, they set up a series of ambushes. After two days, they realized no one pursued. While they saw this as a great victory, they also understood if they remained in the Llano Estacado, the army would hunt them down. Straight Lance sent his men to join Quanah Parker's band in Oklahoma Territory. By the end of our stay, all had come in except Straight Lance, at which point I feared Flynn's men had caught him. When I shared my concerns with Waco, he said, "Unlikely."

On the morning we set out for the Bar 4 C, black clouds haunted the western sky. We rode the entire day with the storm lingering on the horizon. The second night as we camped on the edge of Bar 4 C range,

the weather hemmed us in on three sides —
west, north, and south. While the rain held
off, lightning crisscrossed the sky, and
thunder boomed so loudly it rumbled
within our chests. Legion burrowed close to
Waco, his nose buried under his friend's
arm.

The approaching storm affected all of us.
Nantan fiddled with a carving strung
around his neck. Up to this point, he had
kept it hidden under his shirt. I won't say
he prayed to it. Perhaps he thought it a
lucky charm. Whatever its purpose, he
clutched it in his fist while he mumbled to
himself. Blue Feather held to me as if I were
her salvation. Her doubts infected me. Soon
I beheld shapes darting in every direction. I
told myself this was only a phantasmagoria
of my imagination, that the only things at
play were elemental forces of nature. Rea-
soning helped little. I remained awake, one
hand thrown around Blue Feather, the other
clutching my .44, though a weapon was useless against the fury of the gods. The
strength of the tempest proved downright
supernatural, the kind people once believed
augured the death of monarchs, the kind
Shakespeare conjured up when Macbeth
murdered the old king Banquo. I can count
on one hand the times in my life I have been

truly frightened. This was one of those times.

The rain held off until after we broke camp the next morning. Once we crossed into Bar 4 C territory, the wind whipped across the prairie followed by rain. We donned our slickers, lowered our heads, trudged on, our weapons concealed under our rain gear to keep them dry. Once more, Legion rode with Waco, slumped across Diablo's flank, his body moving in rhythm with the horse. Despite the downpour, we constantly scanned our surroundings, on the lookout for riders who would give away our presence, but wherever they were, they remained cloistered, cowering before the elements.

We rode through the day and all the next night, arriving at the base of Powder Hill two hours before sunup. The hill lay between us and the ranch house. A rock outcropping protected us from the rain. Waco and Nantan planned to scout the buildings, assessing Flynn's strength. With that knowledge, we could work out a plan of attack. Blue Feather and I would wait with the horses. When I protested, Waco laid a hand on my shoulder. "The more who go, the more chance of discovery."

"And if things go wrong?" I asked.

"Neither Nantan nor I will surrender to death easily. Keep Legion here." He glanced at the wolf dog and uttered a single command. The animal sat on its haunches, although he fidgeted and didn't look happy about it.

They stepped off into the rain and disappeared in a wall of water.

I faced Blue Feather. "I know I can never take the place of the Captain. Yet, if I live forever, it will be you I carry in my heart."

She leaned into me, her head on my chest, her arms encircling my waist. "You talk too much."

Chapter Forty-Two

Fifty feet from the barn, Waco and Nantan paused under the naked branches of a cottonwood. Waco held a .44, his thumb playing over the smooth hammer. Nantan pointed his Winchester at the ground to keep the barrel free of water.

The light from a single kerosene lamp shone out the rear of the barn. Perched on a bale of hay, a puncher repaired a harness. Another close by, a smoke dangling from his lips, pointed out ways to improve the work. Each man carried a sidearm, but hammer guards held their weapons secure.

"We begin with those in the barn," Nantan said.

"We came to judge their strength, not attack."

"Your friend would hesitate. He might get us killed. As for your mother — this is a job for men. It is time to strike now. The storm covers our approach."

Waco wavered, caught between their original plan and Nantan's desire for immediate action. Each offered rewards, each contained drawbacks.

Nantan said, "Do you wish to endanger your friend, your mother?"

For an answer, Waco reached under his slicker and brought out his second revolver.

Enough light shone for Waco to see his companion's smile. "You are looking forward to this, Nantan."

"I have hunted at the behest of white men, including your brother. I am an old man. I do not long for Death, but I will meet him head on." He squatted, and scooping a handful of mud, smeared his exposed skin so only his eyes appeared under the hat. "This day, I am Apache. I fight by the side of my Comanche brother."

"We must move fast," Waco said.

"Like the wind."

Nantan flung his rifle across his shoulder, the sling holding it in place. He withdrew the tomahawk and knife from his belt, the metal blades reflecting the light. He dashed forward. For a man well into his fifties, he proved fleet afoot. He had sprinted ten feet before Waco took out after him.

Nantan burst upon the men. The tomahawk flashed, dropping the first puncher where he sat, the weapon buried in his skull. The other puncher clawed at his pistol. Nantan thrust his knife in the hollow of the man's throat, the blade sinking to the hilt.

The smell of blood upset the dozen horses that screamed, reared, kicked out, splintering wood of their stalls. Hay drifted from the loft. A voice said, "What the hell, Dooley? What's all the ruckus — ?"

A head popped over the edge, and a sleepy-eyed man looked down. In a continuous motion, Nantan swung the rifle from his shoulder and fired. The slug tore away half the man's face, blood swirling in a red mist.

Another puncher rose in the loft. Waco fired at the same moment as the man, the twin explosions deafening in the confines of the barn. The gunman toppled from his perch, his body thudding on the dirt floor.

A red stain appeared on Nantan's shirt, spreading in a matter of seconds from the size of a half-dime to a dinner plate. His wrinkles deepened, his eyes narrowed. For an instant, he appeared ancient, ready for death. In that instant, Waco believed the attack had failed. Already, men streamed out of the bunkhouse, their voices raised in alarm.

Nantan struck his chest with a fist. "Do

they think this is the end of Nantan?"

He tore out the front entrance.

Waco ran after him. He emerged into the rain, intent on facing the attackers with Nantan, ready to die if need be. He felt no fear, but he would sell his life dearly.

A single shot rang out from the porch. A burning slug carved a path in Waco's thigh. He spun, his .44s roaring. Pieces of the banister flew off. The man ducked into the house.

At least a dozen men, outlines in the night, rushed forward, pistols blasting. Nantan swayed but remained upright. His rifle spoke, a man dropped and another. Still they came, spreading out, keeping up the barrage.

Nantan collapsed to his knees, bullets ripping into him. He fell forward, his face buried in the mud.

The attackers turned their weapons on Waco. A slug tore into the loose part of his slicker, another nipped the crown of his hat, two splashed water at his feet. The bullets buzzed past him, and he paid them no more heed than if they were fireflies. He focused on the men outlined by the flashes of their weapons, beacons in the night. Easy targets. Easier than the pebbles he tossed in the air.

With a calmness that must have terrified

his antagonists, Waco fired one pistol then the other with such precision and swiftness, the sounds merged. Men pirouetted or crumpled. So easy, so satisfying. He took pleasure as each shot found its mark, as if with each he was repaying the enemy for the death of Lone Wanderer, Motsai, and most of all, Morning Star.

Morning Star.

Even as he spewed death, the thought of her and their unborn child pained him, and each bullet became a personal message.

Here's Mister Death.

Hear him howl.

But too many of the enemy remained. Bullets would soon find him. The end was near. He counted his shots and had but two remaining.

With an unexpected swiftness, Straight Lance charged out of the rain, his voice a scream, high, piercing, ferocious. The Bar 4 C gunmen froze.

The boom of his rifle was a thunder crack, and each time he fired, another man collapsed or spun away, dead before he hit the ground, the action so fast that not one had time to turn his weapon on the Comanche.

When only three gunmen remained, they fled for the open range and disappeared in the rain. Straight Lance fired after them until his rifle was empty.

One man rose out of the mud, and with a shaking hand, raised a .44. Straight Lance drove the butt of his rifle into the man's forehead, which exploded into a red fountain. The man fell back, still clutching his weapon, his eyes open but sightless.

Straight Lance cast his gaze over the dead. A sneer twisted his lips. "Vermin." He spoke the word loud enough for Waco to hear.

Except for the rain, the world had grown loudly quiet.

Blood trickled down Waco's leg, but the wound was a scratch, perhaps an inch long but it barely grazed the skin. He put it out of his mind.

Straight Lance crossed the space that separated them.

"It is good to see you, my brother," Waco said.

"I have been waiting." A smile crossed the Comanche's lips. "I knew you would come."

Waco opened the rolling gate of his .44s, ejected the spent shells, and reloaded each chamber. He looked toward the ranch house. "An enemy still remains."

CHAPTER FORTY-THREE

Gunfire crackled through the pounding rain.

Without a word, without a nod between us, Blue Feather and I leapt aboard our mounts and galloped for the ranch, our ponies splashing water in every direction. Diablo and Legion followed with an urgency that said they shared our fears. I pictured Waco and Nantan, riddled with bullets, Flynn standing over their bodies. If so, we rode to our own deaths.

As we drew within fifty yards of the barn, the gunshots came so fast they blended *onetwothreefourfivesixseveneight.*

This followed by a deafening silence.

We reached the bunkhouse, where an unarmed figure held a single kerosene lamp that framed him in the doorway.

Blue Feather drew rein, cocking a hammer of her shotgun, ready to blast the man. She recognized Enos and lowered her weapon. He was the last of the old hands, the cook. His belly sagged over his belt, and I doubted he'd ridden a horse in ten years. During the decades we worked together, I never once saw him carry a six-shooter or a rifle. His weapons of choice were skillets and pans, his ammunition the meals he cooked for the Bar 4 C riders. Now seeing us appear out of the maelstrom, he gripped the doorjamb as if to keep himself upright. His eyes widened in fear.

I nudged my mount forward into the light.

"You?" His brows came together.

"Come along, Enos. You have nothing to fear from us," I said.

Less than halfway to the barn, we came upon nine or ten bodies scattered over the ground, half with their arms and legs intertwined as if they sought companionship on the road to the Great Beyond. A few yards farther on, we discovered Nantan. In death, he appeared smaller, a discarded puppet, its strings broken, its wooden frame shattered. Yet, his physical size belied his nature, a giant trapped in a small body, a savage with a moral compass, which I once believed mutually exclusive. Since living with the Comanche, since taking Blue Feather as my woman, I had put aside such outdated concepts. The Indians weren't heathens any more than the rest of us. Most embraced a moral code with much more fidelity than most white people embraced theirs.

We reached Waco and Straight Lance and dismounted.

Enos stood apart, gawking at the dead men before casting a glimpse at Straight Lance, whom he may have feared was about to claim his scalp.

Waco said, "Someone in the house took a shot at me."

"Who's in the house, Enos?" I asked.

"It couldn't've been the boss. He's stove up. That Rojas fella is there."

"Rojas." Waco uttered the name in a cold and dead tone.

In the intervening minutes, the rain had slackened to a drizzle, but clouds hung heavy, bathing the landscape in deep shadows, the house an outline, the front porch a cave.

Straight Lance drew the tomahawk from his belt and sprinted toward the rear of the house. Waco approached the front, his .44s drawn and cocked. I lagged behind so we presented less of a target. Waco stepped on the porch, his weight evenly distributed, the wood offering no protest. From the bottom of the stairs, I surveyed the windows, black holes that concealed danger. I worked the lever of my Winchester and crouched behind a wooden pillar. If shooting started, it offered little protection. My hands shook. I had no wish to die. I had too much to live for. Yet, I would have accompanied the kid into hell if he asked. He would have done the same for me.

Waco prodded the door with his foot, swinging it inward, the hinges squealing like wounded squirrels. He stepped inside.

I scampered after him, afraid any moment a bullet would tear into one of us. Down the hallway, a single lamp emitted a muted glow from a bedroom. Pistols pointed straight ahead, Waco glided forward, his moccasins soundless against the hardwood floor. Straight Lance, a mere shadow, entered the other end of the hallway. Together they converged on the room. Fearing an enemy lurked in every black corner, I trailed behind.

Straight Lance and Waco burst into the bedroom. When no gunshots announced their presence, I entered.

The stench of rotting flesh made me gag.

Flynn lay on the bed, his eyes half-open as if we had awakened him. His right leg lay exposed outside the cover. From the knee down, the limb was swollen to twice its size, the skin stretched to its limit, ready to burst at the slightest probe. Gangrene ate away at the knee.

"Rojas?" Waco said.

"The bastard had a horse out back." Flynn sounded as if he had a mouthful of dry rocks. "He thought you had an army. He lit out." He paused as he summoned the strength to speak again. "Get on with it. Finish me. That's what you come to do."

"I told you once I wouldn't kill you, Brother." Waco lowered the hammers of his pistols and holstered his weapons. "I told you I would take something from you, but now there is no need. You have done it to yourself."

Behind me, Enos entered. He sniffed the air, and his expression said he understood the situation. "I figured things was getting bad, Boss, but Rojas said you didn't need me."

"You served with the Captain in Mexico?" Waco said.

Enos nodded. "Sure did."

"You have seen wounds this bad?"

"Worse."

"Can you save my brother?"

Enos studied Flynn before he spoke. "Two choices. Do nothing, he dies. The only other option is to remove the leg. Even then, there's a good chance he'll die. If the gangrene is in his blood, it's already too late."

Flynn seized Waco's sleeve, pulling the cloth, stretching it. "For God's sake, leave me whole."

"Even if it costs your life?"

"Just leave me whole." Tears filled his eyes.

Waco squatted beside the bed and laid a hand on Flynn's. "As long as you are alive, there is hope. Death steals hope."

I had never heard him speak such softness to Flynn, with such empathy, like he was speaking to a sick child who didn't understand pain.

"The next sunrise you see, you will understand." Waco stood. "Straight Lance and I are going now. You three stay with my brother. Do your best."

"Where are you going?" I asked.

"After Rojas."

"But the rain —"

"I have Straight Lance. He can track Rojas to hell if need be."

After they left, Enos searched the house for tools for the operation. In the meantime, Blue Feather saw to Flynn. If she carried a grudge, she refused to show it. Laying her shotgun aside, she wet a rag and washed his face, flushed with fever. He was too exhausted to protest. Tears spotted his pillow.

He cast his baleful eyes on me. "Why are you doing this? You both hate my guts."

"If it was up to me, I'd ride away. You could stew in your hate. I'm doing this because Waco wants it."

I will not dwell on the details. Even after twenty years, it sickens me to recall those hours. We loaded Flynn with whiskey. When at last he drifted into the arms of Morpheus, Enos cut off the pants so Flynn lay naked from the waist down. Twice during the hour, as Enos sliced flesh and tendons and sawed bone, Flynn awoke screaming. In each instance, I forced more whiskey down his throat until he again passed out.

Eros made the cut halfway between knee and thigh, hoping the infection had not spread that far. We sewed together the loose skin and covered the stump in bandages.

Wrapping the severed limb in the blood-soaked sheets, Enos and I carried it to the south field where we dug a three-foot hole, tossed in the remains, shoveled mud over it. We spent twenty minutes at the water pump scrubbing our hands and faces. I don't remember a time when I felt dirtier, more contaminated, more vulnerable. Why? It was only blood, gristle, bone. In hindsight, I see it was the invasion of the flesh, of hacking off a piece of a man, of leaving him less than

365

whole. If under the same circumstances, had it been my leg they took, I would have reacted the same as Flynn.

Yet, Waco's words rolled around in my brain: "As long as you are alive, there is hope." Since that day, whenever the world turned against me, when I lost my most precious gifts, I have lived by that philosophy. I have memories, and in memories lies our world forever abundant, forever populated by those we love.

Later that same morning, we wrapped Nantan in a blanket and carried him to a field where the last bluebonnets of summer glowed in the early light. We didn't mark the spot with a cross. Instead, Blue Feather sang a death song while we scooped in dirt. When we finished, Enos leaned on his shovel and provided a white man's epitaph. "Ashes to ashes, dust to dust."

We dug a mass grave for Flynn's gunmen and rolled in the bodies. Standing graveside, Enos scratched his grizzled beard. "I don't rightly remember their names. They was a hard bunch to get to know. Not a friendly one among 'em."

As we walked to the house, shovels over our shoulders, I asked, "Is Rojas as good as I've heard?"

"He's a damned braggart. But he can back

it up. I ain't seen nobody faster."

During the following week, Flynn drifted between the land of the living and the land of the dead. I doubt any of us expected him to survive, but a day arrived when pain freed him enough for him to tell us he wanted food. By then, much of him had vanished. He was skin stretched over bone. Gray streaked his hair and beard. The scar, larger, more prominent than ever, rose like a mountain ridge in the middle of a forest. Yet, for once, he forgot about his face. The missing limb troubled him more, although "troubled" is far too tame a word.

On several occasions, as I entered his room, I caught him crying. He kept his face turned to the wall, but the intermittent rise and fall of his chest, the sudden intakes of breaths, told the story. Under the circumstances, the more I considered Flynn, the more my disgust turned to pity. He was a man whose dreams were always out of reach. Every time he thought they appeared within his grasp, they slipped away, vanished with the waking. Now he would be forever less than he envisioned.

On a day his waking hours exceeded his sleeping hours, I brought him supper. I laid the tray at his bedside table and was preparing to leave when, with a shaking hand, he pointed me to a chair. I had little desire to converse with him. I was set to walk out when he uttered a word I had until that moment believed missing from his vocabulary.

"Please." His husky, dry voice sounded more like an old man's than a fellow on the cusp of thirty.

I took a seat next to the bed.

After close to a full minute when he failed to speak, I said, "Well?"

"Why is Waco keeping me alive?"

"Goddamnit, Flynn! He's trying to save your life."

"That's not doing me any favors."

"The way he sees it, he is." I pushed myself to my feet, the chair tilting, suspended for a brief second before it crashed to the floor. "You're about the meanest son of a bitch I've ever known. You've caused that boy a lot of misery, though I doubt that bothers you."

"He's a half-breed." He offered this as a full-blown explanation and appeared surprised I didn't comprehend or agree. My mixed blood stared him in the face, but that didn't matter either.

Flynn would never get better. I knew some who returned home from the war with missing pieces, but it was the parts missing inside that took the biggest toll. It would take a man of superior fortitude to prosper under the circumstances. Whatever ingredients made up such a fellow, Flynn lacked them. He might live a month or a year or twenty years, but only on the outside.

While we watched Flynn descend into a morass of self-pity, we worried about Waco. Had he found Rojas? If he had, what then?

On the seventh day after Waco departed, Straight Lance rode in alone.

CHAPTER FORTY-FOUR

Despite the dark morning, Straight Lance had picked up Rojas's trail. Rather than check every imprint, Straight Lance followed the general direction, halting every few miles to make sure he and Waco continued on the right path. By sunrise, when the indentations of the prints showed in the soaked landscape, they knew Rojas had not disguised his flight. The tracks continued eastward, never varying. He was heading for Dobson's Trading Post, where he could secure a fresh mount.

When darkness again overtook them, Waco wanted to push on, but Straight Lance insisted the horses needed rest.

"I will not let him escape," Waco said.

When he nudged Diablo, Straight Lance grabbed the reins. "Killing our ponies solves nothing."

They made camp, taking care of their animals before they ate. Along the way,

Legion had fallen behind. When he dragged himself into camp, his belly bulging, the wolf dog snuggled close to Waco.

Before first light, they rose, ate the last of their rations, and rode on toward the rising sun. By noon, the evidence told them Rojas would make Dobson's well ahead of them. Waco's hopes for a quick ending dimmed. Diablo pulled at his reins, wanting to gallop, but Waco held him in check, knowing that if he allowed the animal its head, he would soon tire. They faced a long day's journey.

As they entered rolling hills, Straight Lance pointed to the tracks, and Waco gleaned the same story as his Indian brother. Rojas's pony had developed a limp, perhaps a stone bruise, perhaps worse. Now on the alert for an ambush, Waco and Straight Lance spread farther apart so they made more difficult targets. They also relied on Legion, whose senses far outdistanced their own. As if Legion realized his elevated importance, his ears perked, his nose tested the air, the fur on the back of his neck stood at attention.

A ground haze limited their sight to two or three hundred yards. A southern breeze arrived, smelling of more rain. In the long run, a storm would only delay the outcome.

Rojas might run, he might hide, he might try to disappear, but in the end, Waco would find him.

The breeze swept away the ground haze. As they crested each hill, the visibility increased until they could see a mile, a mile and a quarter, a mile and a half. When they descended the last slope and the land flattened, Dobson's Trading Post came into view. Here they found Rojas's pony, standing, its left foreleg swollen and unable to bear weight.

Two hundred yards from the trading post, Rojas stumbled forward, slowed by mud that sucked at his boots.

Waco nudged Diablo, but the devil horse needed no encouragement.

Rojas cast a glance over his shoulder, and spotting Waco, broke into a run. When Rojas was only ten paces from the building, Waco lifted his rifle and fired a single round that nipped the heel of the gunman's boot, sending him sprawling. Waco leapt from the saddle, the Winchester leveled. Legion already stood over the gunman, growling, ready to attack, his fangs bared, his muscles tensed. With a single word, Waco restrained him.

Rojas sat up, facing Waco. Wiping his hands on his shirt, he streaked the cloth with red earth. He glanced down at his boot. "A lucky shot, amigo. You removed the heel from my boot." The gunman climbed to his feet, but the missing heel caused him to list.

Waco transferred the rifle to his left hand, the barrel pointed toward the ground.

"You are very foolish." Rojas pushed the sombrero back, held in place by a drawstring. "You had me. Now you have put your life in my hands. No doubt you have heard of me. I am Rojas. And who are you? I like to know the names of the men I kill."

Waco's gaze bore into Rojas, who stood less than twenty feet away. In the far distance, thunder rumbled. A gust of wind fluttered their clothes.

"You have nothing to say?" Rojas's smile turned arrogant, dismissive. "You are a boy. Go home to Momma. Suckle her breast. Tell her Rojas spared your life."

As the seconds fled, the silence unnerved Rojas. His anger grew. "Damn you! Why did you pursue me? I don't know you."

"You killed my wife."

Rojas narrowed his eyes. "Your voice — the ghost —" He grunted a laugh. "I knew we'd meet again. This time it is I who has the advantage."

His hand flew for his pistol, his thumb

curling over the hammer.

Rojas was lightning, the fastest gun in Texas.

Death with a six-shooter.

The blast of the .44 rocked the afternoon.

His brows merging, Rojas appeared puzzled, as if he'd encountered a problem more difficult than he expected. His own .44 had yet to clear of the holster. He staggered like a drunk — right, left, back — before his legs gave out, and he sat down again. Blood poured from the hole in his belly. He lifted his head, his expression full of disbelief. His hand clawed at his .44, but he had grown slow, like an old man crippled by rheumatiz.

Leaning over Rojas, Waco pried the gunman's fingers from his weapon and stuck it in his belt.

"It hurts —" Rojas lifted his eyes to plead with Waco. "Why? I only followed orders."

Waco holstered his pistol and drew the Bowie knife, the blade flashing in the dying light.

In his desperation, Rojas dropped his Mexican accent. "I'm not a Mex. My name is Goodall. I'm a — white man. You have white blood —"

"It is the blood of the Quahadis that should worry you."

Waco grabbed a handful of hair, drawing the scalp taunt, and with a fine, precise cut, drew the blade along the front hairline. Blood flowed down Rojas's eyes and mouth. He screamed and grabbed Waco's wrist with both hands, but he was too weak to offer any real resistance. Waco jerked and pulled, the skin separating from the scalp with audible snaps. Rojas's eyes rolled back in his head, and his body turned flaccid. The stink of urine pervaded the air. Waco released his hold, and Rojas tumbled into the mud.

During the ordeal, Straight Lance stood silently to one side appraising Waco's performance, but now he felt the need to offer advice. "He seeks to escape. Do not let him die too quickly."

Waco squatted and waited until Rojas stirred, his eyes fluttering, before he resumed his attack. Twice more Rojas passed out, and each time Waco paused, the bloody knife hovering before the face of the dying man. When he cut away the last piece of connecting flesh and held the scalp in his hand, Waco found himself disappointed. Quanah Parker had assured him vengeance would prove satisfying, but the event resulted in far less satisfaction than he anticipated. Rojas deserved his fate. No argument there. Waco had meted out justice for Morning Star and Motsai and anyone else done in by the gunman, yet Waco experienced an unexpected hollowness that he fought to understand. Perhaps because the story ended here. Perhaps because he had no one left to hate. Perhaps because he knew of no one who needed killing, and he had grown quite proficient at killing.

Waco dropped his lariat around Rojas, wrapped the other end around the saddle horn, and with Diablo's help, dragged the gunman to river's edge. The gunman still breathed though each breath was labored. A bloodied crown adorned his head. For a brief moment, as his white blood warred with his Quahadi blood, Waco fought off a feeling of disgust.

He kicked the body into the water, swollen by the recent rains. The swift current carried Rojas to the middle of the stream, where he dipped below the surface and disappeared. Waco tossed the scalp after the body. He squatted and dipped his hands in the water, holding them under until the river washed away the blood. Standing, he wiped his hands on his pants.

"I wish you to return to the ranch," he said to Straight Lance. "Let them know I will be there in the days to come."

"You come with me now," said Straight Lance.

"I have a job I must do first."

After Straight Lance departed, Waco led Diablo to the corral where he rubbed him down and fed him oats. Finished, he and Legion entered the trading post.

Molly waited behind the counter, her black hair hanging over her shoulders. Over the past year, she had put on weight. While not yet stout, she was headed in that direction.

Waco removed his hat. "I suppose you saw what happened, Miss Molly."

Her jaw clenched. He thought she disapproved. Instead, she said, "I suspect he deserved his comeuppance."

"Yes, ma'am, he did." Waco rolled the brim of his hat. "I need a favor. Have you and Miss Ginger kept in touch? Perhaps you know where I might find my brother, Dermot."

CHAPTER FORTY-FIVE

I saw Straight Lance from the living room window and went out on the porch to meet him, Blue Feather at my side. In as few words as possible, he explained the events at Dobson's Trading Post.

"But where did Waco go?" I asked.

"Brother Wolf returns when he returns." Straight Lance wheeled his pony and headed north.

I called out. Blue Feather squeezed my hand, telling me to shut up, which I did.

"Where will he go?" I asked.

"He is going home."

"But his home is gone."

"As long as there is a Llano Estacado, he has a home."

For the next month, Enos, Blue Feather, and I struggled to keep Flynn alive while we waited for Waco. Flynn ate little, his grunts replaced conversation, his body shrank even more. His face had fallen in on itself, his skin translucent. If the light fell at the certain angle, I swear I could see his skull. Each day we replaced the bandages that covered the stump, trying to prevent infection from setting in again. Despite all of Blue Feather's efforts, despite the use of all her potions, his condition failed to improve.

Then early one June day, Waco showed up, leading a wagon driven by Dermot. The ex-whore Ginger sat next to him, her belly swollen to such an extent I wondered if she would deliver before nightfall.

Waco had tracked them to Twin Forks, a dusty town on the banks of the Trinity River halfway between Dallas and Fort Worth. With the money he took from Flynn, Dermot had purchased a gunsmith shop. When Waco walked into the store, Dermot believed he came to kill him. Instead, the kid told him of Flynn and asked him to return with him.

Blue Feather and I helped Ginger to the ground. Waco led Diablo off to the barn, the wolf dog tagging along. By the time I caught up, Waco had unsaddled the devil horse and was rubbing him down. I informed him of Straight Lance's leave-taking.

"Tomorrow, I go to find my brother," he said.

"What of the ranch? Somebody needs to take charge."

He ceased brushing and stared at me with an expression I can only describe as perplexed. "I thought you understood. I never wanted the ranch. Dermot knows. He has given me money. He says there is more if I need it. I do not."

"You can't live the rest of your life on the Llano Estacado. There's no future there."

Legion sat at Waco's feet, and he must have felt the kid paid too much attention to Diablo. He whined. Waco squatted and scratched the wolf dog behind his ears. The animal turned his brown eyes on me as if to say, "See, he loves me as much as Diablo."

"The future —" Waco was talking to the wolf dog and the devil horse now, not me. "What shall we make of it?"

IF TOMORROW —

By the time Pappy finished his story, evening shadows filled the Four-Square Emporium. A finger of whiskey remained in the bottom of his glass, which he downed. I imagined his throat dry from the telling, yet he wasn't finished.

"Dermot gave Blue Feather and me the gunsmith business he'd bought in Twin Forks, which was decent of him. We ran it for a couple of years until the good people made it clear they didn't approve of a colored man and an Indian woman sharing their town. We sold out and came to El Paso, hoping it better suited us. It did." He rolled the shot glass between his palms as he studied his image in the mirror behind the bar.

"Did you ever see Waco again?" I asked.

Leaning an elbow on the bar, he faced me. "I did."

The book he gave me lay on the bar

between us. He tapped the tatty cover with a forefinger. "I said this is mostly a pack of lies, which it is. Mostly. There are a couple of things the author got right. Now Miss Lily, if tomorrow, you'd like to hear the true story of *The Comanche Kid on the Trail of the Six —* "

ABOUT THE AUTHOR

James Hitt holds an MA in history from North Texas State University. In addition to his many magazine articles, he is the author of *The American West: From Fiction into Film,* which critics have called the definitive monograph on the subject. He is also represented in *The Louis L'Amour Companion.*

Carny, A Novel in Stories won the 2011 Grand Prize for Fiction from the Next Generation Indie Book Awards. His novel *The Courage of Others* (2016) was nominated for the Pulitzer Prize. *Roundup Magazine* hailed his latest book, *Bodie* (2019), as "the kind of Western that every traditionalist novelist seeks to pen." He is a member of Western Writers of America. He has also served as a guest speaker at the Gene Autry Museum.

The employees of Thorndike Press hope you have enjoyed this Large Print book. All our Thorndike Large Print titles are designed for easy reading, and all our books are made to last. Other Thorndike Press Large Print books are available at your library, through selected bookstores, or directly from us.

For information about titles, please call:
(800) 223-1244

or visit our website at:
gale.com/thorndike